"I introduced them. This is my fault."

Instinctively Teague reached across the table and put his hand over Laney's. "You didn't know."

He needed to know more about what had triggered her worry.

"Tell me what about your friend's texts you felt were off. You showed them to the police?"

She grimaced again as she nodded. "They thought it was just drunk texting. I know better."

"Because?"

She reached into the low front pocket of her shirt—when had scrubs become somehow sexy? he wondered—and pulled out a phone. She tapped it a few times, then held it out to him.

He took it and read the message:

Take care of Pepper 4me, pls? He's such a gd dog. Thx

"Seems innocuous enough," Teague said.

"Yes. Except for three things. Pepper? A cat. And a she." She took a deep breath. "And she's been dead for ten years."

Cutter's Code: Men of honor offering the ultimate in private witness protection

Dear Reader,

I once set up a friend on a blind date. While they were out doing the traditional dinner and a movie, I sat at home in a panic. It would go horribly, they would have a horrible time, they would hate each other and then both hate me, what was I thinking? As time passed and my friend didn't call to berate me, and I couldn't reach her, that writer's imagination that is both blessing and curse went crazy. By midnight I'd decided they'd both been killed in a car accident. By 2:00 a.m., they'd picked up a hitchhiker who turned out to be an ax murderer. By 4:00 a.m., I'd sent my friend into the clutches of a serial killer.

Ten months later, they got married. They'd been talking all that time, and never once thought of me and my wicked imagination. Hmpf.

I recovered, basked in my own cleverness for a while, wore the official title of "matchmaker" at the wedding with some embarrassment, and laughed at those awful moments when I feared the worst. But apparently I never really forgot them, because they resurfaced as I was toying with the beginnings of this book. May this be as close as you ever come to this scenario!

Happy reading,

Justine

Operation
Blind Date

—

Justine
Davis

HARLEQUIN® ROMANTIC SUSPENSE

Recycling programs
for this product may
not exist in your area.

ISBN-13: 978-0-373-27829-9

OPERATION BLIND DATE

Copyright © 2013 by Janice Davis Smith

This edition published by arrangement with Harlequin Books S.A.

For questions and comments about the quality of this book,
please contact us at CustomerService@Harlequin.com.

HARLEQUIN®
www.Harlequin.com

Printed in U.S.A.

Books by Justine Davis

Harlequin Romantic Suspense

Always a Hero #1651
Enemy Waters #1659
†*Operation Midnight* #1695
Colton Destiny #1720
†*Operation Reunion* #1745
†*Operation Blind Date* #1759

Silhouette Romantic Suspense

‡*Lover Under Cover* #698
‡*Leader of the Pack* #728
‡*A Man to Trust* #805
‡*Gage Butler's Reckoning* #841
Badge of Honor #871
‡*Clay Yeager's Redemption* #926
The Return of Luke McGuire #1036
**Just Another Day in Paradise* #1141
The Prince's Wedding #1190
**One of These Nights* #1201
*In His Sights #1318
**Second-Chance Hero* #1351
*Dark Reunion #1452
**Deadly Temptation* #1493
**Her Best Friend's Husband* #1525
Backstreet Hero #1539
Baby's Watch #1544
His Personal Mission #1573
*The Best Revenge #1597
**Redstone Ever After* #1619
Deadly Valentine #1645
   "Her Un-Valentine"

Silhouette Desire

Angel for Hire #680
Upon the Storm #712
Found Father #772
Private Reasons #833
Errant Angel #924
A Whole Lot of Love #1281
**Midnight Seduction* #1557

Silhouette Bombshell

Proof #2
Flashback #86

Silhouette Books

Silhouette Summer Sizzlers 1994
   "The Raider"

Fortune's Children
The Wrangler's Bride

‡Trinity Street West
*Redstone, Incorporated
†Cutter's Code

Other titles by this author
available in ebook format.

JUSTINE DAVIS

lives on Puget Sound in Washington State, watching big ships and the occasional submarine go by, and sharing the neighborhood with assorted wildlife, including a pair of bald eagles, deer, a bear or two and a tailless raccoon. In the few hours when she's not planning, plotting or writing her next book, her favorite things are photography, knitting her way through a huge yarn stash and driving her restored 1967 Corvette roadster—top down, of course.

Connect with Justine at her website, justinedavis.com, at Twitter.com/ Justine_D_Davis, or on Facebook at Facebook.com/JustineDareDavis.

A lonely little girl.
A mistreated pup who needed a home.
A perfect match.

Ten to nineteen, important years for a girl.
He was the brother I didn't have.
My playmate, my confidant.
My comfort through some rough family years.

He showed me the heart hole only a dog can fill.
And the real meaning of unconditional love.

Decades later, and a slew of dogs afterwards,
I miss him yet. Love ya', Scamper!
                                    —Pam Baker

This is the second in a series of dedications from
readers who have shared the pain of the loss
of a beloved dog. For more information visit my
website at www.justinedavis.com.

Chapter 1

Change was coming.

He could feel it in the air, Teague Johnson thought. It wouldn't be long before the trees started to turn. Soon after that there would be a riot of color as the Pacific Northwest said goodbye to summer and settled in for a long, likely wet and maybe cold winter.

He'd missed that. As a kid, all he'd wanted was out of the wet, but after a while spent at Camp Pendleton near San Diego, he'd found the lack of defined seasons oddly disconcerting. It messed with his sense of time passing. And when he'd finally come home, he'd welcomed the shift from summer to fall and winter to spring in a way he never had before.

You never miss it until you lose it.

Terri's voice echoed in his head as the pain jabbed at his gut. He steeled himself against it with the ease of long and frequent practice. The past had been nagging him lately, in all its various ghostly forms. That was usually a signal he'd been living too much in his head, and the cure was something hard, physical and exhausting. Maybe he'd borrow Cutter for a long, mostly uphill run.

"Crazy dog," he muttered, but he was smiling. The uncannily clever beast had quickly gone from being the pet of his boss's fiancée to being an amazingly useful member of the team.

He hesitated for a moment, looking at the small coffee place next door to the groomer's. Another sure seasonal sign; they were putting up the sign for a string of pumpkin spice items. Tempting. He had a silly weakness for them. Maybe he'd pick up a latte and grab a muffin to share with Cutter, who seemed to have an affinity for the particular flavor as well. That would, if nothing else, guilt him into taking that long, hard run.

After, he decided. He continued toward the groomer's, smiling at the image of a floppy-eared dog in a tub of suds painted on the window.

A bell rang as he pulled open the door of the small shop. A humming sound from the back halted just as he stepped inside, and a split second later he heard a woof of greeting come from the back. He couldn't see the dog, but obviously Cutter knew he was here.

"Almost done, be right out."

The female voice calling from the room at the back was low, even husky, but there was another note in it that made his brows furrow. An unsteadiness or something that was noticeable. He shrugged it off; it wasn't his business. Maybe she had a cold. Or maybe the mess Cutter had gotten into—Hayley, said fiancée and the dog's first chosen person, had said he was mud and muck from nose to plumy tale—had required some heavy-duty cleaners, although the only thing he could smell was a faint scent of something that reminded him of cough drops. Eucalyptus or something.

The humming began anew, and he realized it was a hair dryer of some sort. The image that brought on made him smile, but he had to admit Cutter had enough long, thick fur that it would probably take him hours to dry without the electronic assist.

He wandered as he waited, feeling a bit out of place here amid the displays of dog stuff. He'd had no idea there were so many different kinds of food and supplements. The toys were more familiar, and a couple made him smile; one designed as a fire hydrant actually made him chuckle. He noticed, here and there, more pictures like the one painted on the front window, featuring the same dog, with various expressions from mournful—over the diet foods, he noticed with a grin—to silly. Whoever the artist was, he or she had a great imagination, and clearly a good sense of humor.

He walked toward a few pictures he saw on a side wall. Photos from local 5K and 10K charity runs, in which the shop had apparently participated or sponsored a team. Community involvement. He looked at the people in the shots, wondered if the owner was one of them.

He stopped in front of a rack of colorful collars and leashes, each one sporting a fabric pattern of varying designs and degrees of whimsy. He picked up one with fire hydrants on it, and again chuckled. Bark Boutique, the tag said, with a website of the same name. He wondered if they did custom work. A collar with alternating doggie angels and imps would be more in order for the irrepressible Cutter.

On that thought, the dog appeared in the back of the store. Tail up and newly fluffed, he trotted toward Teague sporting his usual attentive expression. With gleaming black fur from his nose to well back over his shoulders, where the thick coat shifted gradually to a rich, reddish brown, and upright, alert ears, he was, Teague admitted, a beautiful animal. But it was the gold-flecked amber eyes and the uncanny intelligence behind them that was his most striking feature. And Teague had quickly learned the intensity in that gaze wasn't effective just on sheep.

"Hey, boy," he said when the dog reached him and sat expectantly at his feet. "Don't you look all spit-and-polish."

He reached down to deliver the anticipated scratch behind the dog's right ear. He remembered that Hayley had told him how impressed she'd been when she'd brought Cutter here the first time, and the owner had carefully researched his breed to learn the proper way to groom him.

"At least, the breed he looks like," Hayley had added with a laugh. It was of no concern at all to her that nobody knew for sure the ancestry of her fey lost waif. "I want to see her make a go of it. I like that she donates groomings to shelter animals, so they can look their best at adoption days."

Teague liked that himself.

"You're Teague?"

The woman called from the doorway to what was apparently the grooming room. Her voice was steady now, whatever he'd heard before gone.

"Teague Johnson," he agreed as the woman approached. She was tall, maybe two or three inches shorter than his own five-eleven, he thought, attractive in an outdoor, bet-she-could-keep-up-with-you-on-that-run kind of way. Participant, not just sponsor, he guessed, thinking of the run pictures. Her long dark hair was pulled back into a jaunty ponytail he supposed was practical for her work, but also fit with her long-legged grace. She wore scrubs, the damp spots showing that was for practicality as well.

"Hayley called?"

She shook her head. "Quinn, actually."

That his boss had made the call himself didn't surprise him; Quinn never considered much of anything in the way of work beneath him. It was one of the many reasons he was so effective. Not to mention that he was stark, raving crazy about Hayley and would lay down and die for her if necessary. Teague envied him that. If it wasn't so clear the feeling was mutual he might envy him Hayley as well; she was a remarkable woman. The kind Teague had begun to think didn't really exist.

"I'm Laney Adams," she said, and held out a hand as she came to a halt before him. He took it, firmly but not crushingly. Shaking hands with a woman was always tricky, or seemed so to him. Too strong and they winced, too easy and some seemed to get offended. Laney did neither, she just met his grip and released after a solid shake.

And didn't seem to feel at all the jolt of awareness that had gone through him at the contact.

He quickly shook it off. Hadn't rained much yet, so it was probably just some residual charge of static electricity.

Cutter rose and went to stand beside her, nuzzling the hand he'd just shaken in the way usually reserved for cheering humans up; obviously the dog liked and trusted this woman, and Teague had learned to trust the dog's judgment about people.

"You work with Hayley?" she asked.

Teague nodded in answer to her question. And couldn't help noticing the woman's eyes and nose were slightly reddened.

"Dog soap get to you?"

Startled, she swiped at her eyes. "I… No. It's fine." She looked away, then down. "I'm sorry, I forgot his collar and tag. I'll go get it."

She turned on her heel and left quickly. To his surprise, Cutter followed her, although he wouldn't put it past the dog to have understood about the collar.

He barely had time to appreciate the way she moved when it all tumbled together in his head. Red eyes and nose, that undertone in her voice, and the way Cutter had been nosing at her hand...

It wasn't soap. She'd been crying. Unease spiked through him. Female tears unnerved him, like most guys. They made him start looking for something to fix, to make it better, and too often there wasn't anything.

He heard the slight clink of the boat-shaped tag as the now-dressed Cutter approached. According to Hayley, he'd shown up on her doorstep with only that tag, engraved with his name, for identification. All her efforts to find his owner had failed, and in the meantime Cutter had settled in and begun to work his special kind of magic on her grief-torn heart.

And now he seemed glued to Laney Adams. When she stopped again, Cutter stayed pressed against her leg. He nuzzled her hand again, and the woman petted his head as if instinctively.

Cutter looked up, his gaze fastened on Teague. He stifled the urge to read "Well? Fix it!" into the dog's expression, knowing it had to be arising out of his own earlier thoughts.

But there was no denying the intensity of the dog's steady, unwavering gaze. And in the relatively short time since Cutter had come to Foxworth, they had all learned it was wise not to ignore the determined dog when he got "that look."

He didn't want to ask, but did anyway. "What's wrong?"

"Nothing."

"You were crying."

He was a little surprised when she didn't deny it, but simply acknowledged it this time.

"Some women can cry beautifully." She shrugged. "I'm obviously not one of them."

He admired her blunt honesty, but felt awkward. He didn't even know this woman. But Hayley did, she'd said she really liked her, maybe that was why. Friend of a friend in need or something.

He opened his mouth to ask "Are you all right?" then shut it again. Obviously she wasn't all right, or she wouldn't have been crying. Feeling a bit proud of himself for having avoided a stupid question, he felt even better when she leaned down to scratch Cutter's ear briskly.

"I'll see you next time, you lovely boy," she said.

There, another bullet dodged, Teague thought.

"Let's go, dog," he said.

Cutter didn't move.

"Hayley's waiting," Teague said.

Cutter's tail wagged, and he gave the softer version of the happy bark he always greeted Hayley with in reaction to the sound of her name. But he didn't move from Laney's side. And again he gave Teague that look, that compelling gaze that he had no doubt could drive those sheep right off a cliff if that's what the dog intended. Not that he ever would. No, Cutter was a softie, always seeming to find the walking wounded, the ones who needed help.

Often, the ones that needed Foxworth-style help.

Cutter gave a short, sharp yip of impatience. Teague drew back slightly. He did not like how this was shaping up.

With a long-suffering sigh, Cutter finally left Laney's side. Teague let out a long breath of relief. He'd been afraid there for a minute that—

His thoughts were interrupted when the dog, instead of heading for the door, walked behind him and bumped—hard—against the back of his legs. Pushing him rather awkwardly toward Laney.

"Uh-oh."

The muttered phrase escaped Teague before he could stop it.

"Something wrong?" Laney asked. "Hayley already paid the bill, if that's what you're wondering."

"I only wish it was that simple," Teague said, staring down

at Cutter, who seemed to realize he'd finally gotten the message. The dog walked back to Laney, sat this time, and looked back at Teague expectantly.

"He seems restless," she said. "He's usually pretty laid-back with me."

Teague looked back at her. Her eyes were the color of cinnamon, he thought. He hadn't noticed that before.

"Laid-back? I'd have to see that to believe it," Teague said wryly. Then, with a smothered sigh, he gave in to the inevitable. "Tell me what's wrong."

"Nothing." She had herself together now, and clearly wasn't inclined to discuss whatever had been bothering her with a total stranger. He appreciated that, understood it, and normally would have let it end there.

Except that when Cutter got involved, *normal* wasn't a word that got used very often.

Chapter 2

Laney inwardly steadied herself. It wasn't really a lie, she told herself. Not sharing personal pain with a total stranger wasn't lying. Maybe denying anything was wrong was, but not pouring out her heart to a man she'd never met before was simply reasonable. Even if she was disposed to see him favorably because he worked with Hayley, whom she'd very quickly come to like a great deal.

Now, Hayley's fiancé, Quinn, was a man she'd found more than a little intimidating the one time she'd met him. But not this man, she thought. In fact, the easy smile, and the way he'd seemed so relieved when she'd refused to talk about the reason for her tears, made him seem much more approachable than his boss.

Not that he wasn't as attractive, just in a different way. He was a bit taller than she, enough to be appreciated given her own height of five-eight. He looked lean, fit and strong. His eyes were a light, clear blue, and went well with his sandy-brown hair. And besides the nice smile, he had an easy confidence she found appealing. She even liked his haircut, buzzed close on the sides, slightly longer on the top. Ex-military? she wondered. Navy was her first thought, this being a navy region, but army and air force bases weren't far, either.

Cutter nudged her hand again, stopping her musing and making her wonder how long she'd been standing there staring at him.

"See, he knows it's not 'nothing,'" Teague said.

It took her a moment to backtrack in her mind, she'd been so lost in her contemplation of the man before her. That was unlike her, and only added to her unsettled state.

"No," she admitted, "it's not. It's just not something you need to hear." She reached down to stroke Cutter's head once more. "See you next time, Cutter. Nice to meet you, Mr. Johnson."

She turned to head back to her office. And had to stop when Cutter darted in front of her, blocking her path. Startled, she couldn't help but laugh.

"Well, I'm flattered, sweet boy, but your mom's probably missing you by now. You'd better go."

"He's not going anywhere," Teague said.

Laney whirled around. In her state of mind, the words almost sounded ominous. But the man's expression was so glum and resigned any thought of being in danger from him vanished quickly. She wasn't sure what this man did—wasn't sure exactly what Foxworth did, for that matter—but she was sure he wasn't a threat.

You thought that about Edward, too, she reminded herself, the thoughts flooding back, a painful contrast to the pleasant diversion of contemplating an attractive man. *You thought he was harmless, safe to recommend to your best friend.*

"Don't let me see an expression like that and then try to

convince me that nothing's wrong," Teague said quietly. "I may not be as smart as Cutter, but I'm not blind."

She managed a laugh at the joke.

"I mean it. He knows when people are in trouble."

"I'm not in trouble." That much, at least, was true. She wasn't the one in trouble. She was just to blame for it.

Cutter sighed audibly. This time he got up and walked behind Laney, leaned into the back of her legs the same way he'd done to Teague moments ago, an action that had amused and puzzled her. The dog was, she noted, more gentle with her.

She heard a wry chuckle from Teague and her gaze shot to his face.

"Guess he figures I'm more stubborn or more stupid, so he has to push harder," he said, his tone matching his expression.

In spite of her worry, she smiled; she couldn't help it.

"Look, I know this sounds crazy, but he really does know. When people have a problem, I mean."

"I believe it. He's a very perceptive animal. More than any I've ever known and I've known a few."

He seemed relieved that she accepted it. "It's even more than that. He... It's hard to explain. He's like a mind reader, a strategist and an early warning system all in one. He's one of our team now, and we've all come to trust him, rely on him even."

His praise of her favorite client warmed her; people who loved and respected dogs went quickly to the friend column in her book. One who realized how special Cutter was started near the top. But it was the phrase "early warning system" that made her blink.

"What exactly is it that the Foxworth Foundation does?"

"Hayley hasn't told you?"

"She said they help people. I assumed they were some sort of charitable operation."

"They are, when they need to be." He seemed to hesitate, then asked, "Do you have another appointment?"

"Just with my bookkeeping program."

He glanced at his watch, a heavy, military-looking thing with more dials than she could conceive of needing. Then he looked back at her.

"I was about to go get him a pumpkin muffin next door."

She smiled. "He likes pumpkin muffins?"

"I think he'd bite for one. But only the pumpkin. Hayley brings an assorted box in now and then, and that's the only one he wants."

Laney laughed. It felt good after the morning's grim thoughts.

"Join us for a cup of coffee." He smiled crookedly, in a sheepish way that warmed her. "Or one of those pumpkin latte things. My weakness."

That he could admit a liking for the flavored, frothy drink without feeling his manhood threatened was more reason to like him. And she liked his easy humor about it, too. He was racking up points quickly.

And you, she told herself firmly, *are not keeping score. You have enough to deal with.*

But she found herself saying yes anyway. After all, what harm could there be in sitting in a public place with him? She'd have to be wrong not only about him, but about Hayley, Quinn and Cutter for it to be a problem.

She knew she wasn't wrong about Cutter.

She trusted Cutter wasn't wrong about Teague Johnson.

Teague took another sip of the latte. It was probably a good thing they only did this seasonally, he thought, or he'd be twenty pounds overweight, or having to add five miles a day to his runs, which were already long enough.

Cutter, muffin happily consumed, had found the one spot

of sunshine near the outside table and plopped down for a snooze. Now that they were talking, the dog had that mission-accomplished sort of air that Teague had learned to recognize.

"Now that's the Cutter I know," Laney said.

"He only seems to know two speeds," Teague said, indicating the dog with his cup, "that, and full tilt."

"Maybe the latter requires the former," Laney said.

Teague smiled. And not for the first time since they'd sat down here, he felt the urge to just forget what had brought them here, to simply sit here and enjoy a few minutes with an attractive woman, without the undercurrent.

But if it wasn't for that undercurrent, they wouldn't be here. It wasn't like he asked every appealing woman he ran into out for coffee. In fact, he hadn't asked a woman out for coffee, dinner or anything else in a long time. A very long time.

"Problem with your drink?"

Her quiet question made him realize he'd been frowning. "No." He seized on his earlier thought, since he wasn't about to open the door on his pitiful social life. "Just thinking it's good this is only available now."

She smiled. "It might not be so appealing on a hot summer day."

"Did you really use the words 'hot summer' while sitting here in the Pacific Northwest?"

She laughed. It was a wonderful sound, and he wondered why she didn't do it more. Then remembered that the reason was probably why they were sitting here in the first place.

"It does happen," she said. "A couple of years ago we nearly set a record."

"A record heat wave here is a cold snap elsewhere," he said; he was willing to let the chat about the weather continue, if that's what she needed to ease into the real subject. Or maybe she'd flat-out refuse to talk about it, and he could walk away knowing he'd at least tried. Guilt-free.

"Like where you're from?" she suggested.

He gave a one-shouldered shrug of assent. "Where I've spent time," he acknowledged, and left it at that. This was not the time to speak of distant lands of heat and burning sun and sand. "But I was born in Seattle, grew up over there." Time to do a little steering of this conversation. "You?"

"I was born in Phoenix," she said. "But we moved here when I was two, so I practically feel like a native."

"Family?"

"They've retired back to Arizona," she said. "Dad's building dune buggies and mom's taking skydiving lessons."

He blinked at that one. She apparently came by the athletic bent honestly. Laney laughed again.

"You slow down, you die. That's Dad's motto."

"He's got a point," Teague said.

She seemed relaxed now, smiling. "I miss them, but they're having so much fun, and they worked so hard for so long, I can't help but be happy for them."

"What about you? How'd you end up doing this?" he asked, indicating her shop.

"I wanted to be a vet, even started school. I wanted to help animals, but I just couldn't deal with seeing so many sick and in pain. I had to find another way to work with them."

"And you did."

"It's not as important, but it's what I can do."

"I'll bet the dogs who get adopted after you spruce them up think it's pretty important."

She looked startled, then smiled. "Hayley told you."

"She mentioned it, yes. She admires you for it."

"It's what I can do," she said again. And he liked the quiet way she said it. *If everybody took that approach, we'd all be better off.* He watched her for a moment.

Now, he thought. "So what is it you're upset or worried about?"

It didn't quite have the effect of a glass of cold water tossed at her, but it was close, and he wished he hadn't had to do it. He realized with a little shock how much he'd been enjoying simply talking with her. Simply sitting and talking with an attractive woman was a pleasure he'd not had in too long.

"I'm not…"

Her voice trailed away. He felt a twinge of disappointment at the denial after she'd been so honest about the crying.

She tried again. "I'm not sure I should talk about it."

Well, that was better. At least she wasn't denying that "it" existed.

"Why?"

"Because it's not my problem, it's someone else's. Maybe. Or maybe it's not a problem at all. Except in my own overactive imagination. Everything could be fine. Could be wonderful, in fact. But I have this gut feeling there is something really wrong. But everyone else thinks I'm the one who's wrong. So I just don't know anymore."

Teague felt like a guy who'd just had a jigsaw puzzle dumped at his feet, all the pieces scrambled, and he was supposed to make sense of it.

Laney laughed, as if she'd just realized how what she'd said sounded. But it was a different sort of a laugh, not charming and fun, but self-deprecating and on the edge of some deeper, darker emotion. But it cemented Teague's notion that this was not a woman who cried at the drop of a hat, making the times when she did significant.

"I'm sorry. That didn't make much sense, did it? I shouldn't have said anything."

"Or say it all," Teague said. "Whose problem is it, maybe?"

Her mouth twitched into almost a smile at his use of her own words back at her. But still she hesitated. This time he stayed silent, just looking at her, which was no hardship. She stared down into her cup, and Teague noticed the length and thickness of her eyelashes, the delicate arch of her brow, the length of her neck revealed by the pulled-back hair. Her fingers, wrapped around the cup now as if she needed its warmth even on this relatively mild day, were long and slender, tipped with nails cut short; no fancy manicures for this woman who dealt with washing animals every day.

Crazy, he thought. The most common complaint about women he'd heard from his buddies in the corps was that they never stopped talking. And here he couldn't get this one to start. Whether that was a reflection on her, or himself, he wasn't sure.

He was contemplating pressing harder when Cutter intervened. As if he'd sensed the lull in the conversation was a problem, the dog had roused from his nap in the sun. He looked at them both consideringly, then got to his feet and padded quietly over to Laney. He rested his chin on her knee and looked up at her. In a move that seemed and probably was automatic, Laney began to stroke his dark head.

"You are so warm from the sun," she said to him. "That must feel good."

The dog stared at her until she gave an odd little shake of her head. Teague knew just how she felt. He'd been on the receiving end of that steady gaze himself, and he knew the odd feeling it gave you.

"You might as well tell me," he said after a final taste of the flavorful drink. "He's not going to let go until you do."

"Is that what you think he's doing? Trying to compel me?"

"I know it is. I've seen him do it too many times. He's done it to me."

"Giving him a bit too much credit, aren't you?"

"Don't be too sure of that," Teague said wryly. "My boss is the biggest skeptic on the planet, save maybe one—well, two—and even he thinks there's something uncanny about that dog."

"I can't deny he's clever—"

"Oh, it goes way beyond clever. I could tell you stories," Teague said. "But I promise you, he's not going away until you talk about what's bothering you."

She looked from him to Cutter, then back.

"I know you don't know me, not enough to trust me. But you can trust him."

"I know."

"So talk to me. You need to talk to somebody." When she still didn't answer, he leaned back in his chair. "I could call Hayley. Would you talk to her?"

"Oh, don't do that. I know she's busy, or she would have come for him herself."

"Yes. But she trusts me with him."

Her head came up then, and he sensed he'd finally hit the right words. "Yes," she said softly, "she does."

Again he stayed silent, thinking that pushing harder at this instant would be the wrong thing to do. He'd learned from Cutter that sometimes the best thing to do was just stare them down and wait.

"It's my best friend," Laney finally said in a rush, and before he processed the words Teague allowed himself a split second of satisfaction. "Amber. Amber Logan."

"Pretty name."

"Yes. And it fits her." She gestured back toward the shop. "She's a graphic artist. She did the paintings here."

"I noticed those. Cute. She's good."

"Yes. She is." He saw her mouth tighten slightly.

"Has she done something?" he asked. "Gotten in trouble?"

"I think…" Her voice trailed off. She drew in a deep breath and started again. "The police don't believe it, even her folks don't believe it, but I can't shake the feeling something's very, very wrong."

The police? That kicked it into an entirely different category in Teague's mind. He leaned forward, sensing she was on the verge of either blurting it out or withdrawing altogether.

"Wrong how?"

She met his gaze, held it. She was committed now, he could feel it.

"I think she's been abducted."

Chapter 3

Relief was obvious on Laney's face as the words finally came out. She looked as if having someone listen to her without that doubt in their eyes, without that expression that told her they were merely humoring her and couldn't wait to move on, was nearly overwhelming.

She proved his guess right with her next words, spoken fervently.

"You don't know how much time I've spent every day trying to make myself believe that they're all right, that there's nothing wrong, that Amber's just fine and I'm being silly, with an overactive imagination."

She also looked as if she wanted to hug him. Not something he'd particularly mind, but he wasn't about to stray into that minefield. Not now, anyway.

"Why don't you just tell me? Don't worry about how it sounds, just get it all out there. Then we'll sort it out."

Gratitude supplanted relief on her face. She nodded, a

short, sharp motion that spoke worlds about what she was feeling. Even if it really was nothing, she needed to get this out.

She continued to pet Cutter, as if she welcomed the distraction. He could almost see her turning over in her mind where to start. He opened his mouth to prod her along, then stopped; he didn't want to sound like the police who hadn't believed her, but coplike questions were the first thing that came to mind.

He remembered Terri once telling him she had to work up to the real problem sometimes. *And you were a lot of help when she needed you, weren't you, halfway around the world fighting for people who didn't even want—*

He broke off his own thoughts before they galloped down that old path. And grabbed the first neutral question he could think of.

"Tell me about Amber."

"We've been best friends since third grade. I know her like a sister. And love her like one."

"Is that where you met? School?" he asked.

"Yes. Ms. Waters's class. Meanest teacher in school." Laney looked up at him then, gave him a fleeting smile. "I don't mean hard, or strict. I mean...mean. And Amber and I, we bonded together in surviving her."

Now that was something he understood. "Easier to handle stuff like that if you're not alone."

The smile was better this time as she nodded. "We had secret meetings where we plotted her absence in various ways, from changing the number on the door of the classroom, to the address on the school. At eight, logic didn't enter into it much."

He smiled back. "No GPS in cars yet, so who knows?"

She laughed then, and he felt oddly pleased.

"We were best friends from the day Ms. Waters sent us to

the principal's office for passing notes. Which weren't even about her, by the way."

Teague's mouth quirked. "Why do I get the feeling that that part was pure luck?"

She looked startled, then laughed again. And he got that same little jolt of pleasure out of it. Natural, he thought. She'd been crying when he'd arrived, and he'd managed not to make it worse, maybe even a little better. Something any guy would be happy about.

"But the point is, we were inseparable after that. We shared everything. We poured our hearts out to each other. When I had my first crush on a boy, she was the one I told. When her mom got sick, I was the first to know. She's the sister I never had."

"A long time ago, my father used to say there's two kinds of families—the one you're born into, and the one you build yourself."

"Your dad sounds wise."

"At one time, he had his moments." He knew he sounded a little odd, but went on easily enough. "He also used to say that's not something you can pass down to your kids. You have to earn your own wisdom. Usually the hard way." *Too bad he forgot his own lessons,* Teague thought.

Laney grimaced at the words. Thinking of Amber, Teague guessed. It was time for those cop questions. He certainly wasn't about to keep discussing his own family; that was not a topic he lingered on. Ever.

As if he was finally sure things were progressing properly, Cutter lay down. But for insurance, he put his head on Laney's foot. She seemed to take it as a sign the time for idle chatter was over. Teague saw her take in a deep breath, then let it out slowly.

"When did you last talk to her?" he asked.

"It'll be four weeks on Friday."

"That's a long time, for friends as close as you are."

He didn't say 'female friends,' although he at least knew enough to realize there was a difference. Girls seemed to always want to be in touch, whereas with a guy he could go for weeks, even months without any contact, and then run into him and it would be like nothing was wrong. Nothing *was* wrong. But a woman tended to take offense at that kind of benign neglect. At least, that had been his sad experience.

"That," she said firmly, "is unheard of. For us. We talked or texted every day. Usually multiple times a day."

"Wow."

He couldn't imagine that. It had boggled him when Quinn and Hayley had come out of that mess so tightly connected they did the same; neither of them was happy if they went longer than a few hours without contact of some kind. He teased his boss about it, but beneath the joking was a thread of wonder. He'd never felt that way about anyone.

"Now she's blocked incoming calls," Laney said. "I had another friend try, and my mother. Even the police officer tried, I'll give her that, and she was blocked, so it's all incoming calls, not just me."

"Hmm." It was the most noncommittal sound Teague could manage.

"Look, I know how it sounds. I even understand why the police feel the way they do. On the surface, it looks simple. Woman meets a new man, they hit it off in a big way, then head out on a romantic getaway. They want to be undisturbed, so woman blocks incoming calls on her phone."

"But you don't think so."

"No. She just wouldn't, not without telling me. In fact, she'd call me and giggle about it for an hour first. And then there's the texts."

"Texts?"

"The ones that came after my calls were blocked."

His brow furrowed. "So you have heard from her? Via text?"

She sighed. "Yes. And no."

He leaned back. "I think maybe you'd better explain that one."

"I've gotten texts sent from her phone. But they're…off."

"Off how?"

"They just don't sound like her."

"The wording or what she's saying?"

"Yes. And there are mistakes. Things that are just flat-out wrong."

He tapped the side of his now-empty cup with his index finger. "All right. Could she have lost her phone, had it stolen?"

"She would have a replacement by now. Amber wouldn't go from the living room to the kitchen without a phone. And besides, she missed our get-together yesterday, without even a call to cancel. She would never, ever do that. All of this is completely out of character for her."

Which probably explained the tears today, Teague thought.

"I remember my sister telling me about girls who blow off their friends when a new guy comes along," he said, trying to keep his tone neutral.

"Amber's not one of them. Nor am I. We always hated that, swore it would never happen, and it never did."

She was so adamant he decided to leave that one alone. "So she would have told you if she was going to run off with this guy she just happened to meet."

Laney went a little pale. Cutter's head came up, so Teague knew he wasn't imagining her sudden tension.

"She didn't just happen to meet him." He saw moisture gathering in her eyes, saw her visibly fighting the tears. "I introduced them. This is my fault."

"Whoa. Slow down. You knew this guy?"

She nodded. "Slightly. I knew him from my old job, where I learned, over in Lynnwood."

"A bit of a drive, from the U-District."

"My boss specialized in pocket dogs," Laney said. "People came from farther than that."

He smiled at the term, but said only, "Go on."

"So, Edward, he'd even asked me out a couple of times. But I wasn't attracted, and I was too busy with plans for this shop."

"And?"

"Last month Amber and I went to the mall there. She loved to shop. Edward was there with a friend, we ran into him. I introduced them. She seemed interested, and so did he, she'd just broken up with a guy and was kind of down, so I told her she should go, he was a nice guy." She blinked again, more rapidly this time. "I told her she should go, damn it. I practically set her up on a blind date with this guy, and now—"

"Easy." Instinctively he reached across the table and put his hand over hers. "You didn't know."

Not that he was sure anything was wrong himself, not really. He needed to know more about what had triggered her worry.

"Tell me about the texts you felt were off. Did you answer?"

"Yes. But she never responded. Which isn't like her, either."

"What if you initiate a text?"

She shook her head. "I either get no reply, or if I do, it doesn't really answer what I said."

"Example?"

"I ask where she is, she says she's fine. I ask when she's coming back, she says she's having a great time."

Which could, Teague thought, be answers. Just not the ones Laney wanted or expected.

"You showed them to the police?"

She grimaced again as she nodded. "They thought it was just drunk texting. I know better."

"Because?"

She reached into the low front pocket of her shirt—when had scrubs become somehow sexy? he wondered—and pulled out a phone. She tapped it a few times, then held it out to him. "This is the first one I got."

He took it and read the message.

Take care of Pepper 4me, pls? He's such a gd dog. Thx

"Seems innocuous enough," Teague said neutrally.

"Yes. Except for three things."

"Three?"

"Pepper? A cat. And a she." She took a deep breath. "And she's been dead for ten years."

Chapter 4

"Amber has never been *that* drunk in her entire life," Laney said firmly. "Pepper was her pet for eighteen years, from childhood, and she adored her. She cried for months when she died."

It wasn't much to go on. But even Teague had to admit that three such mistakes in a text message fifty characters long was a bit much. Even drunk on her ass, would Amber have forgotten Pepper was a cat not a dog, a she not a he, and that she had died a decade ago?

Teague glanced down at Cutter, still ensconced on the floor with his head on Laney's foot, as if to hold her there until the story was out. He tried to imagine, even drunk, ever forgetting about the dog.

Nope. Impossible. And he's not even my dog.

"Are there more?" he asked.

She nodded. "None as obviously wrong as that one, but

some. Read through them. I cleared out all the non-Amber ones."

He wondered for a moment if there had been some from a boyfriend. But she had said she hadn't been attracted to this Edward, implying if she had been, perhaps she might not have said no. So there couldn't be a boyfriend. Unless she was the juggling type. He didn't think so. If nothing else, he suspected she didn't have time.

And none of that was in the slightest bit relevant, he reminded himself.

He focused on the series of texts. Most seemed innocuous to him, something about being late for the office and catching up later, one about wanting to buy a new car, and a final one about jetting off to Canada. Nothing jumped out at him, but then nothing would have about the first one, either.

He didn't have to ask. The moment he looked up, Laney ran through a list. "Except for days when she meets with clients, Amber works from home. She bought a new car late last year, and the process exhausted her so much she plans on keeping it at least ten years. And she absolutely hates to fly. Canada's way too close to get her on an airplane."

"You told the police all this?"

"Yes." She let out a compressed breath. "Their answer was people newly in love do things they might not otherwise. And I can't argue with that. Especially Amber. She's always…impulsive, especially with men. More than me, anyway."

Teague filed that self-observation from Laney away in the "might be good to remember" slot in his mind. Even as he did it, he silently chastised himself; he needed to be paying attention, not…whatever he was doing.

She lowered her gaze to the painted surface of the small, round table. There was something scratched into the surface, something Teague couldn't read upside down because of the angular shape and unevenness of the letters. A name, perhaps. Carved by somebody as infatuated as Laney said Amber got?

"It's my fault," she said, her voice barely above a whisper. "I was even glad when he seemed even more interested in Amber than he had been in me, after I'd said no all those times."

"Laney—"

She picked at the scratched name with a thumbnail. "I told her to go. That he seemed like a nice guy."

"Did you lie? Did you really think he was a bad guy?"

Her head snapped up. "No! I would never—"

She cut herself off, giving a short, abrupt shake of her head.

"I brought them together. She never would have met him if not for me. I still feel responsible. Maybe that doesn't make sense, but…"

Teague stared at her for a long, silent moment, fighting down the memories that battered at him. "I get it. Believe me, I get it."

When he refocused, Laney was staring at him. "You do, don't you." The way she said it wasn't a question. "You lost somebody, didn't you?"

"My sister. Years ago." *And yesterday.* "But Amber is now. Let's stay there."

For a moment he thought she might persist. And he wasn't about to talk about Terri. He'd talked to no one about her in a very long time, except Quinn, and then only because he'd known he had to be thoroughly honest during the long vetting process for going to work at Foxworth.

As if Teague just thinking the name Foxworth had roused him, Cutter got up. He turned from Laney to look up at him. When he was certain he had Teague's attention, he walked toward where his car was parked. After a few steps he stopped and looked back over his shoulder at both of them.

Teague sighed.

"I guess he's finally bored and ready to go," Laney said. She stood up. "Thanks for listening to my…conspiracy theory."

Teague slowly rose as well, but said nothing. He had a theory of his own about Cutter's sudden movement. A year ago he would have laughed at the idea, but after seeing the dog in action for months now, he knew better.

"Maybe I'll see you again, if he keeps getting into messes," she said with a creditable attempt at cheerfulness.

Cutter yipped. Short, sharp and to the point. Laney smiled. "Now he's impatient. You'd better go."

"I'll try," Teague said. "I think he's got other ideas."

Her forehead creased. "What do you mean?"

"Wait and see."

He started to follow Cutter back toward his car. The dark gray SUV was parked about twenty feet away. He made it five before Cutter reacted.

Tail up, ears alert, the dog turned back. He trotted toward him, then right past him, just as Teague had expected. He stopped in front of a surprised Laney, nudged her hand, then tried the walk and look back routine again.

"What is he doing?" she asked.

"I think," Teague said with a wry quirk of his mouth, "he's saying it's time for us to go tell your story to Foxworth."

This was, without a doubt, the craziest thing she'd ever seen.

She loved dogs, she'd worked with them for years now, but she'd never seen one act like Cutter before. Except maybe in movies or on TV, where the animal did what it was trained to do, no more thought process behind it than a willingness and a need to please.

But this, this was all Cutter's doing, born out of his obviously uncanny canine brain. He had a Plan, Teague had said, and woe be unto the human who didn't get that.

She liked him for that, Laney thought. One of the many things she could like him for; he was a good listener, he didn't laugh at her or make her feel as if she were being silly, to be humored, sent on her way and then forgotten.

Of course, there were the blue eyes, the lean, strong build, the air of quiet confidence, the easy grace and that smile... oh, yes, that smile.

She tried to shake off the feeling that was growing. She had no time for this. She needed to focus on Amber, on finding her, even if she had to do it alone.

But Teague was saying she might not have to do it alone.

"I can't promise anything, except that they'll listen. And take you seriously."

Her first instinct was to doubt that. But Teague had done just that, hadn't he? He would hardly take her to his boss if he didn't think there was something to her suspicions, would he?

"I can't afford to hire anyone."

"If Foxworth takes it on, it won't cost you."

"So Foxworth is a charity?"

"It is, in some ways. In other ways, it's something completely different. Come on, lock up and I'll explain on the way."

"But—"

He gestured at Cutter, who was pacing now, from where they stood outside her shop to Teague's car and back. "You might as well give in, because he's not going to give up."

"So you're saying you're letting a dog boss you around?"

He grinned suddenly. It took her breath away. "Yep."

She found herself grinning back, unable to stop it.

She went back into the shop, Cutter on her heels. He truly wasn't going to let up until she followed him. She went into the small bathroom and quickly switched her scrubs for the jeans and lightweight cabled sweater she'd worn in this morning, grabbed up her keys and her slouchy bag and headed back out. She flipped the Open sign to Closed and locked the front door.

Cutter was clearly happier now, and she followed him back to where Teague was waiting. The SUV obediently chirped twice as Teague unlocked it and he opened the passenger door for her, the door behind it for Cutter, who leaped in then turned on the seat to look at her expectantly. She was nearly laughing as she got in.

Teague walked around and slid into the driver's seat. Cutter let out a soft, clearly happy woof.

"You got what you wanted," Teague said to the dog. "Way back."

Without hesitation the dog jumped over the back of the seats into the cargo area of the SUV.

"Safer for him back there," Teague said as he turned the key.

"This is insane," she said as she fastened her seat belt.

"Yep."

"He's a dog."

"Maybe."

Laney laughed out loud. The relief of having someone actually listen to her worries must have made her giddy.

"Foxworth," she began.

"Is the most amazing place, full of the most amazing people I've ever met."

"Doing what, exactly?"

"A little bit of everything," Teague said. "But it's all aimed at one single goal."

"Which is?"

He glanced at her as they were caught by a light turning red, the newest of the three signals in the small town. He'd pulled into the left turn lane, heading away from the main road toward the next, bigger town.

"Helping people in the right, when they have nowhere else to turn."

She blinked. "That's…quite a goal."

"We do what should be done but isn't, for whatever reason."

"You must have hoards pounding on your doors," she said wryly.

"We work only on referral," he said. "We don't advertise."

"Then how did you find them?"

His mouth quirked upward at one corner, as if he liked the question. "I didn't. They found me. There was this online military forum, and some of us got into some pretty heavy discussions. I used to post a lot. Turns out it was monitored by Foxworth, and they noticed. Thought I might be a good fit."

So she'd been right about the military air. But she thought she heard something else in his voice as well. "You miss it," she said.

"I do. I was a marine," he said, as if that answered all. Perhaps, to him, it did. "The corps was the greatest fighting force in the world."

She wasn't sure what the past tense referred to, but there was a finality in his voice that kept her from asking. Or asking why he'd left, if he loved it so much.

"So Foxworth, what, recruited you?"

He shrugged. "It was pretty clear I wasn't happy with the way things were going. I wasn't re-upping, anyway. I didn't know what I would do. They gave me an alternative."

"So now you work for Quinn?"

"Yes. And Foxworth is a private foundation, so the only limits on what we can do are our own."

"And now you sound very…proprietary."

He gave her a sideways glance, and she saw that grin flash

across his face again. It had the same effect it had had before. He answered as the light finally changed and they made the left turn.

"Yeah, I guess I am. We do good work. I'm proud to be part of it."

She liked that. So many people just griped about their jobs all the time. "How long have you been there?"

"I'm the new guy. Only two years—three if you count the vetting process—but I'm there as long as they'll have me."

She drew back slightly. "A vetting that lasts an entire year?"

He nodded. "Quinn and Charlie Foxworth are very, very particular."

"They run the foundation?"

He nodded as they slowed for a truckload of topsoil pulling out of a side driveway. "It's a family thing. Quinn's idea, mostly, but Charlie makes it possible." He grinned again. "It's nice to have a financial and logistical genius in the family, I guess."

"Are there more Foxworths?"

"Just them," Teague said, sounding suddenly solemn. "Their folks were killed in the Lockerbie bombing. Charlie's a little older than Quinn, and raised him after that. It's why Quinn started the foundation. He hated feeling so helpless when it happened, even though he was just a little kid. And when they let the guy go, he was so furious he vowed to try to help people who felt like he did, helpless to do anything about whatever injustice had befallen them."

"He turned his anger to good use."

"Yes."

He slowed the car then, and Laney realized she hadn't been paying much attention to where they were. She felt a little pang of unease. She was putting a lot of faith in his connection to Hayley, and the fact that Cutter clearly liked and trusted him. And now she was out in a remote area she didn't know well, with a man she'd just met. Her unease grew as he turned into a narrow driveway that wound through thick trees.

It hit her then that perhaps Amber had been the same way. Too trusting. Because her best friend had said a guy seemed nice to her and she should give him a shot.

Guilt flooded her again, and she shivered under the force of it.

There was no getting around it. If Amber was in real trouble, or worse, it was her fault.

Chapter 5

"Laney?"

Teague had noticed her shiver, she thought. He didn't seem to miss much.

"I don't expect you to understand, but I really do feel so damned responsible," she said. "For Amber."

He said nothing as they reached a wide clearing in the trees where a rather utilitarian, three-story green building stood. There was no sign, not even a street number marking it. It was like many places out here, she guessed. If you belonged, you knew how to find it. Off to one side was a large metal building that looked like a warehouse, with a battered-looking silver sedan parked beside it. And beside that was a large swath of concrete with some odd markings. She was puzzled until she saw the bright orange windsock to one side and realized she was looking at a helicopter landing pad.

Teague pulled to a halt in a graveled parking area beside the green building and a larger, dark blue SUV. He put the car in Park. He turned off the engine. He unfastened his seat belt.

Then he shifted in his seat, turning to look at her.

"I understand perfectly," he said, his voice holding a grimness she hadn't heard from him until now. And when he went on, it sounded as if he were digging the words out with a rusty knife.

"My little sister was sixteen when I was first deployed. I was off to the Middle East, excited and afraid at the same time. Dad was stoic, as usual, Mom tight-lipped and silent. Neither of them was happy about what I was doing. Only Terri was proud. Weepy at my leaving, but proud of her big brother in uniform."

Laney could picture it, and marveled anew at the bravery of people like Teague who served voluntarily. And hated that they weren't always treated with the respect they deserved.

"Terri was the one who made me promise to write, call and Skype whenever I could. And she kept to her part of the bargain. I know more than once she passed on a date or a night with her friends or a party because that was the only time I'd be able to reach out halfway around the world."

"She sounds wonderful."

"She was." His voice was tight, harsh.

You lost somebody, didn't you?

My sister. Years ago.

The brief exchange they'd had echoed in her head now.

"What happened?" she asked quietly.

"While I was on my second tour, she vanished. Left for school and never arrived. She was never found. It destroyed what there was left of my family. My father drank himself to death, and my mother is a bitter woman who drives away anyone who tries to get close. Especially me."

The words came choppily, and she wondered when the last time he'd told anyone this was. That he was telling her now, to help her, moved her a great deal.

"Teague, I'm so sorry. But it wasn't your fault."

"No? Tell my mother that. If I'd stayed home, like my parents wanted me to, I might have been able to protect her, or at least find her. So, yeah, I understand. Perfectly."

Laney sighed. "I guess logic loses when stacked up against enough guilt."

"Always," Teague agreed.

Cutter woofed softly, politely, as if to remind them he was still there.

"Sorry, buddy," Teague said, his tone reverting to normal. He hit a button that opened the back of the SUV. Laney turned to look as the dog jumped out, lifted his dark head, sniffed the air for a moment then confidently trotted toward the green building.

"Look," Teague said, drawing her attention back, "I can't promise they'll take this on. But if they do, even if Amber is really just on some romantic escape, we'll make sure of it so you can quit feeling guilty."

"Do they usually take on what you bring them?"

His mouth quirked. "I've never brought anything to them before."

She didn't know whether to feel honored or worried.

He got out of the car, walked around and opened her door. Manners, she thought. Nice.

And then she was distracted by Cutter's actions as he rose on his hind legs at the single door she could see, and batted at a large square button with his paw. He hit it, and the door slowly opened.

Teague saw her look. "Quinn's brainstorm," he said with that killer grin. "Sort of an oversize doggie door. And handicapped access, should it ever be needed. Took Cutter all of three seconds to figure it out. Now he comes and goes as he pleases."

"Is that safe for him?"

"Nearly ten acres here and Cutter knows exactly where

the boundaries are. He never gets too far from his people anyway."

"Why is this place so…anonymous?" she asked as they neared the door Cutter had used.

"Sometimes those people who aren't doing the right thing end up not too happy with us," he explained. "So we don't hang out a sign to advertise where we are. And that automatic door has a cutoff and lock switch in just about every room, in case we have to secure the building."

She blinked at that. Did they really expect some kind of attack here? What had she gotten herself into?

He skipped the automatic door button and simply pulled it open for her. She stepped inside, not knowing what to expect.

To her surprise, the downstairs was furnished as if it were a home, a gas fireplace the centerpiece along one wall, with a leather couch and a couple of chairs arranged around a heavy coffee table in front of it, and a large area rug marking off the space visually. There was a small kitchen area along a back wall with an island separating it. A doorway on the other side stood partway open, showing a bathroom.

"This is…unexpected, from the outside."

Teague chuckled. "Quinn was living here before he kidnapped Hayley."

She blinked. "He what?"

"It's a long story. Ask her sometime."

He led her toward the stairway that ran along the far wall. They went up a flight, past the second floor that seemed mostly used for storage, then another.

"Quinn set up in here so we could watch the eagles," Teague explained. "There's a nesting pair in the woods just across the clearing."

Laney smiled, feeling better at that. The frequent sightings of majestic bald eagles was one of her favorite things about living out of the city. She didn't miss the crowds, the traffic or the noise, either. She had few regrets about moving across the water.

Except Amber.

She only hoped she didn't regret that for the rest of her life.

Laney, Teague noted, had the same reaction many did to Quinn, a sort of awed silence. Despite the casual clothes, the polite words as he greeted them, and the way he was scratching the clearly delighted Cutter's ears, what they called "command presence" fairly oozed from the guy. More than once Teague had caught himself about to salute him, and more often than that had thought if there were more like Quinn in the upper echelons, more brass that had come up the hard way instead of the political way, he never would have left the corps. When they talked about riding into the valley of hell, Quinn was the kind of guy it would take to lead that charge.

"Where is Hayley, anyway?" Teague asked. She wasn't usually far away from Quinn or Cutter for long.

"Shopping."

"Oh."

"Clothes. Charlie," Quinn said.

Teague grinned. "She's still nervous about that, huh?"

Quinn grimaced. "Hell, I'm nervous about that. You know how Charlie can be."

Since he'd had to go through a lengthy interview—more like an interrogation—with Foxworth's CFO/CEO himself, Teague had all the sympathy in the world for anyone looking at their first meeting with the redoubtable Charlie Foxworth.

Quinn gave Cutter a final, roughhousing sort of rub behind both ears, then straightened up and looked at Laney.

"I can see he's fine, and you're not bandaged so I assume he didn't bite you."

Laney laughed, and Teague sensed her relax a little. "Cutter? Oh, no. He's far too well-mannered for that."

"That," Quinn said dryly, "is up for debate. But if not that, what's up?"

The "why are you here?" wasn't spoken, but Teague heard it just the same. They didn't bring people here unless they were already involved in their case, and Teague suddenly realized maybe he should have arranged a meeting somewhere else.

"Laney has...a problem."

Quinn lifted a brow at him.

"One I think we could help with."

"I see." He focused on Laney, who had lapsed back into silence. Second thoughts? Teague wondered. Wishing she'd never agreed to this?

"I'm sorry," she said, sounding intimidated. "Maybe this was a bad idea, maybe I—"

"Maybe you should just tell me what's going on." Quinn's voice was gentle then, calming, encouraging. It was another facet of that ability to command, and Quinn had them in balance better than anyone Teague had ever known.

Quinn walked over to the table that was placed beside the expansive windows that looked out over the clearing to the thick stand of trees. Different shades of green marked the spots where maples and other deciduous trees stood against steady evergreens.

He cleared away some papers, closed an open laptop and slid it to one side. "Sit down," he said, "and let's go over it."

Laney still looked a little nervous, and Teague guessed she was remembering how the police had reacted. She gave him a sideways glance that made it clear going through it all again for the intimidating Quinn seemed overwhelming to her.

So Teague began. In the back of his mind he'd been thinking how to present it all the way over here anyway. He managed a fairly concise assessment, and Quinn listened without comment or interrupting.

"At least you made sense out of it," Laney muttered when he'd finished.

"Not much to go on," Quinn said neutrally.

"I know that," Laney said. "Believe me, I know that."

"I thought maybe we could at least find her, make sure she's okay, put Laney's mind at ease," Teague said, wondering if his first effort at bringing a job to Foxworth was going to be a miserable failure.

"And if she is, Amber will likely be so embarrassed she might never speak to me again," Laney said. "I hadn't really thought that far until now."

"If she gets angry with you for worrying about her," Quinn said, "she's not much of a friend."

Laney's surprised expression told Teague she hadn't expected that. But the cogent assessment seemed to help, because Laney slowly nodded.

"There's one more thing," he said to his boss. "One thing I left out."

"What?"

Teague drew in a deep breath. "Cutter."

Quinn drew back slightly. He glanced over to where the dog was curled up on his bed in a beam of late summer sunlight, snoozing peacefully.

"Uh-oh," Quinn said, much as Teague had back in the shop.

"Yeah. He made it pretty clear."

He described the dog's actions until Quinn held up a hand.

"All right," his boss said. And with a slight shake of his head, he added, "Then I guess we're in."

Laney's startled look nearly made Teague grin.

"Wait," she said, "you decided this because of Cutter's behavior?"

"His instincts are…I won't say infallible, but he hasn't made a mistake yet," Quinn said.

Laney looked from Quinn to Teague and then back again. She spoke slowly, carefully. "I love dogs as much as anyone, and more than most. But you're letting a dog decide this?"

"No." Quinn glanced at Cutter again. "I'm letting *that* dog decide this. Because that's what he does."

"He brings you cases?"

"He finds them. After that it's up to us."

She gaped at Quinn. Teague couldn't resist poking a little more.

"And he trusts us with them, unless he feels we're not moving fast enough, or in the right direction. Then he butts in again."

Quinn chuckled. "Makes you wonder how we functioned at all before he came along, doesn't it?

Laney shook her head. "I think I've fallen down the rabbit hole."

"Nope," Teague said, more cheerful than he had been, now that Quinn had agreed to take it on. "But you are in Cutter's world now. And you'll find things go smoother if you just accept that. He's got his own sort of code, and a way of making sure we all follow it."

"And when we don't, things tend to go haywire," Quinn said, his tone only half joking.

"And when you do?"

"Then things seem to work out."

"You'll see," Teague said at Laney's expression. "But the most important thing is, you'll know for sure about Amber."

And he could tell by the change in those expressive cinnamon eyes that he'd managed to say the right thing.

And Foxworth had a new case.

Chapter 6

"I'm not sure of Edward's last name. His aunt's name was Reed. Nancy Reed." She grimaced. "I always thought it was nice he was willing to help her out picking up her dog at my old shop. Not every guy's secure enough to be walking around with a three-pound Yorkie with a pink bow."

"I'd be afraid I'd break it," Teague said. "Or drop it."

"He was always very gentle with her. I think that's why I…"

Her voice trailed off.

"Trusted him?" Quinn asked.

She looked miserable as she nodded.

Teague couldn't think of a thing to say that would make her feel better. Nothing had ever really made him feel better about Terri, so maybe the words didn't exist.

"Can you tell us anything else about him?"

She'd already given a good description of him to Tyler Hewitt, their tech genius, who had used his own software, tweaked even further by former Foxworth client Dane Burdette's company, to produce a very lifelike image of the man. Two, actually, one with and one without the ball cap with a boat on the front that Laney said he'd been wearing that day at the mall; people tended to focus on things like that. Printed on photo paper, you'd swear they were actual photographs of him. She'd been more observant than she'd realized, once she got into it, Teague thought. She'd remembered not just the cap but a mole behind his right ear and a small indentation over his left eyebrow.

"And I think Peachy may have bitten him once," she'd said. "He had a couple of little scars on his right hand."

"I wish I could be more help about him," Laney said now, sounding upset with herself.

"You gave a great description," Teague said.

"I feel so…self-absorbed. I never really noticed him that much at all, until he asked me out. Colleen, my boss and trainer at the shop there, usually handled the drop-offs and pickups, because she knew all the customers."

Teague's gaze flicked to Quinn, who gave him a barely perceptible nod. He was clearly giving Teague the lead on this, and Teague wasn't sure how that made him feel.

"Did she ever say anything to you about him?"

"I've been trying to remember," she said. "She never gossiped, said it wasn't good business. The only thing I can think of was that once after he picked up Peachy for his aunt, I said how thoughtful that was. She laughed, and said something about him knowing where his bread was buttered. I'm not sure what she meant."

"How about the aunt? Ever see or meet her?"

"Once. She was older than I expected, he's only in his thirties. I think she might be Edward's great-aunt, really." She started to go on, then stopped.

"Laney?" Teague prompted.

"I don't want to be mean," she said. "And it doesn't have anything to do with Amber."

"We need everything you can tell us. For Amber's sake," Quinn said. "Let us decide if there's a connection. It's what we do."

Laney sighed.

"She was older than I expected, but trying to hide it. I think she'd had surgery on her face. It had that kind of tight, wide-eyed look. But her hands...they were old."

Teague flicked another glance at Quinn, saw he'd picked up on the two things Teague had.

"What kind of car did he drive?"

Laney blinked. "I... Uh, a racy little import. You know, one of those classics-brought-back kind of things. Red."

Something in her tone made Teague ask, "You didn't like it?"

"A bit much for me. I'm more of a utilitarian kind of person."

"Did the aunt impress you as well-off?" Quinn asked.

Laney frowned "Wealthy, you mean? I suppose. She lived in a nice neighborhood. She did have diamond earrings, and a big ring on her right hand the one time I saw her, but it's not like she was dripping in them. Nice clothes. I didn't see her car. And if she did have plastic surgery, I suppose she must be. Why?"

"Diamonds, nice clothes, nephew drives a fancy car and knows where his bread is buttered."

Laney's eyes widened as Teague ran through the list. "You think he was just helping her out because he gets money from her?"

"Or plans to," Teague said. "If she's older, he may be playing a long game."

She got there quickly. "Expecting to inherit?"

"It's been done."

Her nose wrinkled in distaste. Teague liked her for that. Or he just liked the cute way she did it.

Slapping that thought back, he made himself focus. "Anything else about him? Did he live with his aunt?"

"I'm not sure. She lived near the U-District."

"The university?" Teague asked. "Good hunting ground if you're a thirty-plus-year-old guy into fresh-out-of-high-school women."

Again her nose wrinkled. She muttered something under her breath that sounded like "ew." Teague suppressed a smile and wondered what the hell he was finding so amusing about all this.

"Wouldn't Amber be too old for him, then? She's my age."

Teague couldn't picture anybody over sixteen thinking Laney Adams was too old. Too hot, maybe.

"Never mind," Laney said, answering herself. "For a woman who looks like Amber, what guy wouldn't make an exception?"

Teague was glad she'd gotten there on her own, because he had a feeling anything he would have said would have come out wrong.

"Did Amber have a passport?" Quinn asked.

"I don't think so. But she had one of the travel ID cards. We used to go up to Victoria sometimes, at Christmas. Figured it was as close as we'd ever get to Christmas in London."

"So she could have made the trip, technically."

"Yes," Laney admitted. "And I'm not saying she wouldn't, just that I can't believe she'd fly someplace that's only a three-hour drive."

"People in love change," Teague said carefully.

"Amen," Quinn said dryly.

Teague grinned at his boss, admitting the statement had been double-edged.

"And thankfully so," Quinn added, with a smile Teague

had come to know, an inwardly directed expression of pure love that made clear his thoughts were of the woman who had so changed his life.

"I know they do," Laney said, her voice tentative, as if she didn't want to interrupt Quinn's pleasant musings. "But Amber never did. And I've been through a lot of guys with her. She's always had guys after her. But she never blew me off for one of them."

"Until now. With Edward. If that's what's happened," Teague added carefully.

"Yes."

"And you didn't go out with him. Wouldn't." Teague hadn't meant to ask that, but he'd been saying a few things he hadn't meant to lately.

"I told you, I wasn't attracted."

Quinn seemed to ponder that. "Good-looking guy, nice car, money, potentially a lot of money."

He sounded like he was only musing out loud, but Laney answered somewhat defensively, "I don't need money, or things, or even looks, but character and kindness and honesty. I'm really picky."

"And Amber isn't."

And there it was, Teague thought. Damn, Quinn was good at this. Laney drew back, looking almost hurt at first, but then thoughtful.

"No," she finally said, very softly. "She isn't. Particular, but not picky. A difference she often pointed out to me."

I'll take picky, Teague thought. *What could be better than knowing a picky woman had picked you?*

He caught himself again, wondering where the hell this tendency to personalize every damn thing had come from. This was work, this was a job, and he'd better attend to it or he was going to royally mess it up.

He'd promised her they'd find Amber, one way or another.

And that was what he intended to do. All he intended to do. Laney was vulnerable, hurting, and his screwy reaction to her was just his protective instincts in overdrive.

To prove it, he focused completely on the matter at hand as Quinn worked out the next steps. Foxworth was on a case, and that was where his unruly mind would stay.

Chapter 7

"Why didn't you tell me?" Hayley asked.

Laney looked at the woman who had so quickly become more than just a client since she'd first brought Cutter to her several months ago. She had stopped in just after Laney had opened up this morning, and had obviously talked to Quinn.

"You seemed really distracted yesterday," she said.

Hayley made a face. "Well, you're right about that. I'm a wreck about meeting the boss for the first time. Somehow I got it in my head the right clothes would make a difference, make me relax. Didn't work."

Laney stifled a laugh, then said, "And I thought Quinn was the boss. Teague said Charlie's the organization, logistics and money side."

"Genius burns," Hayley said wryly.

"And you've never met before?"

"No. Charlie's headquartered in St. Louis, near where they

grew up, and prefers to stay there. Quinn's only here because he loves this part of the country."

"Well, and you."

Hayley smiled then, a bright, flashing smile of pure and utter happiness. "Yes. And me."

Laney felt a stab of…not envy—she liked Hayley too much for that—but perhaps longing. She supposed most women dreamed of having what Hayley had found, a strong, steady man like Quinn who would go to the ends of the earth for her.

And that's what gets us into trouble, she thought. Like Amber.

"We'll find her," Hayley said, accurately reading her thoughts. "I promise. Nobody's better at this than Foxworth."

"I didn't give you much to go on," Laney said ruefully. She'd spent most of last night trying not to get her hopes up. "I know so little about the guy."

"We have an amazing research team that can find darn near anything, or anyone. They can look in places most people don't even know exist."

"That sounds a bit…something."

Hayley laughed. "Foxworth's built up a lot of goodwill in a lot of different places over the years. It pays off."

"What a strange operation," Laney said. "You help anybody who needs it?"

"No," Hayley said. "Not just anybody. People on the high road, who tried to do the right thing in the right way, but ran up against a roadblock they couldn't get over or around, a block that shouldn't be there in the first place. Sometimes groups, but individuals mostly, who have fought hard on their own but can't keep going, financially, physically or emotionally. People fighting decisions made against them for no better reason than political expediency. Or stupidity. The powers that be, or petty tyrants throwing their weight around, or bigger types of corruption. That's what Foxworth fights."

Laney couldn't miss the passion in Hayley's voice. She might be the most recent to join Foxworth, through Quinn, but she was clearly as dedicated as the rest of them. And if that was truly their cause, she could understand that.

"Sorry," Hayley said with a smile. "I didn't mean to launch on you."

"You don't have to apologize for believing in what you do," Laney said, meaning it. "Teague said you worked on referral only, though."

Hayley nodded. "Word of mouth is the best advertising, and the only kind we rely on. Well, and now Cutter, since he seems to have such a knack."

Laney laughed. "I still can't believe Quinn really decided to help me because of what Cutter did."

"It took us all a while to realize the dog knows what he's doing. And the Foxworth crew is an unlikely bunch to put their trust in four paws, but they've learned he's usually right." Hayley shook her head. "Sometimes I think he's not really a dog, but some magical being in disguise."

"He certainly communicates better than any dog I've ever known."

"He knows a lot more human than we know dog, that's for sure," Hayley agreed with a laugh.

Laney picked at a thread that had worked loose on her shirt. "Teague was very kind."

"He's a good guy."

"He really seemed to understand how I feel. Because of his sister."

Hayley went still. "He told you about Terri?"

Laney nodded. "How she vanished while he was deployed, and was never found. And how he feels guilty for not being here to protect her. Of course, his parents didn't help, blaming him."

For a long, silent moment Hayley just stared at her.

"What?" Laney finally asked.

"Teague," she said, "never talks to anyone about that. I don't think even Quinn knows as much as you just said. I certainly didn't."

Laney stared in turn. "You didn't?"

Hayley shook her head. "I knew his sister had disappeared, but I had no idea he felt like that, or worse, that his parents blamed him. No wonder he's not close to his mother now."

"I think she was the worst," Laney said. "I got the idea his father just shut down after."

Even as she spoke, her mind was racing. She believed Teague never talked about his sister, it would explain the painful sound of his voice. She'd had the feeling then he hadn't talked about it in a while, but she hadn't realized "a while" meant never.

And yet he had told her.

It was disconcerting, to say the least.

"Teague is the most cheerful guy I know," Hayley said. "Always with a quip, the one who lightens the mood. I knew there was another side to him, deeper, but he hides it so well...."

She focused on Laney. And the speculation in her vivid green eyes was hard to miss.

Oh, don't go there, please!

Her sudden internal recoil startled her. Shouldn't she be flattered that the guy let down enough to share an awful, painful story? That he felt enough empathy for her, and her situation, to do something he never did, share a part of himself he always kept hidden?

If she was honest, she had to admit she was flattered. Problem was, maybe she was *too* flattered. Teague was an attractive guy, she'd been alone a long time now, and he came with as much of a guarantee as you could get with a guy these days; the benefit of a thorough background check by Foxworth.

Instead of a casual, thoughtless "he seems like a nice guy, go for it" tossed off by an unthinking friend.

It stabbed at her again, the guilt, sharp and merciless. How on earth had Teague survived this for so long? Hayley said he was the most cheerful guy she knew; how did he do it? Was it just a facade, or had he really found a way to…obviously not forget, but live with it?

"It's that guy thing," Hayley said, shaking her out of her thoughts. "Compartmentalization. They really are able to do that, much better than I am, anyway."

Laney drew back, eyes wide. How had she known exactly what she was thinking? "You are as perceptive as your dog. And I trust you to realize I mean that as a compliment."

Hayley laughed. "Oh, I know. And it is a compliment, to be compared to that rascal in the perception department, since he's uncannily good at it."

Hayley's cell phone rang, and from her instant smile Laney guessed the lilting, lively bit of music was assigned to Quinn's calls. She answered, and Laney tactfully turned away, giving her some privacy. But Hayley mostly listened instead of talking. When she finally spoke, it was only to say "I'll tell her." Then a pause, an even wider smile, followed by "I love you, too."

She tucked the phone back into an outside pocket on her bag. Then she turned to face Laney straight on.

"We have a lead," she said.

"I can't believe you guys did this so quickly."

Teague glanced at Laney, who was sitting in the passenger seat of his SUV once more. They were on their way to SeaTac airport with recent photos of Amber in hand. Quinn was a big believer in HUMINT, human intelligence, or as Teague called it, boots on the ground, a holdover from his corps days.

But it was Hayley who had quietly convinced Quinn to add another facet to their approach in non-hazardous situations: letting the involved party participate if that was what they wanted. No one, she said, was as invested in the case as the person themselves, and the urgency and emotion they displayed sometimes nudged people over onto their side, into empathy, by the sheer force of it. It made sense, and Teague had seen it work a couple of times now. He'd already had a lot of respect for Hayley after how she'd handled their actions the night she'd become collateral damage in their operation, and this only added to it.

Laney Adams, he thought, was cut from similar cloth. She might have been crying at first, but not since, and there was a steely determination in her, now that she knew she wasn't alone. He suspected it would be wise not to underestimate her, now that she had a course set. And she'd made it clear she wanted to be involved every step of the way.

He'd reluctantly volunteered to be the one to pick up Laney. It only made sense, given he was the one who had brought her problem to them. And he didn't quite understand his own reluctance. He hadn't been happy about pouring his guts out to her about Terri, but it had seemed necessary at the time. He wasn't much for looking backward and dwelling on things he couldn't change, a lesson learned in the hardest of ways with his sister. But he was still uneasy, and if it wouldn't have been odd enough to draw attention, he would have opted out.

He'd even thought of suggesting Hayley, using the girl thing as an excuse, but Quinn had so obviously assumed he'd want to be handling this one that it made him stop and wonder why he didn't.

Maybe it was just that this one reminded him too much of Terri. True, Amber was an adult, not a sixteen-year-old girl, and there had been some contact, at least, via the texts, and they had a clue who she might be with....

Yeah, right. Cases are exactly alike, he thought wryly.

That excuse shattered, he wasn't sure where that left him. Except in the car alone with Laney Adams, who unsettled him far too much. And as much as he didn't want to admit it, that was likely what had him wishing someone else would be doing this. Somewhere along the line he'd turned into a coward, wanting to avoid a situation that made him uncomfortable.

"Teague?"

He'd never answered her, he realized. In fact, he had to think for a second to remember exactly what her words had been.

"Sorry. Thinking." *Don't ask me about what.* "Yes, our guys are good."

"It helps that they even looked." Her voice was harsh, even a touch angry.

"The cops are understaffed, they have to play the odds," he said. "And the odds say that an adult who's still, as far as they know, texting her best friend, is okay."

"And the friend who thinks something's wrong with those texts is imagining things."

"They have to justify the time they spend on cases. They have a lot on their plate. When they're dealing with murders, shootings, robberies and the like, there's not a lot of time left for..."

He'd been about to say "lesser things," but managed to bite it back before the words got out.

"I get it. I know they have priorities. And they did try. They took the report, entered it into their system, put out flyers and released them to the press. But it pretty much ended there. I don't really blame them, and I wouldn't be upset if I weren't so worried." She sighed audibly. "I would have hired a private investigator, if I could afford it. But everything I have went into starting the shop."

"Well, you've got in essence a team of them now," Teague said.

"And you really do this for nothing? How does Foxworth afford it?"

"Charlie."

"Charlie," Laney said, "must truly be a genius."

"In many ways. Plus being the only person on earth I've seen Quinn intimidated by."

"That is a frightening thought."

Laney laughed as she said it, and Teague was grateful the moment of tension seemed to have passed.

"I still can't believe Amber got on a plane to Vancouver, though," she said. "She seriously hates to fly. She got groped really badly once, and she's never flown since unless she had no other choice."

"All we know for certain is she bought a ticket," he cautioned. "Or at least, her credit card did."

Laney was looking at him; he could feel it, without even taking his eyes off the road in front of them. And when she spoke he heard the underlying note of fear in her voice, although he could tell she was trying to hide it.

"Are you saying somebody else bought it in her name?"

"The ticket was purchased online."

"So all they needed was the card in hand."

"Yes."

"If she is with Edward, why didn't he buy it?"

"Good question."

"They said it was a round-trip ticket, though, right?"

Teague nodded. He didn't point out that anybody paying attention these days would know a one-way ticket, especially one for an imminent flight, automatically drew more attention.

"So she would have been back by now, if she really had taken that trip."

"If she kept to that schedule, yes. It's taking our team a bit longer to find if the ticket was actually used. Passenger manifests are kept pretty close these days."

She went silent then, but Teague sensed her mind was still racing. It was as if having Foxworth on her side had helped her go from helpless flailing to critical thinking, and now she was catching up in a hurry.

"It's asking a lot to hope some ticket or airline agent will remember having seen her two weeks ago, isn't it?"

"Yes. But there's always a chance."

"She is kind of distinctive." She paused, gave him a sideways glance. "By that I mean beautiful. Stop-you-in-your-tracks stunning."

He'd seen the photo they'd chosen to show, seen the others Laney had. He couldn't deny Amber was a beautiful woman. Hair the golden color of her name, hazel eyes also more gold than anything. He preferred the warmth of cinnamon-brown, himself, but there was no denying Amber would have been noticed by any guy around.

Amber and Laney together would be enough to turn heads.

"You two must have looked like flip sides of the same coin."

"Amber's much prettier," she said. It sounded like a reflex, an automatic response. Because she believed it? Because she'd said it so many times it actually was a reflex?

A third possibility occurred to him.

"If you were fishing for a compliment, consider it landed."

Out of the corner of his eye he saw her head snap up. "No! I wasn't. It's a simple fact. I'm all right, but Amber is exquisite."

He couldn't deny the genuineness of her quick response; she really hadn't been fishing. But what she said still surprised him.

All right? Is that really what you think, that you're just "all right"?

It wasn't just him, he told himself. Any guy breathing would think she was a lot more than "all right."

But any guy wasn't working for her—that's how they were taught at Foxworth, you were working directly for the client—so he'd better keep his head straight.

No matter how difficult the woman sitting beside him made that.

Chapter 8

You two must have looked like flip sides of the same coin.

His words kept echoing in her head. Even though he had graciously said it was a compliment, she knew he was just reacting to her own words, in that reassuring way some men had. She appreciated it, but she also had a mirror. And dozens of pictures of her and Amber together. Reality was.

He had meant, of course, her hair, as dark as Amber's was light. And her eyes, she supposed, ordinary brown where Amber's were a striking golden-brown that matched her name.

He had to have meant that, because to think he'd meant to say she, also, was beautiful would open a door that had best stay closed. No matter how tempted she might be to not just open it, but to race right through. Because he was the kind of man who stopped her in her tracks.

They drove across the newer of the two—she never thought of them as twins, because they were so different—Narrows bridges. They didn't stop for the toll, so she assumed Fox-worth had a pass account.

She stayed silent, using the distraction of the expansive view of the waterway for a brief escape. She tried to tell herself this was just because she was finally doing something concrete to look for Amber, that that was what had her all wound up and on the edge of her seat. But she tried to always be honest with herself, at least, and had to admit it was more than that.

Stop it. You're not some brainless teenager all fizzed up over hanging with a good-looking guy. You need to be thinking about Amber, and Amber alone.

On the other side he negotiated the traffic and transitions to the northbound freeway easily, reminding her he'd grown up here, on the city side. He seemed willing to preserve her silence, not surprising if he really thought she'd been hoping for some flattery before.

"I truly wasn't fishing for a compliment." The words slipped out, and Laney was wide-eyed with disbelief that she'd actually said them.

"Okay."

"People look at Amber. Not just men, but women. Who can be pretty catty about it, frankly. But I reconciled myself long ago to the fact that Amber has what makes people notice her."

"So do neon signs."

She blinked.

"Some men—not boys, but men—prefer a little subtlety," Teague said, his eyes on the road, as if this were simply some conversation to fill the time until they got to the airport. "The kind of slow realization of beauty, and an inside that's more attractive than the outside."

Laney swallowed. "Wow. If that's a line, it's a hell of a good one. I'll bet it works wonders."

He flashed her a glance then, and she saw the gleam of

humor in his cool blue eyes, and it was confirmed by the up-ward curve of one side of his mouth into a crooked smile.

"Think so? I'll have to try it."

"Do," she said, happy she hadn't been self-deluded enough to believe it.

"Helps that I meant it," he said.

Okay, so she was happy she hadn't been self-deluded enough to believe it was meant to apply to her.

She relapsed into silence, wondering what it was about this man that had her so edgy. She realized on the thought that she had part of the answer right there. This man. For he was that. Not one of the boys he'd referred to rather dismis-sively, but a man. One who had come through hard times, loss, even war. One who had worked hard to get where he was. One who had gone through all that and grown past that carefree sort of youth that she saw so often in men Teague's age and even older.

Never having faced what he faced, they had stayed young, callow, immature.

Teague had grown up.

They pulled into the short-term parking structure at SeaTac, found a spot not too far out, made sure they had the photos of Amber and Edward, and headed into the terminal. They made their way to the check-in desk at the airline Am-ber's credit card had showed the purchase from, waited in a thankfully short line this weekday afternoon and finally got up to the counter.

The first woman, young and pretty in an Amber sort of way, eyed Teague appreciatively, and gave Laney the kind of assessing once-over she'd been more used to getting standing beside Amber. She knew the look, Laney thought. *Checking for a ring first, then deciding if I'm attractive enough to hang on to this hunk, or if she might have a chance.*

And that was another difference, she thought. If it was

Amber they knew there was no chance, these predatory females. With her, there was always a shot. It hadn't always been easy, being Amber's best friend. But she had such a generous soul, and never played up her advantage, at least not in Laney's presence, more than once using her considerable charm and attractiveness to include Laney where she might otherwise have been ignored. She was the very best kind of friend, and that's all that mattered now.

She focused on that, crowding out the crazy thoughts that wanted to romp through her stupid brain at the very thought of hanging on to the hunk beside her in any way.

But it seemed they were getting nowhere; nobody recognized the photos. They went to each agent working today, learned that many had this shift on the day of the flight Amber's purchase had listed, but no one remembered the striking blonde.

Despite knowing it had been a long shot, Laney had let her hopes build; she knew by the way she was feeling more disheartened with every negative answer. She began to let Teague take the lead, ask the questions, while she inwardly dealt with her disappointment.

"Wait, you said you were from Foxworth?"

The way the man at the last window said it snapped Laney out of her personal misery.

"Yes," Teague answered.

"I know you guys. You helped my cousin a couple of years ago. Made the case against the guy who killed his dog because he crossed a picket line to drive a delivery truck."

Laney smothered a gasp at such cruelty.

"The chemo," Teague said, clearly knowing exactly what the man was referring to.

"Yeah. Who knows how many might have died eventually if he hadn't made that delivery, but that didn't seem to matter." He smiled. "Except to you guys."

"Still sorry about the dog," Teague said. "Actually, even more now. I didn't really realize back then just how much a dog could mean."

Cutter, Laney thought. He did now because of Cutter. Had the poor man never had a dog in his life? She couldn't imagine that, even though she knew there were millions who didn't. Teague just seemed like the type who would have a good dog at his side, hunting dog maybe; one who would love him with that unconditional devotion only dogs could give.

People love was so much more complicated, with feelings and baggage and overthinking involved.

She stopped her own thoughts sharply. Teague was here helping her to find Amber, and there was no time for silly inattentiveness just because she was in prolonged proximity to an attractive man for the first time since she'd moved "to the country," as her mother persisted in calling it.

"—give me one of those, and I'll make sure everybody on every shift sees it. Skycaps and gate people, too. There's one guy, Willy, he's a hound, if a woman who looked like that went by him, he'd notice."

"Thanks," Teague said, handing the man a copy of the photograph. "Phone number's on the back, if you find anything."

"Thank you," Laney echoed.

The man shrugged. "You guys were there for my family. Least I can do. You want, I can put it on the employee bulletin board. Somebody I miss might have seen her."

"That would be great," Teague said.

The man tapped the picture against his fingers as he met Teague's gaze. "You Foxworth guys did all that for nothing. Amazing."

"Not for nothing," Teague said with a smile. "Now you're helping us because of it. That's how it works. Why it works."

"What an awful story," Laney said as they moved on.

"It was. That was my first case," Teague said.

"And he still remembers and wants to help. Does that happen often?" Laney asked.

"Sometimes it happens that way. Sometimes we call on people ourselves. We keep track of particular skills or knowledge the people we've helped have. They're usually more than willing to help out if they can. Nobody forgets what it feels like to be in the kind of position Foxworth helps them out of."

"I certainly won't." She said it quietly, but fervently.

"We will find Amber," he said. "And we won't stop until we do. Ever."

She looked at him as they headed toward the baggage and transport area on the lower level. "Ever?"

"Once Foxworth takes on a case, we keep going until we get results. They may not be exactly what the client hoped for, or the news we find may not be good, but we will resolve it. No matter how long it takes. Unless the client tells us to stop."

"Has a client ever done that?"

"Once or twice. For their own reasons. And since they're in charge, what they say goes, barring any criminal activity being involved."

"And if there is?"

"We have a very good relationship with law enforcement. We intend to keep it that way."

Curious now, she tilted her head as she looked at him. "What's the longest case Foxworth has had?"

"Years. Quinn's got one from three years ago that was never resolved. He still lugs it around in his head. And Rafe…"

He stopped, shaking his head. They were at the ground transportation kiosk, and he was into the routine with the photo again before she could ask who Rafe was. Again, no one remembered seeing the striking blonde, and at least one of the guys fervently agreed that if he had, he would have remembered.

They stopped at the baggage claim and did the same with the skycaps, and Laney finally remembered something she thought might be useful, describing the bright, hot-pink leather luggage tags Amber had favored.

When at last they stepped outside, Laney looked with dismay at the lineup of cabs and busses. "This could take a while."

"We don't have to check individual drivers. Quinn's got a contact at each of the licensed companies, and he'll have Ty or Liam do that by email. I just wanted to—"

He stopped as his cell rang. He and Laney stepped to one side, out of the flow of pedestrians along the wide sidewalk in front of the terminal as he answered. He glanced at Laney as he listened to the caller, said "okay" a couple of times, then glanced at his watch. Then he said goodbye and disconnected.

The next thing he did was slip the remaining few copies of Amber's photo they had left into the inside pocket of his battered leather jacket.

"Why do I get the feeling we're done here?"

He gave her a reassuring smile that normally would have done just that. If it were anything less than Amber missing and in trouble...

"We are," he said. "Tyler was able to confirm Amber's ticket was never used, her name wasn't on any passenger manifest, and Charlie just let Quinn know there's no record of Amber entering Canada."

Laney was disheartened but tried to hide it, to keep her tone light. "The ubiquitous Charlie again?"

"Charlie's got contacts high up in Canada." Teague flashed her that grin that so turned her insides upside down. "Hell, Charlie's got contacts everywhere."

She smiled, but her heart wasn't in it. She'd hoped they'd find the answer here, that someone would have remembered seeing Amber happily boarding a plane, her distaste for flying overwhelmed by the joy of falling in love. She should have known it wouldn't be that easy. Clearly Teague hadn't expected it to be; he didn't seem at all upset. And that seemed to help, somewhat to her surprise.

"We're just getting started, Laney," Teague said gently. "This is just the eliminating of possibilities."

"I know. I just...hoped."

It sounded silly, now that she'd said it. Naive. Things just didn't work out that tidily in life.

Not in hers, anyway.

"Quinn wants us back at Foxworth."

She nodded, not wanting to risk speaking just now.

"We'll go back on the ferry," he said decisively. "We can grab something to eat aboard."

"I'm sorry," she said, feeling suddenly contrite as she realized Teague had already put in a lot of time on this, from the time he'd tried to do Hayley a favor to now. "I didn't realize how late it was getting. What time do you get off?"

He flicked her a glance and a grin. "Whenever Quinn says I do. When we're on a case, there are no limits."

She blinked then frowned. Foxworth might work for free, but the people who did the work had to eat. "You do get paid, don't you?" she asked.

Teague nodded. "And it's a great gig. Sometimes we work like crazy, long hours, sometimes 24/7, for weeks on end, but sometimes we go for a couple of weeks with nothing but free time."

"Sounds...unpredictable."

Teague laughed. "It's no nine-to-five, that's for sure. I like it that way."

They continued toward Seattle, taking the off-ramp toward the ferry to one of the islands on the other side, and from there they'd take the bridge to the peninsula and then on to Foxworth. There was a bit of traffic, enough that Laney was glad she wasn't driving, and she stayed silent to let him pay attention to the process.

His cell phone rang again just as they were negotiating the turn into the ferry holding lots. Again he answered, listened, acknowledged and disconnected, this time all through an earpiece he slipped over his right ear.

He waited until he'd paid the fare and they'd been directed into the line to wait. He glanced at his watch, said they had about ten minutes to go before loading. Then he turned off the engine and twisted in his seat to look at her.

"We know who your guy is," he said.

Chapter 9

Laney might have been disappointed they hadn't found answers at the airport, but she was still astonished at how quickly Foxworth was putting pieces together.

"You found Edward?"

He nodded. "We think so. Tyler put all the pieces together in his own little piece of the web, and came up with the right name. Photo's almost a perfect match to your sketch."

"His sketch, you mean. He's the one who did it."

"From your description. He's sending a copy of his driver's license photo."

He glanced down at his phone, nodded then held it up for her to see. Even prepared, it was a little shocking to see the man's face.

"Yes! Yes, that's him, that's Edward."

"His full name is Edward Page."

"Yes," she said again, this time with a sharp nod. "I

couldn't remember before, but now that you say it I remember Barbara once calling out to him with that name."

"Then we have him. I'll call Quinn back and confirm, then it will be only a matter of time."

Her mind had kicked into overdrive again, Teague could see it. He wondered how long it would take her to reach the conclusion his mind had leaped to when Quinn had said the airplane ticket to Vancouver had never been used. Not long, he suspected. She was smart, and quick, and always thinking.

It was when they were onboard the ferry back to the other side—in addition to the availability of food, he'd thought the pleasant boat ride might be soothing for her—when she finally said something about it, and her words told him she'd realized right away, maybe as soon as he had, the implications of the unused ticket.

"Will the police think this was enough? Would buying a ticket and not using it tip them over into believing something's really wrong?"

"Might get them to do another round of press releases, might move it a bit higher on the list."

"Might."

"Depends on what their caseload is right now. And I'm guessing with that string of shootings downtown, their focus is there."

She sighed.

"They have to staff for the likely, not the possible," Teague said.

"I know, I know. Sometimes I even have myself half-convinced I'm overreacting. But it just nags at me, because Amber wouldn't do this. If it truly was a normal romantic getaway, she'd have been texting me at the least, all about it. We would have made a shopping expedition for clothes. She would have wanted to share her excitement. That's just who she is."

"So we keep looking."

She gave him a sideways look. "I'm going to feel pretty silly if it all turns out to be my best friend having met the love of her life or something."

"It's a lot better than some of the possible alternatives." He probably shouldn't have reminded her of that, Teague thought. But when she answered, her words and tone eased his qualm.

"And I'll be delighted to feel silly. Not to have wasted your time, though."

"If you're put at ease, it's not a waste."

"Foxworth is a most unusual organization."

"Yes."

He left it at that, because it was the simple truth.

They left the car and went up from the car deck inside to the small restaurant, quickly selecting a couple of bowls of the famous clam chowder. When they were done with the rich soup, they stepped outside to watch the water slip by. The wind had picked up on the middle of the sound, kicking up whitecaps, but the wide, solid boat churned through with a minimum of fuss or reaction.

"These are the only boats Amber will voluntarily get on," Laney said. "Anything else makes her violently seasick."

"They are pretty steady," Teague acknowledged.

"Amber's the only person I've ever seen who could get queasy standing on a dock."

Teague chuckled. "It's all about the idea for some people, I guess. Or maybe the visual."

Laney smiled. Lifted her hand to brush back an errant strand of dark hair caught by the breeze of their passage. Tilted her head back to lift her face to the sun, still warm in these last days of summer. For a moment she closed her eyes.

She had to be tired, Teague thought, free for the moment to study her openly. Tired of feeling helpless. And responsible. He knew too well how wearing that was. And yet she'd insisted on coming along, when she could have just as easily stayed home and waited. He admired her quiet determination, the fortitude that had enabled her to start a business at a time when there were few riskier things to do, her loyalty to her friend, her gentleness and love for the animals she cared for, her generosity to the creatures not lucky enough to have a home. He admired many things about Laney Adams.

And in that moment, there in the sun, with her thick lashes resting on her cheeks, her thick, dark ponytail waving slightly, Teague admitted there was more to his urge to help this woman than that it was just what Foxworth does.

The warning bell that went off in his mind then was oddly distant, would have been easy to ignore, if it hadn't been for the fact that she was, in fact, a client. That was a line he didn't dare cross. He didn't know how Quinn would deal with that, and he didn't want to be the first to find out. Hayley may have softened him a bit personally, but the leader was as tough as he'd ever been. He had high standards for Foxworth, and that hadn't changed a bit. Teague doubted it ever would. It was one of the things that made him proud to be part of it all.

They were two-thirds of the way over when his cell chirped a text message. There was a stretch in the middle of the crossing where reception was almost nonexistent, so he checked the time sent. It had been, in fact, about eight minutes ago. He quickly read the message. When he finished, Laney had opened her eyes and focused on him.

"More confirmation," he said. "She didn't go to Canada."

"What?"

"Those texts you got were sent from here. Or there, rather," he finished, gesturing with a thumb over his shoulder, back toward Seattle.

She took the news steadily.

"Charlie again?"

"No. This was from Liam. You haven't met him yet, he's

been off at a seminar, but he's got ways we don't even ask about so Quinn asked him to check this out."

"Handy guy to have around."

"On your side, anyway. He's a tech head, almost as good as Ty, but also field-trained. He's our best tracker, both virtually and in reality. Looks as innocent as a puppy, and he uses that, too. He could have easily gone the other way if Quinn hadn't plucked him out of a mess of trouble and put him to work for us."

"Your Quinn seems to have a very good eye for talent."

He blinked. Had that been a compliment, in a subtle way? Or was she just being polite, making conversation?

Doesn't matter. Eyes on the prize, and that does not *mean her.*

Chiding himself seemed to work, for the moment at least. Odd, he'd never had a problem keeping things cool before. Of course, with Quinn and Hayley fairly trumpeting love and joy all over, and watching their last two clients, Kayla and Dane Burdette, who had been in love since childhood, nearly lose themselves then put it back together again, he supposed it was inevitable that everyone not settled would feel a bit unsettled.

And that last phrase sounded so silly even in his head that he clamped down further on his errant thoughts.

As they disembarked from the ferry and headed toward Foxworth, Teague pondered the fact that Laney hadn't mentioned going back to the police with this latest bit of information. He wondered if she thought it wouldn't make any difference, or if she was concerned about how they'd gotten the data.

"Our concern is finding Amber," he finally said once they were on the road that led back toward the less populated areas. "And only that."

"Thank you for that," she said, her voice wobbling just slightly. Teague went on as much to reassure her as to explain.

"Chain of evidence or procedural protocols aren't limitations for us. We do things aboveboard and in ways that will help the police when we can, but our bottom line isn't theirs. We worry about the victims, not what will stand up in court."

That seemed to steady her. She nodded in almost fierce agreement.

"What about the bad guys?" she asked.

"We have our own ways of dealing with them, too. Quinn's the toughest guy you'll find when it comes to people who hurt innocents."

"Because he was one of the victims, once," she said.

"And he doesn't like anybody feeling the way he did then. Helpless. Like nobody's doing the right thing, like nobody cares about anything except their own agenda or advancement. Backroom deals that make the dealers feel good but hurt the people they're supposed to protect set him off like nothing I've ever seen."

"I think I quite admire Quinn and his foundation."

"So do I," Teague said.

"You're rightfully proud to be part of it."

He smiled at that as he made the last turn, onto the road that would take them back to Foxworth.

"Did that make it easier to leave the service?"

The unexpected question threw him. "Nothing could make that easy," he said, his tone sharp.

"I didn't say easy. I said easier."

Abashed, he muttered a quick "Guess I'm still a little touchy about it. But yes, if it wasn't for Foxworth I probably would have stuck it out. And had to numb myself to the realities of what was happening around me."

She said nothing more, and a few minutes later he was parking in Foxworth's gravel lot outside the green building. In less than a minute the door swung open and Cutter came racing out. Seconds later his dark head was at her window, his intense gaze fixed on her as she smiled at the dog.

"Is he always the first to greet visitors?"

"You're not a visitor to him. You're his personal concern until this is resolved."

She blinked. "You really do take him seriously."

"We've seen what happens if we don't," Teague said wryly. "Liam's family breeds dogs.... He grew up with dozens of them over the years. He says Cutter's not really a dog, he's some sort of alien form of intelligence that's taken on dog form."

Laney laughed as she opened the door and Cutter greeted her happily with a swipe of his tongue over her chin, a wag of his tail, and a short, excited little dance on his paws. She reached out and stroked his head, then curved her fingers to get to that spot below his right ear that made him practically wiggle when she scratched it.

She definitely had the Cutter stamp of approval, he thought.

And he'd be crazier than a loon to make something out of that.

"Teague?"

Quinn's voice boomed down the stairwell as they stepped inside.

"Here," he called back.

"Thought that was your bark. Come on up, we've got something."

"Your bark?" Laney asked as they started up the stairs, Cutter leading the way.

He laughed, pointed at the dog, whose reddish-brown tail waved with every step. "He's got one for everybody. Well, almost. Hayley's got her own, of course, and Quinn. And Rafe rates his own somehow. The rest of us share one."

Laney laughed in turn. "And people say I'm too tuned into dogs. But there is something special about him," she agreed.

"We don't dwell on it too much anymore," Teague said. "That way lies crazy, as Rafe says."

She shook her head, an amused but slightly amazed expression on her face. "Definitely a most unusual organization," she said, echoing her earlier words.

Teague liked the way she said it. He liked the way she looked when she said it. He liked that she looked at him dead-on when she said it.

What he didn't like was the realization of how much he liked it.

Chapter 10

They reached the third-floor office and meeting area, and found Quinn and another man waiting. Cutter trotted ahead, stopped at the table where they'd sat before and waited. Only when they'd joined the two at the table and, at Quinn's gesture, taken seats on the other side, did Cutter walk to his bed beneath one of the expansive windows and curl up comfortably, a dog whose job, for the moment, was done.

"Laney Adams, Tyler Hewitt," Quinn said by way of introduction.

"Hello," Laney said in surprise. She'd thought she'd recognized him; this was the man who'd done the composite of Edward with her, but they'd done it via an online connection. He looked even younger in person, like a kid just out of high school, a little skinny, hair looking like he ran his hands through it a lot, and a small patch of—or a try at—beard under the center of his lower lip.

"I thought you were in St. Louis," she said.

"I was. I got on a plane right after we finished," the young man said. "I'm installing the new work station. While it's going through its own diagnostics, they put me to work on your case."

He sounded excited, Laney thought.

"We'll make a field agent out of you yet," Teague said.

"No, thanks." Tyler gave a shudder that was obviously for effect. "I leave that to you outdoor types."

"Good thing we have Liam, then," Teague shot back. Clearly this was a familiar routine to them both; there was an undercurrent of humor in both their voices.

"Hah." Tyler waved a hand in mock dismissiveness. "He's good enough for an end user of the system, but if you want one *built* you need the real expert."

The reference to the Liam she'd heard about had the tone of a longstanding friendly competition, with the emphasis on the friendly part. It made her believe all the more in the feeling she'd gotten that Foxworth was indeed a family sort of operation, and not one limited by blood.

"You children through?" Quinn asked with a lifted brow. The teasing back and forth stopped instantly. Quinn turned his gaze on Laney. "Sorry. Tyler doesn't get out of St. Louis much, so it's an occasion when he does."

"I didn't mind," she said, meaning it. The quick back and forth had amused her more than anything. At least, as much as anything could when the thing truly consuming her was worry about Amber. "I never had brothers, so I missed out on the male sibling rivalry."

Tyler laughed and gave her a genuine smile, not the slightly awkward one he'd proffered at first. "Quinn said you were really nice. He didn't say how pretty you were, though."

Laney smiled; it was impossible not to in the face of the simple compliment. Teague, meanwhile, made an odd sound, as if a little brother had said something to embarrass him.

"Maybe he assumed," Teague said, "that you would be capable of seeing that for yourself when you met her."

Laney blinked at that. Tyler's compliment had been sweet; Teague's subtler one had sounded more like a challenge. She just wasn't sure who the challenge was aimed at. Fortunately for her peace of mind, Hayley arrived before she could spend too much time dwelling on it.

Laney watched as Quinn greeted Hayley, felt the warmth between them as if it were so big and encompassing it spilled over onto others. She felt a twinge of longing she quashed firmly; this was not the time to moon over what she didn't have.

"Go over what you found, Ty," Quinn said when Hayley had pulled up another chair and joined them.

"Oh. Yeah. Okay." The young man reached for a tablet computer that sat in front of him. "I did some digging after we found out who the guy was." His gaze flicked to Laney. "The Edward guy, I mean. That is his real name."

She kept her wince inward. It hadn't occurred to her he might have lied about that, and she didn't like feeling so naive.

"And he works at North Country Enterprises, just like he said."

"Well, that's something, after that elaborate story he gave me about his office being so beautifully remodeled." She was feeling a bit of relief that she hadn't been completely conned.

"In fact, that's what got me started. Quinn pointed out that with that big government grant they got last year, he should be making decent money, but there wasn't much sign of it. He lives in an apartment in back of his aunt's house, and drives a car that's in her name, judging by the parking tickets I found."

"Maybe she asked him to live there, to help her out," Laney suggested. "And the car's a sort of payback."

"We can't say that's not part of it, it may well be," Quinn agreed. "But tell her the rest."

Tyler went on then. "I found a string of ATM withdrawals of cash. Lots of cash, sometimes thousands at a time. And if there wasn't enough cash to cover it, he went for a cash advance on the credit card linked to the account."

Laney frowned. "From whose account? His own?"

Quinn gave her an approving nod, as if he were pleased she'd asked. "His aunt's. Household account, mostly used to buy groceries, pay for repairs, that kind of thing."

"You think he's ripping her off? His own aunt?"

The idea left a nasty taste in her mouth. From Teague's grimace, she gathered it did him, too. He leaned over to look at the display on the tablet.

"Can't prove she doesn't know," Quinn answered. "He has full access, so it could be with her knowledge."

"We need to talk to her," Hayley said.

"Yes," Teague said. Quinn nodded, but told Ty to finish first.

"It's where the withdrawals were made that turned out to be interesting," Tyler said. "I didn't get it, because I'm not from here, so the names didn't mean anything to me. Except that I couldn't pronounce half of them right."

Teague had been reading the list, and just as Tyler finished speaking he let out a low whistle.

"Casinos," he said.

"Exactly," Quinn agreed.

"So he's gambling with this money?" Laney asked. She wasn't sure if that made her feel better or worse.

"And he's in deep," Tyler said. "Those cash advances, the interest alone would pay my car payment."

"And yet he keeps doing it," Teague said with a shake of his head. "He's headed for big trouble. He can't not see that."

"Willful ignorance?" Quinn said. "Or addiction."

Laney leaned back in her seat. "He's obviously got a problem. But how does this tie in to Amber's disappearance?

Money? It's not like she's rich. She has a small trust fund from her grandfather, but she doesn't get all that much from it. And she can't access the principal for another five years yet, when she's thirty-five."

"That's tough," Tyler said.

"Amber didn't think so. He made his money the hard way, he didn't want her to have everything just handed to her," Laney said. "She used to complain, but as she got older, got the satisfaction of making it on her own, she realized it was for the best. But the trust is rock-solid, there's no way anybody could get at it."

"Let's make that call to his aunt," Quinn said. "We'll keep it low-key and anonymous for now, don't want her warning him if she's in contact."

They decided to have Hayley make the initial call to Edward's aunt—or great-aunt, whichever she was—to keep Laney out of it for now, on the chance Edward might have complained to the woman about her turning away his interest. She would make the call as a prospective client of Laney's mentor.

"I'm a big-dog girl," Hayley said with a laugh, "you'll have to quickly educate me on the appeal of the little ones."

Laney answered several questions from Hayley, things that would let her sound as if she knew what she was talking about. And then she sat and listened as Hayley made contact, and slowly but cleverly worked the call around from her own nonexistent Yorkshire terrier to Mrs. Reed's nephew.

"She's pretty protective of him," Hayley said a few minutes later as she disconnected the call. "She wanted off the phone in a hurry."

Quinn looked thoughtful. "Too protective?"

"You mean like she knows there's something to protect him from?" Laney asked, trying not to read too much into it.

"More like she doesn't want to hear anything bad about him, I think," Hayley said.

"Which makes you wonder if she suspects she might, if she listened," Teague put in.

"Sometimes people know things, in their gut, that they won't consciously acknowledge," Quinn said.

"Because the price of knowing is too high," Hayley said. "Sad. But the only worthwhile thing I got was that she's a little peeved with him just now. He hasn't been calling as he should, and apparently hasn't been home in days. I think she's worried."

"Collateral damage," Teague muttered.

"We may have to go back at her again later," Quinn said. "We'll keep Laney in reserve for that."

Laney nodded.

"What's this?" Teague asked suddenly, pointing at the tablet, where he'd swiped through a couple of pages of Tyler's research.

"Just an automatic notification. I sent him an anonymous generic type email from an ISP stripped address, just to see what happened. That's what I got back, just before you guys got here."

"Teague?" Quinn asked. "What? I haven't seen what he got back."

"It says Page will be out of the office until further notice."

Laney's breath caught. She was trying very hard not to jump to conclusions, but her mind was screaming this was proof they were together. What it didn't resolve was the question of whether Amber was there voluntarily.

Teague read the displayed automated response again as he pulled out his cell phone. He glanced at the time, then dialed a number he was apparently reading from the bottom of the email.

"Hi," he said when someone picked up, "Edward Page, please."

There was a pause while he listened.

"He didn't say anything to me about this. He's supposed to be handling a transaction for me."

Again a pause.

"This is really irritating." He sounded exactly like a demanding customer who was not pleased. "When do you expect him back?"

He listened for a moment longer, muttered a thank-you that sounded less than sincere, and disconnected. Laney was impressed. Whoever had answered, confronted with an apparent unhappy customer, would focus on calming them first. Which meant they were much more likely to answer questions than if he had simply called looking for the man.

But her feelings shifted quickly to dismay when he spoke, his voice grim.

"He's on an unscheduled, unexpected leave as of two weeks ago, something about taking care of a sick relative. They're not sure exactly when he'll be back."

Laney's breath stopped in her throat. Two weeks ago. A week after she'd introduced him to Amber.

And almost exactly when the odd texts had begun.

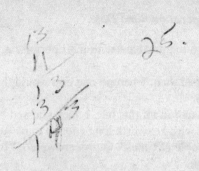

Chapter 11

"It can't be coincidence that he takes off on an unplanned 'vacation' right when Amber goes missing," Teague said.

"Seems unlikely," Quinn agreed. He thought for a moment, then seemed to reach several decisions at once.

"Tyler, do a run-through of our records, see if we have anyone in the database with a connection to North Country, up through third degree. I'm going to go talk to them about Page, and I'd like to have a reason for them to cooperate."

"Third degree?" Laney asked, the first words she'd spoken since the discovery that Edward, too, had, in a way, vanished without warning. She was trying desperately to focus on something else, anything else.

"Someone in house first, a direct connection second, third is somebody with a connection to somebody with a direct connection," Teague explained.

"You keep that kind of information on all your clients?"

"And their families," Teague said.

"They only go into the database with their permission," Hayley added.

"After you've helped them when no one else would, has anybody ever said no?"

Teague glanced at Quinn for that one, Laney guessed because he hadn't been with Foxworth long enough to be sure of the answer. "A couple of times," Quinn answered. "But with very good reason."

"If Quinn called them himself, they'd help out, they just can't risk being in a database. Our security's the best, but nothing's unhackable," Tyler put in.

Laney guessed that Quinn had an interesting catalog of people in his head to reach out to if need be. Probably more interesting than the average sorts Foxworth seemed to help most often.

"You two," Quinn said, indicating her and Teague, "go talk to Amber's family. I know you've spoken to them several times on the phone, Laney, but sometimes a face-to-face has a different effect. You can read reactions that might lead to the right question. Maybe they know something they don't know they know."

"They're in Spokane," Laney said, "or I would have done that already."

Quinn nodded. "I remember. Teague, take the plane." He glanced at his watch. "It's late, but you'd better go today. Weather on the way in by tomorrow."

"Yes, sir."

Nothing seemed odd to her, but something passed between the two men, a split second of something, lifted brow by Quinn, half-sheepish quirk of the mouth from Teague.

"Plane?" she asked as they headed back out to the parking lot.

Teague nodded. "And a sweet one. Cruises at better than two hundred knots. We'll be there in a couple of hours instead of five driving." He gave her a sideways glance. "You okay with small planes?"

"I don't know," she said frankly. "I see them all the time, it's impossible not to around here, but I've never been on one."

"Almost as many seaplanes as seabirds around here," he agreed with a smile. When they were back in his car he added, "It'll be fun, Laney. And a heck of a distraction, which I'm guessing you could use right about now."

She couldn't deny that, she thought. What she wasn't so sure of was if she wanted to be alone with him for as long as this might take. She was all too aware that her reaction to him was uncharacteristic, to say the least.

But it wasn't his fault if the first thing she thought at the idea of flying off with him somewhere had little to do with why they were really going, and everything to do with her suddenly too vivid imagination. When had she started having heated, daytime fantasies about a man she'd just met?

"So Foxworth has a plane and pilot on hand?"

"Don't forget the helicopter."

Laney shook her head. "Amazing."

And it did amaze her. All this equipment, all these people, knowledgeable and well trained, and all for one goal. An honest, honorable goal, in a world that too often looked upon such words as cheesy or out of touch.

"We'll go by your place," Teague said, snapping her out of her thoughts. "Pick up whatever you might need in case this takes longer than expected."

"You mean like…overnight?"

"Yeah. I never take weather in the northwest for granted, especially traveling over the Cascades."

Wise, she was sure. The weather Quinn had mentioned that was forecast for late tomorrow could just as easily pick up the pace and arrive tonight. But somehow all she could focus on was the idea of being stranded somewhere overnight. With Teague.

She wasn't sure if that excited her or terrified her. And finally decided it did both.

She'd been quick about it, Teague thought. She'd changed clothes, added a sweater over a T-shirt, thrown a jacket over her arm and put on sturdier shoes. Whatever else she thought she needed had gone into the canvas bag that was smaller than the purses he'd seen some women carry every day.

He'd been waiting in her small but cozy living room, looking around with interest. The colors were the soothing greens of the outdoors brought inside, but with splashes of yellow that seemed to brighten things the way the occasional sun break did during the long gray days of February. The TV was in one corner, fairly small and unobtrusive; the music system, with a slot for her smartphone, was a bit more prominent. Most prominent of all was the large bookcase on one wall, full of actual books, which was telling, he guessed. No e-reader for her...or maybe she had one of those, too.

He hadn't realized she lived behind the shop, in a small, one-bedroom apartment attached to the main building. She was truly doing everything she could to make a go of it, sacrificing her own comfort to the building of her business. He appreciated that kind of dedication to a dream. He'd had it once.

And thanks to Quinn and Foxworth, he had it again.

"What about you?" she asked as she added a bottle of water from the fridge to the bag.

"We'll have more aboard," he said, indicating the bottle. "And I've got my go bag in the car."

She looked up from zipping the bag closed again. "Go bag? As in always ready?"

He shrugged. "You never know."

"A holdover from your time in the service?"

"More a requirement for Foxworth. Quinn wants us ready to jump fast if we have to. In his way, he's as good at logistics as Charlie. Well, almost," he amended, looking up as if for a lightning strike.

She laughed. "I begin to see why Hayley's nervous about meeting the infamous other Foxworth."

"Better her than me," Teague said with a feigned shudder. "Charlie scares the hell out of me."

He'd gotten her to laugh, and that made him feel good. So good it also made him a little nervous.

You'd better hope that weather holds off, he thought. *You get stranded with her overnight and you'll be in big trouble.*

And that realization truly scared the hell out of him. Which scared him even more. Fear compounded fear. And he was acting like some idiot schoolkid who'd just discovered girls were different for a reason.

He was grateful for her silence as they headed out toward the small airport. If they'd been really rushed they could have taken the chopper to the airport, but unless Quinn flew them himself, that would have put both it and the plane out of service, and they tried to avoid that if possible. And right now, although he would never tell Laney this, there wasn't that much of a rush. If they were closer, if they had a better lead on where she was, then Foxworth would pull out all the stops. Right now they were still in the information gathering stage, and while the sense of urgency was there, it wasn't overwhelming yet.

He hoped it never got to that. For Laney's sake, he hoped they found out Amber was simply off on a romantic jaunt, acting oddly because she was all wrapped up in her new guy. Some women got like that. Or so he'd been told; he'd never run into it firsthand.

Would Laney be like that? So besotted that the way she acted with even her best friend would change? He couldn't picture it. She seemed the kind who would be rock-solid loyal, unchanging, barring some unforgivable offense. The kind of woman you could count on and could trust on every level.

And that was a hell of an assessment to reach in two days, he thought ruefully.

They'd reached the interchange, turning to put the Naval Shipyard behind them and heading toward the airport just three miles farther on, when she spoke.

"Should I call them? Let them know we're coming? Or would it be better if they didn't know?"

Teague thought about that one for a moment. "What's the likelihood they'd be gone?"

"Not much. They play a lot of golf, that's about it, otherwise they're homebodies."

"Health? You said they moved there for the weather."

Laney frowned. "They're fine. They just wanted the heat after years of living on the rainy side. Why?"

He shrugged. "Just wanted to be sure nobody would keel over if you showed up out of the blue."

She clearly hadn't thought of that. "They're going to realize how worried I am."

"Yes."

"And that will worry them, in turn."

"Probably. But don't call. If they know something they're not telling you for some reason, the surprise might work to our advantage."

"They wouldn't. Seriously."

"All right. You know them."

He made the turn onto the airport, kept to the fifteen-mile-per-hour limit as he headed toward the large hangar Foxworth leased. The slow speed allowed him to take a longer look at her. She was staring down at her hands, where she was rubbing at her fingers one at a time. Something about the angle of her head, the half-lowered lashes, the way her ponytail brushed her nape and the concern in her troubled expression made him want to reach out and touch her, comfort her somehow, even though he had no idea what to say.

But he had to say something.

"Do you really think they're not worried at all?"

Her head came up. She didn't look at him, but out through the windshield toward the long stretch of runway marked by tracks of dark rubber left by countless landings. After a moment, she let out a long breath.

"No. If they haven't actually spoken to her, either, then they're worried. She talked to them at least two or three times a week." After a moment of silence, she added quietly, "Thank you."

He wasn't sure what he'd done, but he'd take it.

Chapter 12

He hit a button on the console above his head, and Laney saw a door on the large hangar at the end of a row of them start to open. It was fully open by the time they got there, and they drove right into the cavernous building.

The first thing she saw was the sleek blue-and-white airplane. It seemed big to her, larger than some of the planes tied down outside, but certainly much smaller than any commercial plane she'd ever flown in. The wide windshield was divided, and there were generous windows on each side of the cockpit as well, followed by three smaller rectangular windows along the side. The swath of dark blue, accented by a ribbon of light blue, flowed over the white body from the bottom, sweeping up toward the tail as if caught by the wind.

"Told you she was pretty," Teague said with a laugh as he parked toward the back, well clear of the airplane.

"Definitely an eye-catcher," Laney said, feeling both a thrill and a touch of nervousness at the thought of making the trip over the mountains in something this much smaller than the usual commercial jet.

They got out, Laney shouldering her bag while Teague opened the lift gate and grabbed the smaller of two backpacks from the back of his SUV.

"Two?" Laney asked.

"Long-term, short-term," Teague said.

"And you just keep them like this all the time?"

"Except for rotating the rations now and then, yes."

She blinked. "Rations?"

"You never know," he said again. And as if reminded he said, "Snacks are on the plane, plus water and sodas, but if you want coffee you'll have to do it yourself."

"I'll be fine without."

They stopped beside the plane.

"She's a bit unique in the light aviation world. A prop plane with a pressurized cabin. We'll go over the Cascades like they were foothills. All due respect, of course."

She liked that, that he expressed respect for the mountains. She wouldn't have trusted someone who disregarded a mountain range full of volcanoes and that held the fourteen-thousand-foot Mount Rainier along with ten other peaks over nine thousand feet tall. Her parents still talked about the day Mount St. Helens had left that group in one huge explosion that sheared off the top thousand feet.

She looked around the rest of the hangar with interest. There was a row of what looked to be offices and storage across the back, one with windows open to the main hangar bay.

"Backup," Teague said when he saw her looking. "That's why the hangar's really bigger than we need for just the plane. We can operate all of Foxworth out of here if we have to."

"Have you ever had to?"

"Not yet. But Charlie's a big believer in redundancy of systems."

Laney felt a pang of sympathy for Hayley. Even she was feeling intimidated by the impressive Charlie Foxworth, and she didn't have to cope with the thought of being related.

Teague walked toward what looked like a small tractor and fired it up. He was heading toward the front of the plane when a fuel truck appeared outside the doorway. He waved at the driver, who stopped, then backed up slightly.

She watched what was obviously a familiar routine as Teague hooked the small tractor up to the plane.

"Can't start the engine inside the hangar, airport rules," he said when he saw her watching intently. "I get it, safety-wise, but it's a pain in the backside when it's pouring rain."

She managed not to ask how often they flew in that kind of weather. Obviously in the northwest if you only flew when it was dry you didn't fly much.

The plane seemed smaller to her after it was rolled out of the hangar into the open air. It gleamed in the late summer sun, and she found herself following the rather rakish curve of the three-bladed prop with her eye. The silver cone in front was polished to a high shine, the nose looked long and racy, and she had the whimsical thought that the plane looked eager to fly.

She glanced around at the other planes tethered outside several yards away. Some of them looked downright clunky next to the sleek lines of this one. Wings above and below, she was used to seeing that, but she rarely saw the planes stationary so noticed other differences.

"Why the different propellers? Two blades, four, but this one has three?"

Teague laughed. "Just open up the trickiest part of aerodynamics, why don't you? We could spend the whole flight on propeller theory and barely scratch the surface."

"Oh." She felt a little sheepish. She'd thought there might be a simple answer, like the size of the engine or something. And belatedly, the obvious began to dawn on her.

"But to answer what I think you're asking," Teague went on, "Quinn went with three for takeoff performance, since we don't always end up at wide-open airfields. Four tends to keep the engine cooler, but he figured up here that was a decent trade-off, since we don't usually have much ambient heat to deal with in this region."

The fueler went about his business briskly while Teague walked around the aircraft, checking things whose function was beyond her. Tires, that was obvious. Flaps she figured out and the thing on the tail that went side to side. But he seemed to go over the thing inch by inch, taking his time, with all the care of a surgeon prepping for an operation.

And he was the surgeon. She felt foolish for not realizing sooner. The absence of anyone else around should have tipped her off right away, before the way he talked about the plane had. When Quinn had said "Take the plane," he'd meant it literally for Teague. Take it as in fly it. Himself.

The fuel truck finished and departed, and Teague walked back into the hangar to pick up his bag.

"Ready?" he asked her.

"I guess," she said, sliding him a sideways look. "You really fly this thing?"

"Nah. She practically flies herself. I just steer now and then."

She smiled at that, watching as he reached up and grabbed a handle on the side of the plane's fuselage and pulled. A clamshell door opened, each half lifting and lowering smoothly. The lower half held two wide, comfortably deep steps that looked easy to negotiate.

"She seats six," Teague said as she lifted her foot to the first step. "Pick your spot." He gave her a considering look.

"You can sit up front if you want, or if that will bother you, or you want more room to relax, you've got four to choose from back here. There's a stowaway desk over there, if you want it."

She hesitated, then jumped. "I'd like to start out up front."

He grinned that crooked grin, and she wondered how flying could flip her heart any more than that.

"You can move back later. In the meantime, you can always close your eyes if it freaks you out."

"No stunts, okay?"

The grin vanished. "In this? Charlie would have my head. And rightfully so."

There was no mistaking his seriousness. When it came down to business he was as steady as Quinn. That made the last of her reservations fade.

As it turned out, the flight was smooth and uneventful, exciting only because she'd never done it and had never felt so close to the process. He did angle the plane once so, on this severe clear day, she could look down the range of mountains and see the string of volcanoes that were the crown jewels; Baker to the north, to the south majestic Rainier and the remains of St. Helens, reminding everyone of the power of the giants that they lived with. From Canada to California the string of fire stretched.

Then the jagged peaks were behind them and they were on the dry side, and she was so busy looking she forgot to be nervous. That she spent as much time watching Teague smoothly handle the controls, and the rather fearsome-looking electronics in front of them, was something she told herself was purely for her own edification.

Sooner than seemed possible they landed at a small airfield northeast of the city, along the Spokane River. As she was coming to realize, Foxworth's planning genius wasn't limited to the infamous Charlie. There was a rental car waiting for them.

"Navigate or drive?" Teague asked.

She liked that he asked, but the decision seemed obvious.

"I'd better navigate. I know where they live, but I'm not used to coming in this way. When I've come out to visit with Amber, we came in commercial, at the big airport."

Laney quickly oriented herself with the map on her phone and set them on their way. She guessed he could easily have done the same, probably even with turn by turn voiced directions, judging by the high-end phones all of Foxworth seemed to have. She wondered if he'd done it just to give her something to do, something else to think about. If he had, it worked.

At least, it did until they made the last turn onto the cul-de-sac where Amber's parents lived.

There was a police car parked in their driveway.

Chapter 13

There was no mistaking the delight in the woman's face when she opened the door and saw Laney, Teague thought. Or her stark disappointment when she saw him.

She'd been hoping it would be Amber with Laney, he realized. He took no pleasure in being right; they were already worried.

Under normal conditions, Teague guessed it would be easy to see where Amber got her looks. He knew from Laney Amber's mother was only a couple of years younger than her father's sixty-two, but if she said she was less than fifty he wouldn't really doubt it. Laney had said they'd moved for the weather, and the woman's tan seemed to show they enjoyed it.

But now she didn't look like a slim, fit, attractive middle-aged woman. She looked like what she was, a worried mother. Still, she didn't seem distraught. Not yet anyway.

And, he quickly realized as she ushered them inside the

small but immaculately maintained house, she'd made an assumption about him. Them, rather.

"Well, so you've finally brought us a young man to meet? About time, young lady." Laney tried to speak but the woman seemed on a roll, and turned her attention on him. "Aren't you the handsome one?"

"No, no," Laney finally managed to get in. "It's not… he's not—"

"I may be getting old, girl, but my eyesight's fine. He most certainly is." She smiled widely at Teague, who suddenly couldn't resist keeping his mouth shut, just to see where this would go. "You've quite the treasure here, you know. You take good care of her, or you'll have us to answer to first, since we're closer than her folks now."

"I mean we're not together," Laney said. "Not like that."

Did she sound regretful? Or was it his imagination? And if so, why the hell was he imagining that?

"Too bad," Mrs. Logan said with an appreciative once-over that make Teague smile, just barely. "You might want to rethink that."

"I might," he said, even though the comment had clearly been meant for Laney. He wasn't sure what had gotten into him. Something about the assumption they were together seemed to have set him off. "Teague Johnson, Mrs. Logan," he said, holding out a hand. Saying it was a pleasure to meet her seemed wrong under the circumstances so he left it at that.

The woman shook his hand rather delicately, but she smiled, and in that smile he again saw the younger woman from one of the photos Laney had shown them. A bright, beautiful smile. Somehow it made things more ominous instead of better.

"Sorry," Laney said, apparently in apology for her lack of manners in not introducing him. Had Mrs. Logan's assumption flustered her that much? The inward satisfaction he felt at that thought was unsettling.

"That's all right, dear, I embarrassed you. I didn't mean to."

"Mrs. L.," Laney said, changing the subject by pointing out the obvious, "there's a police car in your driveway."

"Yes." The troubled expression again furrowed her brow. "Lisa's a neighbor. She stopped by to give us some advice about Amber."

Teague could almost feel Laney's pulse leap. "Have you spoken to her?"

"No." The furrow deepened. "You haven't yet, either?"

"No."

Teague could tell Amber's parents hadn't progressed to where Laney was. She seemed concerned but not panicked, and hadn't yet connected her daughter's lack of contact to Laney's appearance on her doorstep.

"That's why we're here," Laney said. "Teague, I mean the people he works for, are helping me try to find her. Make sure she's all right."

That did it, Teague thought. Ratcheted up the worry several notches. "You think there's something really wrong?"

"I'm just worried," Laney said. "You know it isn't like her to not talk to either of us for so long. I just want to be sure she's okay, that she's really off on some romantic getaway."

"Romantic getaway?"

Laney sighed as the woman's puzzled expression made it clear she had no idea what she was talking about.

"You'd better come into the den with Lisa and Jim," the woman said.

It was a small room, with a couch, a couple of recliners that served as comfortable seating in front of the flat-screen on one wall. Not huge, but new-looking. Teague watched as Laney greeted the silver-haired man who rose quickly when he saw her, and decided Amber had had the luck of the draw on both sides. Jim Logan was a handsome man, in a distinguished sort of way.

The uniformed officer that went with the unit outside was young, blonde and lively-looking. She gave him a once-over much more thorough than Amber's mother's assessment, and he guessed like any cop, she was doing just that, assessing.

"Foxworth?" she said when it came up. "I've heard of them. Didn't one of your guys take a bullet taking down that cop killer in Seattle?"

"My boss," Teague said.

"He okay now?"

"Fine. He was lucky."

She nodded. "You think there's something serious going on?"

"We're involved to ease Laney's mind," Teague said. "I'm hoping that means we find Amber is fine, and annoyed at us for interrupting her fling."

"I've told the Logans how tough it is when the person's an adult and theoretically still in contact, and there's no evidence of foul play."

Teague nodded. "That's why we're in."

"Anything I can do from here?"

"Probably not, but it's early yet."

The woman nodded. She reached into a pocket and pulled out a business card. Lisa Valpraiso, Teague read.

"Call me if there is." She turned back to her neighbors. "I've heard good things about these people. You're in good hands."

She excused herself and left. Teague let Laney explain what they knew, let her decide what to tell these people who were clearly like second parents to her. She told them most of it, including the odd texts.

"We don't text, so I can't say," Amber's father said. "We did get an odd email from her, though, a couple of weeks ago.

We didn't think that much about it at the time, but when we didn't hear from her after that…"

"Do you still have it?" Teague asked.

"I'm sure," he said, rather wryly. "Audra never deletes anything."

"Jim, stop," his wife said.

The exchange held the tone of being oft-discussed. Amber's mother got up and went to a small desk in one corner where a laptop computer sat. It was already on; he guessed they'd already checked for anything new from their daughter. It took her only a moment to find the email in question, and before he had to ask she had printed it out.

"See, you never know when you might need something. If it had been up to you, it would be already gone."

"And if it was up to you, we'd need another hard drive just for mail," her husband answered.

Normalcy bias, Teague thought. Neither of them seemed as worried as Laney, because they couldn't let themselves believe anything was truly wrong. They clung to the world as it had been; the normal world they knew, because to acknowledge the possibilities was unbearable.

He didn't blame them. Understood it all too well. Too bad it always smacked right into the immovable wall of reality. He understood that, too.

He realized that somewhere along the line his own view had shifted. He'd begun this with the goal of proving Amber was just off on a jaunt with a new love, simply so that Laney would stop worrying. Now he realized he wasn't just thinking about finding her, but finding her in time. There wasn't a lot more evidence something was wrong than they'd had before, except for the plane ticket, and yet he'd somehow become convinced. As if Laney's worry was infectious.

And maybe it was. To him, anyway.

Audra Logan handed the printed page to him. Laney leaned over to read it with him.

"See?" the woman asked. "It's all choppy and full of those silly shortcuts I hate. CUL8R? Really?"

"She never used those in email to us," Jim put in. "She knows we hate it."

"Sent from her phone," Laney said.

Teague nodded. He'd seen the line at the bottom indicating that.

"And I have no idea what she's talking about there, our anniversary was six months ago," Mrs. Logan said with a glance at Laney. "You know that, you came for that lovely party she threw for us."

"Yes," Laney said, softly.

She looked at him then, and he saw the fear back in her eyes. She was more convinced than ever that something was very wrong.

"May we have a copy of this?" Teague asked.

"Of course. Do you want me to forward the email to you as well?"

"Yes, please." He reached for his wallet.

"You can just send it—" Laney caught the barely perceptible shake of his head, and stopped midsentence.

"—to this address," Teague said, finishing her sentence smoothly as he held out a business card, as if that had been the intention the whole time.

Jim took the card and nodded. He studied it for a moment. "It doesn't say on here what you do."

"If it listed everything we do, it would be a business book, not a card," Teague said.

"Lisa trusts them," Audra said to her husband, who made a noncommittal sound, but sat down to forward the email.

Audra turned back to Laney. "You're worried, aren't you?"

It was finally getting through that Laney hadn't come all

this way just to say hello. "I got those odd messages like yours, too," Laney said. "I just want to know what's going on."

"This isn't like her."

"No. That's why I—we are trying to find her."

Amber's father stood up. "It's sent," he said, then held up the card. "But I'll just hang on to this, if you don't mind."

Laney didn't miss the slight undertone of suspicion in the man's voice.

"It's all right," she began.

"Didn't you say you flew here in a private plane? You can't afford to be paying some fancy P.I.," he said with very fatherly concern. Teague kept his expression even, although *fancy* was not a word he'd ever heard applied to himself.

"I'm not paying them. They do this for free."

"Free?" The suspicion went from an undertone to a trumpet. The man glared at Teague.

"Now, Jim," Audra began.

"It's all right, Mrs. Logan," Teague said. "He's absolutely right. Nothing's really free."

Laney looked at him then. Was she wondering if she really was going to get a smacking huge bill at the end of this?

"We don't take money from the clients we choose to help."

"Choose?"

He nodded. He glanced at Laney, saw her expression, knew she was wondering if he was going to try to explain Cutter. He wasn't. She'd told him on the flight here that Amber's father had been an old-school engineer who had retired reluctantly when technology began to move in leaps rather than steps. Teague didn't figure he'd be receptive to the idea of taking cues from a dog, no matter how uncannily clever he was.

"We have our own criteria. A process and a research team. As my boss says, it's amazing how many people seem on the side of the angels until you do a little digging."

"Well, Laney is definitely that," Audra said firmly.

"Yes, sir," Teague said, barely managing not to glance at her again.

"If you don't take money, what do you take?" Jim asked, obviously still not quite convinced.

"What we do take is their knowledge, their connections, because we never know what might help us help someone else later on down the line."

"A network," Jim said, still looking a bit wary. "But what do you get out of it? You get paid, right?"

"I do. A decent but not exorbitant salary. And a tremendous, unusually high amount of job satisfaction."

Jim studied him carefully. "Were you in the service?"

"Yes, sir. Marines."

"Well, then. Why didn't you say so? Thank you. A lot of fine men in the corps."

"There are." *The problem's from the top down, not the ground up.*

"I worked more with DOD than any one branch, but I have a lot of respect for the marines."

Teague went still. "You worked with the Department of Defense?"

"My company did. Grimholt Guidance Systems." He grimaced. "That was back when they were a lot simpler than they are now."

Teague absorbed that. And wondered.

Could Amber's father's work have anything to do with this?

Now that, he thought, would make this a whole different bowl of dog food.

Chapter 14

Laney knew Teague was thinking, thinking hard. Something about what Amber's father had said had sparked this. When Audra insisted they join them for a home-cooked meal and bustled off to the kitchen, followed by her husband, she held him back with a hand on his arm.

"What?"

He didn't try denying it, which she appreciated. She'd meant what she'd said when she'd told them she wanted the truth every step of the way.

"Just wondering." He took out his smartphone and began to text something.

"What?"

"If her father's work could have anything to do with this."

Laney drew back, frowned. "But he's been retired for nearly three years."

"That's what makes it unlikely. But it's a blip I hadn't expected, him working with the DOD." He backed up and corrected or shortened something to fit, then sent the text.

"You're not thinking this is some…espionage thing?" she said, stunned at the very thought.

"Not really. It doesn't have that feel. But we don't get the results we do by not covering all the bases."

She couldn't argue with that.

"If there's anything to find, Tyler will find it. Or Liam, if he's back."

Laney was careful throughout the time at the table, not wanting them to worry any more about Amber than they already were, trying to make her visit seem more like just that, a friendly visit. Teague asked questions about Amber, but he somehow made them sound merely friendly, always relating them to Laney or even himself. He was good at this, she thought, when she wasn't wondering if all—or any—of the stuff he was telling about himself was true, or just a way to get Amber's parents talking. He even managed to get her father talking about Amber's dislike of the water, and the childhood incident involving him and his small fishing skiff that had likely caused it.

She hid her restlessness, the need to get back and keep looking, knowing that would only make them realize how seriously she was taking this. Besides, it could still well be nothing. It was most likely it was nothing. She almost convinced herself by the time they were looking at a slice of Audra's wonderful apple cake, a treat that had always been Laney's favorite.

It was after the meal, when Teague mentioned leaving ahead of the expected weather, that the awkward part started.

"You can't head back over the mountains now, it's too late," Audra said.

"We flew," Laney reminded her.

"I know, and in a little plane. I'd be terrified. And it's nearly dark now. You should stay. Use the guest room."

Audra was focused on her, and for a moment Laney wondered if she'd forgotten all about Teague.

You might want to rethink that.

Her words at the front door came back to Laney. No, she hadn't forgotten at all. She didn't dare look at Teague, not when the very idea of sharing a room with him made her cheeks heat.

"Twin beds, dear. You're both adults, you can manage."

No. No, we can't. I can't, Laney thought. She wanted to glance at Teague, but she had a suspicion his face wouldn't betray a thing. Perhaps because there was nothing to betray. It was possible, in fact likely, that she was the only one fighting this sudden battle of awakened hormones or something.

Besides, for all she knew, he had a girlfriend. Just because he hadn't mentioned it didn't mean she didn't exist. It wasn't like he owed her any explanations of his current personal life. And she couldn't imagine any woman who got a chance with a man like Teague not hanging on for dear life.

Jim, who had disappeared into the den for a few minutes, reappeared. "Too late," he said. "Cascades are getting slammed. Thunderstorms headed this way."

"Welcome to the end of summer in the northwest," she muttered.

Teague pulled out his cell phone. She took the chance to look at him then, while he tapped a series of selections. His jaw seemed tight, and his forehead was furrowed as he looked at the screen.

The weather, she told herself. He was just worried about the weather. He wasn't all chewed up inside at the idea of sharing a room with her. She was the only total fool in this operation.

A weather map appeared on the phone's screen, half-covered with an ominously large swath of green, yellow and far too much of the darker colors that meant seriously heavy weather. At nearly the same moment the chime announcing a text message came through, and he quickly switched over to read it.

He let out a compressed breath then glanced up at her. "Quinn. He says stay. It's twelve hours early and nasty. But fast-moving. Should be clear by morning."

Morning. Wonderful.

"I'll get you set up," Audra said cheerfully, and headed off to the guest room.

Laney smothered a groan. At least, she thought she had, but Teague took her to one side.

"I'll go crash at the airport. I can sleep aboard the plane."

"That doesn't sound comfortable."

"It's not that bad. I've done it before. The back row of seats recline."

"With a storm coming? That's silly when there's a perfectly good bed available."

The words were out before she realized the absurdity of it all. She'd been the one so uncomfortable with the very idea of sharing close quarters with him, and now she was practically demanding he do it? When clearly he wasn't any happier than she'd been about it?

"I'm sorry. I didn't mean to push. If you're not comfortable sleeping in a strange place—"

His short laugh cut her off. "Honey, I've slept on my feet in Afghanistan. Doesn't get much stranger than that."

After the jolt of the unexpected endearment wore off, Laney just stared at him. Sometimes she simply forgot his history. He was generally so cheerful, so upbeat; it didn't seem possible that he'd seen the dark things she knew he must have.

"I'm sorry," she said again, this time less flustered, more heartfelt. "Do enough people thank you?"

He blinked, drew back.

"Thank me?"

"Like Amber's dad did. For serving."

He lowered his gaze. "Some do," he said.

"More should. Including me. Thank you."

She turned on her heel and followed Audra into the guest bedroom, leaving him to decide whether to stay or go without any pressure from her.

He stayed.

It was all about context, Teague thought.

He, for instance, was wearing a pair of sweats that had been in his go bag for the duration, and a T-shirt. He could have been going to the gym. Laney was wearing a pair of flannel lounge pants and a T-shirt of her own, which covered as much as her work scrubs had. Nothing in the least provocative.

Well, except for the fact that the T-shirt clung to curves that were more generous than he'd realized, and the pants rode a fraction of an inch lower than the hem of the shirt. And that she'd pulled her hair free of the ponytail, and it flowed down past her shoulders in long, silky waves that gleamed.

Between that sweep of hair, legs that seemed a mile long and that tiny, occasional flash of skin above the utilitarian blue plaid, he was where he'd sworn he wouldn't be. Lying wide-awake in the dark, staring at the ceiling, as aware of Laney's soft breathing as he would have been of an enemy patrol working in their quadrant. As aware as if his life depended on it.

Because Laney wasn't in her scrubs, working. She was lying warm and inviting in a bed a bare three feet away, and no slinky nightwear, no revealing lingerie could make him any more aware of that fact.

Even with the buffeting wind and rain, he would have been smarter to have headed back to the plane.

But then, it would have been smarter to have just walked out of her shop and let it all be.

He had the grace to laugh inwardly at that one. The dog had been so determined there had been no ignoring him. Not that Cutter was a dog you could ever ignore, but when he set that quirky canine mind on something, he was an immovable force.

And a good partner. He'd have made a hell of a war dog.

Laney's quiet words about being thanked enough echoed in his head. He wondered if she had any idea how much they meant. How much such words from random civilians meant to anyone who served.

He thought she just might. She was perceptive, sensitive, and smart.

You miss it.

She'd known that, even though he'd said nothing, and rarely let it show. And she'd let it stop there, hadn't pried, hadn't probed the sore spot. He was grateful to her for that, for being willing to let it drop. Typically many weren't. Especially women, who seemed to have that digging, relentless need to know every personal thing immediately.

But Laney wasn't typical.

And lying here next to that impassable three feet of floor between them, knowing she was so close and yet off-limits, was going to drive him crazy. Staying was the worst decision he'd made since…well, since he hadn't walked out of her shop.

You're both adults, you can manage, Amber's mother had said.

He wasn't feeling very adult right now. He was feeling more like a hormone-crazed teenager, or a deprived soldier who'd gone without for too long.

And if he kept thinking about this, about her, and how

tempting she was, how much he wanted to bury his hands in that thick mane of hair and explore that tiny strip of skin that shouldn't have been nearly as provocative as it was, he was going to lose it.

It took every bit of discipline he'd learned in the field, when you truly had to sleep when you could, coupled with the knowledge he had to fly in the morning, to clear his mind. He shoved his unruly thoughts into a cage and locked it, silently ordered his body to behave. He summoned up the old image, that picture that had gotten him through so many long nights, including the ones when he had purposefully slept on his feet, so that he wouldn't go so deep he wouldn't hear an enemy approach. It formed in his mind, that image of a peaceful, glassy lake reflecting a huge mountain, the most beautiful place he knew.

He fought off one last errant thought that he'd like to take Laney there.

Face it, you'd like to take her anywhere. In all senses of the word.

He slapped that all too true assessment into the cage with the rest. And finally, restlessly, slept.

Chapter 15

Laney smothered another yawn.

It was the full tummy, she told herself as they drove toward the airport. Audra had produced a breakfast that would have fed a dozen. And she so rarely indulged, usually grabbing something quick before heading to work, she had eaten some of everything, and clearly too much.

And even as she thought it she knew she was kidding herself. Her yawning had little to do with that, and everything to do with the fact that she'd lain awake half the night.

That Teague hadn't seemed bothered at all, while she had only kept from tossing and turning by the knowledge that he'd hear it, should be enough to keep her rambunctious thoughts in check. But instead, here she was, tired but restless, anxious; feeling like a bath-hating dog who knew one was coming.

Teague had been up and out when, after finally dozing off at some after-midnight hour, she awoke. He had apparently had no problem sleeping, she'd thought grouchily. But her mood had softened when, up and ready herself, she had followed the scent of fresh coffee to the kitchen, only to find him working alongside Audra, scrambling eggs in a skillet.

"Always room in my kitchen for a handsome man who can cook," Audra was saying.

Teague laughed in a way that made Audra smile, and Laney would have forgiven him almost anything for that. "I'm not sure scrambling eggs qualifies, but thank you."

Audra paused in her mixing of what appeared to be pancake batter. "You will find my girl?"

"We will," Teague said. "I can't promise when, but we will. Foxworth doesn't quit."

Audra still looked troubled, but nodded.

"And when we do, I want a picture of you both to add to our records. Since it's obvious where Amber got her looks. And charm."

He sounded utterly sincere. Audra blushed and reached out to tap Teague on the arm. "Hush, you."

"Pure truth."

Yes, Laney thought now, remembering, she would forgive him just about anything for that.

Not that there was anything to forgive him for, other than the fact that he'd slept while she couldn't. And that was so childish she hated to even admit to the thought. No, he'd been the perfect gentleman last night. Kept to himself, not speaking a word after a quiet good-night. She'd been the one wide-awake, strung tight by his presence, fighting not to let that moment when she'd caught a glimpse of him changing his shirt in the room's dresser mirror as she'd come back from the bathroom take over every inch of her consciousness.

If he hadn't been built to perfection, it would be easier, she thought. To her perfection, anyway. He had that lean, rangy yet muscular build she liked. She didn't know what kind of conditioning the marine corps put people through, but it was obviously effective. And he also obviously hadn't slacked off since.

And probably had no shortage of women lusting after that body, she told herself.

"You all right?"

Laney sucked in a quick breath; what had her expression looked like as that parade of unwelcome thoughts had marched through her mind?

"Just tired," she said, hastily adding her first excuse, "all that food."

"She just kept going," Teague said with a laugh. "You'd have thought Hobbits were coming to feed."

The reference caught her off guard, and she laughed.

"You can nap on the flight," he said. "It really isn't bad in the back. Or there's an air mattress stowed somewhere, if you want to stretch out on the floor."

Laney felt her cheeks heat. Her thoughts really must have been obvious if he was that desperate to get rid of her.

"Maybe I will," she said, working to sound casual.

The skies had cleared as promised, only a few lingering clouds on the horizon left as a reminder. There were damp spots on the airfield, but no puddles, and except for a couple of small branches and some leaves strewn about, there was little sign of the storm that had passed.

The plane seemed to have weathered it well, although she noticed he took extra time going over every inch of the craft, testing every mechanical system twice, poking, prodding, searching for any damage that might not be apparent at first glance. At last they boarded, and he went through a lengthy checklist inside, also twice, after the storm.

She shelved her pride and took a seat in the back, letting the seat recline as far as it would, and as he'd requested, loosely fastening her seat belt. She hadn't really expected to sleep, doze maybe, but after they were airborne the steady, low hum of the powerful engine seemed almost lulling.

She awoke to two surprises. They were descending, and there was a soft, knitted throw tucked around her.

That simple thing flooded her mind. How? Had he put the plane on autopilot just to do this? He had also lowered the pleated shades in the side windows, giving her if not darkness, at least the illusion of it. Why had he even thought of it? And how had she, so hyperaware of him, possibly slept through it?

That she was regretting having slept through it set off a new set of alarms in her head.

She sat upright. And chastised herself for being reluctant to shrug off the throw. It wasn't at all cold in the cabin, but she knew the extra warmth had helped her sleep. And she did feel better. More awake, anyway. Of course, that could be just the thought of him doing something so caring.

And rather intimate.

She made herself tug the throw, made of some soft, snuggly, fuzzy yarn—she suspected Hayley's fine hand there—free and folded it carefully. Not knowing where it went, she put it on the seat next to her.

"Feel better?"

She looked forward. He had the pilot's headphones on, so she wondered how he'd known she was awake. Unless he'd been checking on her, which was almost as unsettling as the throw.

"Yes," she answered, somewhat belatedly.

He turned to look at her for a moment; he had the headset off one ear, rather awkwardly, so they could converse. "We'll be down in about twenty."

"I didn't mean to sleep so long."

"Obviously you needed it."

There was nothing in his tone to make her feel so embarrassed, yet she did. As if he'd somehow guessed she hadn't slept much at all last night. And why. But if that were true, wouldn't he be sounding…smug, maybe? Like any guy who knew a woman was lusting after him?

She felt her face flush and was grateful for the dimmed cabin. But she always tried hard to be honest with herself, and she couldn't deny it was true. It was easy for her to recognize, since it happened so rarely. As in never. Not like this, anyway. She'd never reacted to a man like this before.

Of course, she'd never met a man like this before, she thought wryly.

"Want to come up front for the approach? On a clear day like today, it's beautiful, coming in over the sound. You'll need to belt in tighter for landing either way, though."

She hesitated, then schooled herself to calm. This was ridiculous; she wasn't some teenager who couldn't hide her emotions.

"Thanks," she said as she made her way through the narrow space up to the cockpit. She belted in as instructed, then settled in to look around. It was, as he'd said, beautiful. The water reflected a deep blue today, and the islands looked like deep green gems scattered about.

She had just spotted the Naval Shipyard when they shifted direction. In what seemed like just moments they were paralleling the state highway that ran beside the airfield. And then she could see it in the distance, the wide, cleared patch of land, the heavy white lines marking the start of the main runway, and the second runway angling off to one side.

She glanced at Teague. He was intent now, focused, and she stayed quiet. She heard him talk, saw him look up once, scanning, then nodding as he apparently spotted some other aircraft on approach. There was no control tower here, she knew that much, but how things functioned beyond that she had no idea. Obviously there was a standard plan, rules of flight or some such, and she had no doubt Teague was a pro at this.

The touchdown was so smooth she smiled at his skill. He made it seem so easy, so safe.

More quickly than she expected the plane was back at the hangar and she was back on solid ground, tote bag over her shoulder. And surprised at her own feeling of disappointment. She could see how it could become addicting, this very personal kind of flying.

She headed over to put her bag into the SUV as Teague was talking to a young man in coveralls, who apparently helped maintain the craft, keeping it ready to fly on short notice. She had just set the tote on the floor when she heard Teague's cell ring. From across the hangar she watched as he answered. She couldn't hear what he said from here, but his demeanor changed entirely; he went from casual to intense in an instant. And as he did, so did she, wondering what he was hearing and if it was related to Amber.

He shoved his phone back in the pocket of his battered leather jacket, said a few more quick words to the young man, then turned on his heel and strode toward her. His car keys were already in his hand and that alone told her something urgent was up. She ran to the passenger side and climbed in, and had her seat belt fastened by the time he got there.

He wasted no time in opening the back hatch, just tossed his go bag over the back of his seat onto the backseat floor, got in, quickly fastened his own belt and started the engine.

She waited until he'd maneuvered the vehicle past the parked airplane and out the hangar door, even though it was winding her up to not ask. But as soon as they were clear and on their way out to the highway, he answered the question she hadn't asked.

"Quinn has something."

"About Amber?"

He shook his head. "Her phone. As in where it is. Tyler tracked the cell towers it's using."

Laney's breath caught. "You mean right now?"

He nodded.

"Where?"

"He thinks it's on a ferry. Headed this way."

She dived for her own phone to check for messages or texts she might have missed. Nothing.

She looked at Teague again.

"I don't know," he said before she could ask.

She didn't really need an answer. She knew there were only two options. Either Amber was on that ferry, and for some reason wasn't communicating with her, or someone else was on that ferry. With Amber's phone. The phone she never let out of her sight.

Laney didn't like either option. But she'd rather have Amber not talking to her for some voluntary reason than all the ugly possibilities someone else having her phone could mean.

They were out on the highway now, free from the airfield speed limits. Teague hit the accelerator, giving her the one thing that could ease her tension just now.

Speed.

Chapter 16

"Ty was monitoring the phone and he picked it up in Seattle, hitting a tower near the docks," Teague explained. "Then it dropped out, then reappeared on the other side. Several carriers have a dead zone for a few minutes in the middle of the sound, about halfway through that crossing."

"So Amber's phone was in use?"

He nodded.

"Call or text or data?"

"Call."

She lapsed into silence as she contemplated his answers. She had been amazingly calm so far. And she'd reacted quickly, realizing before he'd said a word that something was breaking. She'd also not peppered him with questions he couldn't answer, which he appreciated. But then, she was clearly smart enough to figure out the ramifications herself.

When she did finally speak again, it was simply to ask "What now?"

"We head for the ferry landing." He glanced at the clock in the dash. "We're still a good half hour away, but Quinn's probably nearly there. And the ferry's just docking now."

"But how will we ever find who has it, if it's not Amber? There have to be hundreds of people onboard."

"Maybe not, this time of day, but yeah, it's going to take some doing." He tried to reassure her. "Quinn'll think of something. He always does."

He dodged a traffic stoppage near an accident on the freeway portion of the road, taking the closest off-ramp and diverting to surface streets. It would be about even, cutting off some distance to compensate for the slower speeds. And he figured it was more important for Laney to have a sense of movement. Sitting in a traffic backup would probably drive her crazy just now.

Laney was silent again, and he could only guess at what she was thinking. He doubted this was as simple as Amber not speaking to her lifetime best friend for some reason. He couldn't imagine anyone being that mad at Laney. She was just too nice, too loyal, too caring, too…many things. Admirable things. Attractive things.

And there he went again.

His mind flashed back to those moments aboard the plane, when he'd turned it over to autopilot and gone back to put that blanket on her. He'd been seized with a fierce wish that he had the right to always look after her like that, that she was his to care for. And the moment he'd thought that, he'd been blasted with the inner realization that if that were true, the reverse would be, too, and he had a feeling he had no idea what it would be like to have a woman like Laney care about him the same way.

Would it be like Quinn and his Hayley? That rock-solid, unwavering steadiness spiced with a passion that electrified the air around them? Could it be?

He should remember last night, he told himself ruefully. The atmosphere in that room last night had been pretty darn charged.

No, forget last night. Stay focused, Johnson.

He glanced at her as they hit a stoplight. She was frowning. As he watched the frown deepened, and she grimaced.

"What?" he asked, wondering if she'd thought of something.

She gave a half shake of her head. "I was just trying to think if there was anything I said or did that could make Amber so upset she'd just walk away without a word."

"The kind of friends you were? Not likely."

"That's what I thought. We shared everything. We were each other's first call when anything happened, good or bad. We laughed together and cried together. She was my sounding board, and I hers. We didn't always agree, but we always listened."

Hey, Teague, got a minute? I need a sounding board.

Drake's oft used phrase echoed in his head. How many times had he heard it? Usually about some project or idea the guy had in mind, sometimes wild and silly, sometimes downright brilliant. It had been Drake who had thought of a way to rig a movable tent over the working end of the wall they'd been building, giving them some relief from the elements, Drake who had thought of making a stand for his tablet computer by simply cutting a groove in a two-by-four, Drake who had used forks jammed handle-first into the sand to hold the wiring diagram for a broken down vehicle between the tines.

He'd heard it so many times it had become almost a joke between them.

"Teague? Are you all right?"

So much for his poker face, he thought. Usually they ragged on Liam for having the worst of all of them.

"Just thinking," he said as the light changed and they moved on.

"About?"

"Not Amber," he said, meaning to be reassuring. Then he realized she probably wanted to think he was completely focused on her friend at all times. Which he should be, he told himself sternly.

"I just meant…I was thinking about my best friend. He was always saying that, that he needed a sounding board."

"Was?"

"He died."

"I'm sorry. Truly. What was his name?"

He hesitated. He never talked about this. But she needed the distraction. And the thought that she could very well end up in the same ugly boat spurred him out of his reluctance.

"Drake Hansen," he said. "But everybody called him Edison."

"Why on earth?"

"Because he was always coming up with brilliant ideas. Sometimes a little twisted, but always brilliant. He could solve anything."

She smiled at that. "Sounds handy to have around."

"He was."

"What happened, Teague?"

He *really* never talked about that. "He died. I told you that."

"But not how."

"Does it matter?"

"Obviously it does to you."

His hands tightened around the steering wheel. White-knuckle tightened. Nearly as tight as his jaw.

"I'm sorry," she said. "I didn't mean to pry. I just thought you might actually want to talk about it."

"The woman's answer to everything? Talk it to death?"

She drew back, shifted in her seat, but said nothing. His

sharp words hung in the silence, hammering at him as if they'd been recorded and played back in a loop.

He sighed inwardly. "That was out of line. I apologize."

"My mom says that when you talk about someone who's gone, it's not only a way of keeping them with you, but that they know somehow that you're still thinking of them, still love them."

He slid her a quick, sideways look. It was the most fanciful thing he'd heard in a while, and he'd left the capacity for that somewhere in Afghanistan. Along with the belief that dead was anything but dead.

"Nice idea," he managed to say, glad she'd apparently accepted his apology, knowing she was only trying to help, and still feeling guilty for the way he'd snapped at her.

"So what happened with your Edison?"

He braced himself. She might be sweet, kind and loyal, but she was no pushover, and clearly could be tenacious when she had to be.

Or wanted to be.

"An RPG," he finally said. "It took out our personnel carrier."

It took her a moment. "Afghanistan."

"Yes."

"And you were with him?"

"Yes." He was done with this. He had to stop her. "It took more pieces off him than we could find. He bled out in my arms before the medic could even get to him."

She paled, and while he was sorry for the image he'd painted for her, it did the job. She shivered, but she didn't speak. Not until they saw the first sign for the ferry landing.

Then, as if she felt she had to acknowledge it before the shift back to her own problem, she said quietly, "So you carry that, too. Along with your sister."

"It's different. That was war."

"A different kind of guilt. But still…" She drew in a deep breath. "I was wrong. There is no way to thank you guys enough. Not if we did it a thousand times a day."

"Laney—"

"And I'm sorry about Edison. Sorrier for you, he's not hurting anymore."

"I don't want your pity."

Again he snapped at her as she poked at festering places he usually kept deeply buried.

He'd apparently found her breaking point, because her voice turned icy. "Pity and sorrow are not the same thing, Teague Johnson. And if you can't accept someone's heartfelt sympathy, can't take someone hurting because you're hurting, then you're as crippled as he would have been had he lived."

To his shock, her scathing indictment stung more than even the much more distant memory of Drake's death. He told himself she was wrong, but couldn't quite vanquish the nagging thought that if she hadn't been on target it wouldn't have jabbed at him so hard.

Before he could respond, which was probably a good thing since he couldn't think of a damned thing to say, he spotted Quinn's car in the parking lot for walk-on passengers. And next to it was a plain, dark blue sedan that screamed unmarked police car to him. He spotted an empty spot a row away and quickly headed the SUV into it.

Before they even got out, Hayley was there waiting; she'd apparently been watching for them. She went quickly to Laney.

"No sign of Amber," she said quickly, answering the obvious first question before they could ask.

He was sure Laney had to be disappointed, that she must have been hoping even if it seemed unlikely, but she hid it well.

"The phone?" Teague asked.

"That, we have. And," she added, putting a gentle hand on Laney's arm, "the person who had it."

Laney visibly sucked in a quick breath at that.

"Who?"

"We're still working on that," Hayley said. "What I can tell you is he's just a kid. Maybe sixteen."

Teague frowned; that didn't fit. Not with anything.

"What?" Laney asked, reading something in Hayley's expression.

"He thought he was being accused of stealing the phone." Hayley glanced at Teague. "Detective Dunbar is here, helping us out with this."

That explained the unmarked car, he thought.

"He helped us on a prior case," Hayley explained to Laney. "He's a good man, a good cop."

"So because he's a cop, the kid thought he was busted?"

Hayley nodded. "So he was maybe more forthcoming than he might have been otherwise."

"Forthcoming with what?" Laney demanded.

Teague saw surprise flicker across Hayley's face at Laney's tone, and wryly thought he was to blame for that. He was the one who'd put her in such an edgy mood.

Again Hayley touched her arm. Laney let out a breath. "Sorry. But—"

"I know. What he said was that a man gave him the phone and paid him to use it. To send texts the guy had already written out, at set times. Indefinitely."

Teague let out a low whistle. "Clever."

Laney had gone pale. She'd gotten there as quickly as he had.

"The texts really weren't from Amber."

Hayley didn't try to soften the truth. "We're not sure yet where hers ended and the kid started, but no, the last ones were not."

"But they were enough to make the police think she was alive and well," Teague said. "And keep them off his back."

The three of them stood there for a silent moment as Laney and Teague absorbed the ramifications of the new information. There was no doubt any longer that something was very wrong. Amber was in serious trouble.

If, Teague thought grimly, she was even still alive.

Chapter 17

"I was supposed to only use the phone for those texts," the boy said, sounding miserable. "But it's so much cooler and better than my phone."

"So you couldn't resist using it for your personal stuff."

Laney watched the boy carefully. He looked as distraught as he sounded. She wasn't surprised. There were three of them and only one of him. And Detective Dunbar was towering over the kid as he sat on the hard plastic chair in the office they'd borrowed from the head of terminal operations, a man Dunbar had apparently dealt with before.

She'd been a little surprised when Hayley and Quinn had exited, but she supposed it spoke to their faith in the detective, and in Teague, who in turn said Laney should be present in case the kid said something about Amber only she might catch. She was grateful to him for that; she didn't think she could stand being shut out right now. And he was clearly able to put the tension that had sparked between them aside for the sake of the case.

Dunbar himself was a tall, rangy man who moved with an ease that spoke of solid strength. Laney guessed he was as tough as he needed to be, when he needed to be. The touch of gray at his temples seemed at odds with a young face, but matched the shadows in his eyes. She didn't like thinking about the things he must have seen to put them there. Just as she didn't like thinking about what Teague had been through. His sister vanishing while he was halfway around the world, his best friend dying in his arms while he watched helplessly. She couldn't imagine.

Sometimes she wondered why anyone would want to be a cop. Or in the military, she thought, with a glance at Teague. She didn't have an ounce of that kind of nobility in her, to sacrifice what they did to serve.

Hayley had told her Dunbar wasn't just a good cop, he was a good man. "I don't know his whole story," she'd said as they headed toward the port building, "but he's a man who understands pain, and a man who listens."

"Maybe I should have gone to him first," Laney said, her willingness to forgive overworked city cops a bit singed now that she knew Amber was truly in trouble.

"He would have heard you out. But based on what you had…"

"I know," she said. "I had nothing. Nothing but a bad feeling."

"And years of knowledge of your friend," Teague had pointed out. She'd liked him for that. And for not staying mad. As if she needed more reasons.

"So," Detective Dunbar was saying now, "you want us to believe this man you'd never seen before just hands you this phone—"

"I never said I'd never seen him before, just that I didn't know him."

The kid sounded scared now. He was small for his age, a little skinny yet, and something about that fear in his voice made Laney see him as a person, not just someone who had something to do with Amber's disappearance.

As if he'd done the same, Dunbar suddenly shifted tacks. He pulled another chair over, reversed it and sat with his arms crossed on the back. Giving the kid a visual barrier between them, she realized. A tactic, just as bringing him inside had been; less likely to try to run, Quinn had said. Outside, people, especially kids, always seemed to think they could get away.

"Okay, Pinch," he said, using the nickname the kid had given them, "why don't you just tell us the whole story? Get your side out."

"I didn't steal it," the boy insisted.

"So you said. Start at the beginning. When and where did this man approach you?"

"At the wireless store at the shopping center near my house. He was, like, hanging outside. A couple of weeks ago."

A couple of weeks, Laney thought. Amber had vanished three weeks ago. Had the first texts she'd gotten truly been from her? It was all she could do to stay quiet and let this man Foxworth trusted handle it.

"And what exactly did he tell you?"

"That he'd pay me five hundred dollars to take the phone and send this list of texts he had written down, at the times it said on the list."

"You didn't find that odd?"

The boy shrugged, as if at the oddities of adults. He seemed a little more at ease now; Dunbar's change in tactics had apparently worked.

"And did he say why he needed you to do this so much it was worth five hundred bucks to him?"

"He said he and his girlfriend were taking off together, but her folks didn't like him and he wanted to hold them off. I get that. This girl I like, her parents hate me."

"You didn't think it a little strange that a grown man would be worried about that?"

The kid shrugged again. "I figure parents keep hassling you as long as you live."

That answer was almost profound. And from the slight smile that flashed on Dunbar's face, she guessed he felt the same way.

"You still have that list?"

"Yeah. It's on the phone, in the notebook app."

Teague spoke for the first time. "Did he tell you when you could stop?"

Again the shrug. "When I got to the end of the list. Like, in about a week."

That made it a month, Laney thought. A total of a month since Amber had disappeared.

"If you want me to believe this, believe you didn't just steal this phone—which could be worth enough to make it grand theft and land you in jail for a good long time—you're going to have to help me here."

The mention of grand theft and jail made the already light-complexioned kid go even paler. "I'm a juvenile," he protested.

"You're seventeen," Dunbar said. "Close enough that my recommendation could probably get you tried as an adult. So help me out. What did this guy look like?"

"He was just a guy. An old guy. Not as old as you, but older than her," he said, pointing at Laney.

That fit, Laney supposed, even as she questioned the wisdom of calling the cop questioning you old. But she figured

to a seventeen-year-old, the forty she guessed Dunbar might
be or be pushing would seem just that—old.

"Tall? Short? Dark hair, light hair, bald, what?"

"I don't know, he was just a guy!" The kid's voice nearly
squeaked. He was genuinely scared now.

"Close your eyes, Pinch," Dunbar said.

"What?"

"Close your eyes. Picture that day he came up to you. What
was he wearing when he handed you the phone?"

"Oh. Uh…"

Pinch complied, seeming relieved that Dunbar wasn't still
hammering at him. Which, Laney guessed, was part of the
tactic. The man really was good.

"A jacket," Pinch said. "Black. It was, you know, that slick
stuff, that makes all the noise, like a windbreaker."

"Right hand or left?"

"Right."

"Any rings on that hand?"

"No."

"Other hand?"

"No."

"Shirt."

"Blue. Like one of those golf-type shirts. And jeans." The
kid's eyes snapped open. "And he had the phone in a baggie.
You know, like you put sandwiches in and stuff."

Dunbar drew back slightly. It didn't take much to guess
why. The man had probably wiped it clean before handing
it over to the kid.

"Hey. I remembered." He sounded pleased with himself.

"Yeah. You're doing fine," Dunbar reassured him. "Now
try it with his face."

The boy gave them a description that could have fit any
five people who had just walked off that ferry, and probably
every other guy over thirty they found on the street. Dunbar

looked at Teague and lifted an eyebrow. Teague nodded and pulled out his phone.

"Look at these. Is he one of them?" Teague asked, holding the phone out as a slow slide show of four images rotated. All similar, yet different. The third one, she saw, was the driver's license image of Edward.

"Maybe," Pinch said, "but he could be any of them. I was looking more at the phone, you know?"

And in the end, that was all they got, that "maybe." It could have been Edward, but maybe not. The money had been cash and already spent, and any suspect fingerprints on the phone had apparently been wiped. But it was more than they'd had.

"If he's only had the phone two weeks, then those first text messages weren't ones he sent," Laney said as she and Teague headed back to Foxworth in his car.

"No."

"So maybe they were really Amber, trying to send a message with the odd references and syntax, trying to signal something was wrong."

"Could be."

He sounded so oddly neutral she knew he had to be making an effort at it. And it hit her quickly.

"Or they were odd because they were sent by Edward, before he gave the phone to Pinch."

"Yes."

"But how would he have even known her cat's name?"

"She might have told him. Innocently, the kind of thing you tell someone you're getting to know. He might have pumped her for information, intending to use it that way."

Laney suppressed a shudder. The thought that Edward might have planned this all along, that he might have worked Amber for details just so he could use them to fend off her friends and family, made this all seem even more horrific.

"Detective Dunbar believes something's wrong," she said.

"Yes. And he'll get the wheels turning."

She should be happier. All she'd wanted was for her worry to be taken seriously, for someone in authority to believe that she wasn't just imagining things, that Amber could really be in trouble. But in fact, she'd been happier when they hadn't taken it seriously. Because if the police didn't believe anything was wrong, it was always a possibility they were right, and Amber was fine.

And now she'd lost that. Now she had to admit that Amber was truly gone, and that she could be in very serious trouble. That she might never be found.

And suddenly she understood Teague's oddly neutral tone. He suspected Amber was already dead.

Chapter 18

Cutter, who had apparently been wandering the field in back, spotted them instantly. He was headed for them before Teague could even park.

"Probably not happy he got left behind," he said as he got out of the car.

"I still worry there's no fence here," Laney said.

It was the first thing she'd said since they'd left the ferry landing, so Teague went with it.

"We all did, at first. Liam says no dog's one hundred percent reliable on recall. Give 'em a squirrel or a deer to chase, and they're gone, tunnel vision turned on, running as if they couldn't hear you calling them at all. But Cutter's as close as you'll get. And he really doesn't like getting too far from his people."

"Which is all of you."

"He has kind of adopted all of us. Some more than others," he said, thinking of Rafe and the different sort of bond that had grown between the dog and the man who had the darkest past of them all. "And he goes kind of nuts if he stays cooped up too much."

"They're a high-energy sort of dog," she said.

Teague watched as Cutter slowed his run just long enough to alter his course. He headed directly for Laney. As if he sensed she was the one who needed his attention.

"And right now, that family includes you, especially," he said.

She'd held up until now. He hadn't pushed her to talk, hadn't known what to say, hadn't known just how much she'd processed what Pinch had told them. Hadn't known if she realized all the ramifications. But now, as she crouched to hug the dog, burying her face in his thick fur, he realized she'd understood it all.

Cutter whined, a soft, worried sound he rarely made unless someone he loved was in distress. Which said it all, Teague thought. His own stomach was knotting up at the sight of the tiny shivers that went through her, at the way she was gulping in air as if trying to keep from crying.

He wished Hayley would hurry up and get here. He was no good with crying women. Hell, that was what had started this. All the more reason to avoid them.

But if he'd walked away that day, where would she be now? Alone, and still frantic about her friend. And from what he'd seen of her so far, she wouldn't be able to let go of that. Which meant she might well keep poking at it and end up in hot water herself. End up in the same boat as Amber apparently had, in the hands of a man whose motives, while unknown yet, were clearly less than aboveboard. And quite possibly dangerous.

Or deadly.

And that thought made his knotted stomach a little queasy.

He heard her take another strangled gulp as she fought to

steady herself. And couldn't stop himself. He knelt beside her. Cutter, for all his focus on her, spared him a glance that so clearly said "Fix it!" that he grimaced.

I wish I knew how, buddy, he muttered inwardly. Then said the only thing he could think of.

"Laney, if you want to go home—"

"No. No, I can't. I need to know something's being done."

He got that. Completely.

Laney stood up. Teague followed.

"And I need to feel like I'm doing something." Her mouth tightened and he saw the wetness on her cheeks. She hadn't quite succeeded in stopping the tears. But she'd certainly given it a valiant try. "Even if it's worthless."

"It's not worthless, Laney," he said.

She looked up at him then. The pain he saw in her eyes jabbed at him, dug deep. Instinctively he reached for her, put his arms around her at the same moment Cutter nudged him in that direction.

She felt better than he'd ever imagined. And, he admitted to himself, he'd been imagining quite a lot.

But even he realized this was not the moment to be indulging in errant thoughts; comfort was what she needed now, and what it was his job to provide. Even Cutter knew that, the way he'd nudged him toward her.

Comfort. Right. That's it. That's what he was here for.

Even if he wasn't very good at it.

He didn't know what to say, so said nothing. If nothing else, he'd learned that sometimes silence was the best option. Cutter, after all, didn't need words, and he was the best antidote to worry and stress that Teague had ever seen. And managed to communicate perfectly, in ways that were unique but unmistakable. The least he, stupid human, could do was learn from the clever animal.

So he simply held her.

And she let him. She didn't pull away, didn't insist she was fine, didn't ask him what the hell he thought he was doing. Instead she rested her head against his shoulder, leaned into him with that lithe yet curved body he'd admired, and after a moment, slipped her arms around him in a move that surprised him. Not so much because she'd done it—it was, after all, a natural response, to return a hug—but because of the effect it had on him.

Warning bells went off in his head, but they had to fight to be heard over the sudden racing of his heart.

Let go, his brain shouted.

Hang on, his body countered.

It was a battle he'd not fought in a long time, and for the first time in even longer, he wasn't sure which side he wanted to win. And no amount of telling himself she was a client, this was wrong, and Quinn would have his head seemed to help matters. His body had raged to life, more quickly than he could ever remember. He tightened his hold, needing her even closer. When she hugged him closer in turn, the ache of need became nearly unbearable.

Cutter's sudden happy bark jerked him out of dangerous territory. And made Laney jump back.

"Hayley," he said. His voice sounded thick, harsh. He cleared his throat and tried again. "They must be here."

"I know that bark," Laney said, not looking at him. "I've heard it when she comes to pick him up. I didn't realize it was just for her."

She sounded like a woman glad of the distraction. Or maybe that was just his own guilt speaking.

The sound of tires on gravel proved the dog right. Quinn's big, dark blue SUV came out of the trees and pulled up beside them. Cutter raced over, danced with eager anticipation outside the passenger door until Hayley emerged and he greeted her joyously. Then he darted to Quinn, who leaned down to scratch his right ear thoroughly, earning a sigh of happiness.

"Thanks for guarding, boy," Quinn said.

Cutter yipped then sat, looking up expectantly. Like a marine waiting for orders, Teague thought.

"Stand down," Quinn said. "Relax."

With another short, expressive bark, Cutter stood, wheeled around and trotted back to Laney. For a moment he just stood there, looking up at her.

"I'm all right now," she said, stroking his head. "Thank you, my furry friend."

The dog looked at Teague then, and no matter how ridiculous it seemed, he would have sworn there was approval in the dog's steady gaze. And it warmed him.

Okay, you're over the edge. Basking in the approval of a dog?

Well, not just a dog. Cutter. That made it different.

"You were a wizard or something in another life, weren't you?" he muttered as he scratched that right ear.

Cutter gave a soft woof, then trotted toward the green building. Teague straightened, saw Laney looking at him. Saw she was smiling, probably at his silly words. He knew they were silly, but sometimes…

More importantly, they'd made her smile. That was worth something. In fact, right now it was worth a lot.

"What's Dunbar going to do with Pinch?" Teague asked as, once inside, they settled around the meeting table. Quinn had stayed to talk to the man after he and Laney had gone.

"The kid was just a dupe, that's pretty obvious. He's going to turn him over to his parents. And when they arrive to get him, he'll run the photo by them, just in case."

Teague nodded.

"Laney? Can we see your phone?" Hayley asked, so gently Teague knew she'd somehow sensed Laney's emotional state.

"Of course."

She pulled it out of her purse, a worn leather satchel Teague knew held, among many other things, dog treats. And yet Cutter had shown no interest in them, not since this had begun. *No treats while you're working,* Teague thought with an inward smile. Cutter's code. He didn't doubt for a minute the dog had one. And that he was working. He had been since Laney had started crying in the grooming room of her shop.

"We want to compare the texts you got right after Amber vanished to the ones when we now know Pinch started sending them," Hayley said.

Laney nodded, but with a furrowed brow. "But we don't really know if she sent any of them."

"No," Quinn agreed. "So why don't you go back to that last one you're certain came from her, and we'll work forward from there."

She'd shown them that point in the long string of texts before, but willingly went back to it again. "I'm glad I didn't clear these out," she said as she called it up and set the phone down and slid it across the table to Hayley and Quinn. "I know this was her, because we talked about it the next day."

Teague remembered the text had been something about a hard-to-please client.

"Do you know the name of that client?" Teague asked.

Laney shook her head. "She just called them Their Highnesses. I know they were semilocal. Greater Seattle area, anyway."

"We'll get Ty on that," Quinn said. "Give him a chance to break in his new toys before he heads back. Which reminds me, he just found some evidence that North Country's in trouble. Maybe even headed for bankruptcy."

"Figures," Teague muttered.

"If Edward knew that," Laney began.

"He could be desperate," Quinn finished for her.

"Or maybe he's been stealing from them, too, and is afraid he's going to be found out in a bankruptcy audit," Teague said.

"Also possible," Quinn said. He turned back to the phone and the text messages. "Now, which one first sounded off to you?"

"There were a couple that were…not odd, but very short. Amber's not a succinct sort of person. She tends to ramble a bit. But she will do short if she's jammed for time, so I can't say it doesn't happen. So the first one that was really off was the one about Pepper."

"The dog. Which was actually a cat," Teague said.

"Yes."

"Other than the obvious mistakes, did it sound like Amber?" Hayley asked. "Meaning the phrasing, the abbreviations, the emoticons?"

Laney nodded. "It did. It was only the content that threw me."

Teague exchanged a glance with Quinn.

"So it could have been her," Hayley said. "Trying to send a message."

"To maybe the only person who would immediately know something was wrong with it," Teague said.

Laney shivered visibly. Teague reached over and laid a hand over hers. Her fingers curled, clasping his, as if she welcomed the contact. It had been automatic, this need to again comfort, and only after he'd done it did he realize how it might look from across the table.

But then there was little room for such concerns. The same jolt at the contact shot through him again, as if he'd grabbed a live wire. Which, in a way, he had. But he hadn't been able to resist; the pull was as certain as a magnet's.

Cutter woofed from his spot at their feet, as if he'd somehow felt the electric charge that had surged between them.

He searched her face, looked for some clue, but she was

looking down at their hands and he couldn't read her. But she didn't let go, didn't pull back. He had to be satisfied with that, for the moment.

And for the moment, he'd damned well better shove the images that shot through his mind at the word *satisfied* back into their cave.

The warning bells rang again. But they were even more distant this time.

Chapter 19

"It's really true."

Laney knew her voice sounded tiny, shaken, but it was how she felt. Even knowing Foxworth would continue the search as promised didn't help just now.

"Something's wrong, yes," Teague said, never taking his eyes off the road. Probably didn't want to look at her, for fear she'd be crying. Again. It was a wonder he hadn't turned and run that first day in the shop. If he hadn't been there for Cutter, maybe he would have.

It was odd. Almost unfair. She rarely cried. When things went wrong, or got tough, she usually just dug in and kept going. Determined, her father said. Stubborn, her mother said.

"Whatever that thought was, hang on to it."

Teague's words echoed in the car. Had she thought he wasn't watching her? He hadn't turned his head, so if he'd caught a shift in her expression he must have peripheral vision as wide as the sky.

"My parents," she said. "My father always said I was determined. My mother called it stubborn."

"Stubborn is good."

"Stubborn is good?"

"Sometimes it's the only thing that gets you through."

She didn't miss the implication that there were tougher times ahead. And her words weren't a question. "You're saying I'm going to need it."

"I think you already know that."

She only nodded, because she could think of nothing to say.

She directed him around to the back where the outside entrance to her small apartment was. She avoided looking at the window of the shop with the Closed sign hanging somewhat forlornly in the center of the door glass. She had managed her two already scheduled appointments but hadn't made any new ones. She knew she was risking damaging the business, but—

"Let us do what we do, Laney. You need to be here, take care of business," Teague said. Laney's head snapped around as he practically read her mind. It wasn't the first time, but it was no less unnerving.

"I'd be afraid I couldn't concentrate. I don't want to hurt an animal because I'm not focused."

"You didn't hurt Cutter."

"Only because he's the most patient dog I've ever groomed."

"Cutter? Patient?" Teague sounded laughingly disbelieving.

"He is," she insisted. "He's perfect for me, every time. Even when he's blowing coat and it takes an extra hour, he's incredibly patient."

"You'll have to teach us the trick," he said as he pulled his car in behind hers; there wasn't room to park beside it. "He runs out of patience with us all the time, and when he does, everybody knows it."

His tone was so rueful she had to smile. It felt strange, and she realized how grim she'd become in the last few days.

"Maybe it's because I do what he wants."

Teague chuckled. "Well, that could be it. We're probably slower on the uptake. I think he gets impatient because we can't read his mind the way he seems to read ours."

The fact that he sounded amused but accepting of Cutter's unusual talents made her smile again.

Yes, she had been unrelentingly grim of late, she admitted to herself as they got out of the car and walked the short distance to her door.

"I don't usually cry a lot."

She wasn't sure why she'd felt compelled to say it, to explain to him that the teary-eyed woman he'd first met wasn't the usual her. Nor did she want to analyze the compulsion just now. She tried to concentrate instead on getting her door unlocked and open. It was inordinately hard for some reason, the key slipping from her fingers, then seeming to not fit the lock.

"You have reason," Teague said as he reached out and took the key from her and slid it into the lock without fuss. And she just stood there and let him.

The door swung open on its own, as it always did. For a moment she just stood there. It seemed impossible to step inside, where nothing had changed, where there was no sign of the chaos that was churning around inside her. How could it be so impervious, so unaffected by her life being turned upside down? It didn't seem right, there should be some sign.

"Yes," she said, "I do have reason. Amber's my best friend, and I miss her so much. I miss talking to her." Her mouth twisted slightly. "Venting to her. I suppose guys don't do that to their friends?"

"Sure we do, only we call it unloading and there's usually

alcohol involved," Teague said. "It's a necessary function that keeps us from going airborne now and then."

It so perfectly described how she'd been feeling that she nearly laughed herself. Which again reminded her how far she'd been from feeling anything pleasant since Amber had disappeared.

"That's it, exactly," she said. And then, before she really thought about it, she said, "Will you come in? I can make coffee."

He hesitated. Long enough that she felt embarrassed at having made the offer.

"Don't feel you have to. I'm not going to shatter if you leave me alone."

"I never thought you would. Stubborn," he reminded her.

"I was holding up all right before you and Foxworth came along. Despite the crying."

He nodded. "Funny, isn't it, how help sometimes makes us weaker?"

"Weaker?"

"I wasn't saying you're weak," he said hastily.

"I know."

What was funny, Laney thought, was how she was so certain he wasn't casting any aspersion on her with that. He wasn't calling her weak, because he wouldn't. He just wouldn't. In fact, she had the distinct feeling he was speaking more of his own experience than her situation.

But it made him step inside and close the door behind him, even if it was only so he could explain.

"I just meant if you're in a rough spot, and you hold it together, then if you finally do get help, all of a sudden you can't do it anymore."

Yes, he was talking from personal experience, Laney thought as she took the keys back from him and put them on the small table by the door, placed there for that purpose. She wondered again what horrors he had seen, had been through. What he'd been through with his sister vanishing and his parents' resulting blame and destruction was bad enough. But then his best friend dying like that. That was an image she shied violently away from; it hit far too close to the bone for her just now.

But she guessed there were probably more. She knew there had to be more. Horrors of war and all that.

"Maybe," she said, "it's just that you're too tired after holding it together, if it takes all you've got. You have to let down when you can, when there's finally help."

He looked at her for a moment, and she thought she saw a trace of surprise in his eyes before he nodded. Had he not expected her to understand? Or had he just not thought about it like that?

"Maybe."

He sounded almost grateful, and it hit her that he had been worried she had really taken offense at the thought of being called weak. And she thought it was nothing less than a miracle that he was as sane and normal as he was. It spoke to a strength she wasn't sure she herself had, no matter what her folks said. Here she was, so rattled by this, when he'd been through much, much worse and was still functioning. Was, in fact, helping others. That said a great deal about who this man was. No wonder she was so attracted to him, she thought, admitting it in so many words for the first time, albeit silently.

And that admission brought with it the answer to her own earlier question about why she'd been so set on him realizing she wasn't just some weepy woman who *was* so weak all she could do when confronted with a problem was continually cry. She had wanted him to see her as more than just the woman Foxworth was helping.

When she set the mug of coffee on the eating bar in front

of him, the sharp sound of it felt like punctuation to a new determination.

"No more crying, I promise," she said. "It's useless."

"Crying is fine as a release. Sometimes I envy women because it's easier for them. And I get it when they say they feel better after." He took a sip, nodded as if in approval of the taste, and set the mug down before adding, "But as a long-term strategy, yeah, it sucks."

Laney stared at him for a long moment. "You," she finally said, "are almost as good at this comfort thing as Cutter is."

She didn't know if it was the sense of what she'd said or the unfussy way she'd said it that made him laugh, but she'd take it either way.

"Not something I'm often accused of. I usually have no idea what to do or say."

"You did back at Foxworth," she said, then wondered why on earth she'd brought that up. If that flooding warmth she'd felt when he'd put his arms around her, if that shocking zap she'd felt when he'd touched her hand later in the office only went one way, then she was opening the door to some pretty serious humiliation here.

"I know you were only trying to make me feel better, not so alone, I know that that's all it was, don't worry, I won't misinterpret, I mean I didn't think you were—"

"That's how it started."

His flat statement cut off her ridiculous spate of words. She usually didn't chatter mindlessly, either; that was more Amber's department.

And then the sense of his welcome interruption hit her. "Started?"

"I know it was out of line, and I apol—"

"Don't." She cut him off as he had her. "Don't apologize."

For a long, silent moment she just looked at him. Her common sense warred with need, a need unlike anything she'd felt before. As if the few men before him were just practice, and finally she was feeling the real thing. She told herself it was that she was so off-kilter, so worried, and he was strong and solid and everything she wasn't just now. That was what pulled her to him so powerfully. She needed his strength, his calm, that was all.

"I needed exactly what you gave," she said, certain she'd resolved to simply thank him and move on. What came out next was totally different. "But I wanted more."

"Laney—"

"I'm not one to live dangerously. I'm the cautious one."

"Then stay that way," he said, and there was no mistaking the warning in his voice.

"That was before I met you."

"Don't stir this fire, Laney."

Her heart leaped at his words. Did he mean there was a fire to stir, that he felt it, too, this electric connection? Was that what he'd meant when he said he'd started out only wanting to comfort? That it had changed, for him as well as for her, into something much different? Much…more?

"I know this is— I know I'm a job, a client."

"Ethics," he said, his voice tight. "Quinn's big on that."

She hadn't quite thought of that. That he could get in trouble if they crossed whatever line Quinn set for dealing with clients. It was like stepping into a cold shower. Or back from the edge of a precipice from which there was no return. Where nothing else had succeeded in tamping down this strange new feeling, the thought of getting him in trouble with his boss did.

The emotional trouble she could have gotten herself into didn't seem to matter at all.

Chapter 20

"It could have been me."

Laney's quiet words drew him out of his brooding contemplation of his nearly empty coffee mug. He wondered if he was really resisting taking that last sip because once the mug was empty, he had no reason to stay and every reason to go.

And he didn't want to go.

"I know that's incredibly selfish of me to even think about, but..."

Her voice trailed off. Teague barely managed not to reach out and take her hand once more. They'd come perilously close to throwing gas on that fire already tonight.

"It's not," he said, keeping both hands wrapped around the mug, a blue-and-green stoneware piece that looked as if it had been handmade. It went with the colors in the apartment. The kind of touch only designers or women seemed to think of; his own small place was utilitarian and safely neutral in color. "It's only natural."

"He seemed nice enough. I could have said yes and gone out with him."

Teague ignored the stab in the gut the words gave him.

"If I hadn't been so busy with the shop, trying to build it up, I might have."

"No other reason not to?"

Her expression changed, to a worried frown. She shook her head slightly. "I swear, he seemed nice enough."

That hadn't been what he'd meant. And now he felt guilty, for trying to ferret out if there was another man in her life while she was still so worried about her friend.

Another man?

Get your head out of your backside, he ordered himself. *You're not in her life, not like that, and you're not going to be.* At least, not until this was resolved. After that? He didn't want to admit how fiercely he was clinging to that thought.

"I didn't get any weird vibe from him that made me say no, if that's what you mean," she said. "I just wasn't attracted."

He nodded, as if that was what he'd been trying to ask all along. And suddenly he realized he had his answer anyway. He'd been right all along. There couldn't be anyone serious in her life, or she wouldn't have even considered going out with someone else. She just wasn't the type. He wasn't sure how he knew, why he was so certain, but he was. Laney Adams was a one-at-a-time kind of girl. No playing a wide field for her.

"Not consciously, anyway," she said, staring into her own mug now. After a moment she looked up again, meeting his gaze with her own troubled eyes. "God, you don't think maybe I did? That maybe I sensed something under the surface that some part of me knew he was dangerous, and that's really why I said no?"

"It can happen," he said, keeping his tone carefully even. "Quinn says that's what instincts often are. That in fact you're processing information so fast your conscious mind skips a few steps, so what seems like intuitive jumps are really just the end of a lightning-fast thinking process."

"But if that's true, then why would I tell Amber he seemed nice?" Her voice had risen slightly as her tension at the idea ratcheted up.

"Laney, it takes time to learn to trust those instincts. And in normal, everyday life for most people, unless you're in dangerous territory, it's not necessary."

"But if I sensed something was wrong about him, and then turned around and told Amber he was okay—"

"Stop," he said, sharply. He'd traveled the guilt road too often himself to want to see her career down it. "You already said it, Laney. If it was there at all, it was subconsciously. You couldn't act on what you weren't consciously aware of."

"But you do." It was building; he could hear it in her voice. He couldn't see her eyes; she was staring down into that mug of coffee as if it held all the answers. He knew because he'd just been doing it himself. "People who are trained, like you, I mean. You act on those instincts."

"*Trained* being the operational word. In your world, you're trained not to follow them. Instincts, intuition are often ignored for the sake of being polite and civil, or politically correct. Because in your world, your life doesn't usually depend on it."

"But Amber's did."

She was there, full-blown guilt.

He'd been where she was right now, for so long, it tore at him to see her do this to herself.

"Don't go there, Laney." His voice broke slightly on her name, but he made himself go on. "It's a damnable place to live."

She lifted her head to meet his gaze.

"It's not your fault," he insisted.

Something changed in her expression then. It shifted, softened somehow. "Your sister wasn't yours, either."

It stunned him that she would think of that, try to ease his long-ago pain in the midst of her own.

"And I can't believe your parents really blamed you."

His fingers tightened involuntarily around the heavy mug. "I'd promised. To take care of her, look out for her. I was her big brother, it was my job."

"And theirs."

He couldn't stop the harsh, compressed sound from escaping. "Well, I abandoned them, too. I abandoned them all, going off to pursue a dream. The dream my mother hated."

"Hated? She should have been proud!"

"That would go against her beliefs, and nothing matters more to her."

"Surely your father, at least, was proud?"

He let out a short, sharp laugh. "He barely spoke to me. I found out later he told his friends he didn't have a son anymore."

"Teague, no. That is all so wrong, so awful. They were wrong. You know that, don't you?"

"In my head, yes." With an effort, he reined the emotions she'd somehow triggered back in. "Don't go there," he said again. "You don't need that nightmare of guilt and self-recriminations. They can take years to cage."

She was quiet for a long moment, and the pure empathy in her eyes was more soothing than he ever would have imagined possible.

"And sometimes they still threaten to break loose, don't they?"

"Yes." There didn't seem any point in denying the obvious. He hadn't meant to let it show, but then he hadn't meant to tell her any of this in the first place. It wasn't something he easily discussed. It wasn't something he usually discussed at all.

But with Laney, it seemed different. Many things seemed different.

"It was more their responsibility than yours," she said. "They were her parents. They probably blamed themselves. And took it out on you."

"My mother has never blamed herself for anything in her life. Responsibility is not her thing."

She stared at him. Set down her mug. "I don't think I'd have liked your parents much."

He gave a half shrug. "That's okay. I didn't, either."

Something flashed in her eyes. He looked away. If she was feeling pity, he didn't want to see it.

When he looked up again, she was looking at the battered leather jacket he'd slipped off and laid on the bar. It was indeed in rough shape, scraped here, some odd darker spots there. Spots outlined with tiny holes, where patches had once been sewn. Unit patch, the flag patch and some other, less authorized patches that expressed opinion more than identification.

"You always wear this?" she asked.

He shrugged. "A lot."

She reached out, fingered a small tear in one arm. "You could get that repaired, so it doesn't get worse."

"No."

"Sure. There's a shoe repair shop in—"

"I meant I don't want it repaired."

She yanked her hand back as if the sudden edge in his voice had startled her. He let out a compressed breath.

"It was Drake's," he said.

Understanding flooded her voice. "Oh. No wonder, then."

She blinked, and he saw the sudden welling of moisture in her eyes. She nearly jumped when he reached out to her, lifted her chin with a gentle finger.

"What's that for?"

"For him. For you. For all of you."

His stomach knotted, but not in a bad way. He swallowed tightly. The memories hovered, ready to swoop down, and he had the crazy thought that if he let them she would somehow feel them, as if they were so powerful they would brush her in passing.

She slipped from the counter-height seat. He noticed it wasn't much of a reach for her, with those long legs that he tried not to think about too much. And then she blasted that effort to bits when she crossed the two feet between them, pushed the swivel chair around and put her arms around him.

He nearly dropped the mug to the counter. As it was, it hit with a heavy thud.

She was holding him, so close her heat was searing him, burning away the remnants of the painful memories that had been stirred up. Her head rested against his chest and he could smell the scent of whatever shampoo she used, something light and faintly citrusy.

He realized with a little shock his arms were around her in turn. He hadn't realized he'd done that. And now, no matter how he tried, he couldn't stop himself from sliding out of the chair so he could stand and pull her closer.

He would have sworn he could feel every inch of her, in his mind he could see every inch of her, his suddenly explosive imagination able to supply every detail he'd never seen.

"If your parents were truly not proud of you, then they were fools," she said softly.

He fought for control in a way he hadn't had to do in years. She was simply returning the favor as it were. He had to remember that that's all this was, that she didn't mean anything more by this. Just a kind soul offering comfort and understanding.

What he couldn't understand was how this had turned

on its head, how his urge to ease her distress had somehow turned into her comforting him.

And then she kissed him.

He was sure she'd probably meant it to be a peck on the cheek, but he'd moved to pull her even closer and their lips brushed. The spark was instant, the fuel his imaginings of every hour since he'd met her, and the blaze caught and flared so quickly any thought of control was too late. His mouth was on hers.

He felt ravenous, a starving man who'd found sustenance at last, a man dying of thirst who had at last found clean, fresh water and a taste of sweetness unlike anything he'd ever known.

It was a heady brew, and he felt himself slipping further out of control as he deepened the kiss. The more he tasted the more he wanted, and the blaze flashed into an inferno.

The fierceness of it startled him. Some part of his passion-numbed brain was aware of one crucial thing: she was responding with the same fierceness he was feeling. She was tasting, probing, not tentatively but with an eagerness that took what little breath he had left away.

If she'd been hesitant, if she'd shown the slightest resistance, he could have pulled back. He would have pulled back. But she didn't, and restraint was beyond him.

His hands traced the curves he'd imagined, found he'd been a bit off, her waist nipped in more than he'd thought under the sweater, making the curve to her hip the perfect spot for his hands. He tugged her closer, wanting the feel of her body pressed against him even as he knew it would drive him crazy. And still the kiss went on, deep, fiery, maddening.

He slid his hands upward, over her taut rib cage, until his fingers encountered the soft, warm flesh of her breasts. This somehow seemed the point of no return. If he did as his body demanded, if he cupped those curves, caressed them, and if she responded with the same intensity as she had to this kiss, he'd be lost. Completely lost.

Or found.

And he would be on a path he shouldn't even be thinking about. And those warning bells were finally loud enough he couldn't ignore them, or the message they sent. If he went down this path, there'd be no turning back.

Chapter 21

Laney felt his hesitation. Thought she understood it. Told herself she should take advantage of it, pull away.

She didn't. Couldn't.

"Laney."

His voice was rough, harsh, and the difference sent another rush of heat through her. She leaned into him, her body suddenly awake and tuned to a fever pitch. She savored the heat of him, the hard, lean strength. Wanted more of it. Wanted more of his mouth, his hands, his body.

She wanted it all. Now.

This was insane, this so wasn't her. She didn't do this, didn't get swept up with a man she barely knew, didn't have to fight off thoughts of leaping into bed with him three days after meeting him.

But then, she'd never, ever had a man make her feel like this. As if the decision were out of her hands, as if fate and nature and biology had all conspired to make this happen and it was useless to fight it.

And as if she would regret it her entire life if she stopped now.

She ran her hands over him, wanting to learn him as he was learning her. She slipped up under the edge of his sweater, nearly gasping at the feel of him, smooth skin over taut muscle, and savoring the way he sucked in his breath at her touch.

She'd always laughed at the idea of sex as an imperative. A nice fantasy, but hardly day-to-day reality. She wasn't laughing now. She was burning up. Being consumed. Feeling as if she would die if she didn't have him.

When he tugged at her shirt she let him, when it got tangled, she helped him. She heard the low, very male sound he made when it dropped to the floor, saw the heat in his eyes when he cupped her breasts so they swelled over the top of her lacy bra. And she swore if she hadn't been in such a hurry to get that sweater off him she would have unhooked the bra herself.

When the sweater was gone and she got her first real look at him her knees nearly gave out. He was as beautiful as she'd known he would be from that glimpse she'd gotten before. Solid, broad shoulders, narrow waist and that flat stomach she'd been touching with such eagerness. A faint dusting of hair graced the center of his chest, narrowed as it trailed down his belly. Her suddenly overactive imagination supplied the rest of the image, but it wasn't enough. She wanted to see, to touch, in a mad, hot, insane way that was the most consuming thing she'd ever felt.

Somehow, they wound up on the floor. She felt the softness of the throw rug at her back. It wouldn't have surprised her if she'd fallen, but he'd managed to ease her down gently, even as she clutched at him, fingers digging into those shoulders.

She couldn't reach his mouth just then, so she pressed her

lips to his neck, trailing kisses down the strong corded muscle to the hollow of his throat. She felt him suck in another deep breath so she lingered there, kissing, tasting. But her hands strayed farther, reaching the waistband of his jeans, fumbling with the button, then the zipper.

And then freezing when she realized what her fingers had encountered, realized just how aroused he was in turn. It made her shiver, not in fear but in anticipation. She traced the rigid flesh through the soft, worn denim.

"Laney."

It was all he said, but it came as if it were ripped from him. And the sound of it, the deep, rough tension of it, was all she needed to hear.

All thought fled as his thumbs brushed over her nipples. It wasn't a firm, demanding stroke, just a light caress, but it didn't matter. Sensation swept through her as if it had been his mouth on that aroused flesh. And at that thought, her body clenched with the need for it to be just that, for his mouth to be on her.

She moaned under the pressure that was building, arched beneath him, reaching, asking, pleading. He answered. He lowered his head, kissed the swell of her breasts. He reached behind her, managed to unhook her bra, quickly enough that she didn't go mad, yet not so easily it made her wonder where he'd gotten all the practice.

And then his mouth was there, his tongue circling, flicking until she nearly screamed. She arched again, twisting, straining to get closer. Vaguely realized he'd unzipped her, as well. With his mouth still teasing her nipple, his fingers slipped lower. She only realized how completely she was responding to him, how suddenly the arousal had swamped her, when he finally reached his goal and stroked her.

The ferocity of her own response to just this stunned her;

if it was like this now, what on earth would it be like when they were actually joined, when he was inside her?

On the thought she echoed his action, sliding her hand farther, tracing the path of that arrow of hair.

"Stop."

The harsh command barely penetrated the haze. She couldn't really have heard that. Who would want to stop this?

It was more forceful this time. "Laney, stop."

Teague would, apparently. Still caught up in the whirling sensations, she looked up at him in puzzlement.

"Damn," he muttered under his breath.

He closed his eyes. She saw his jaw clench for a moment. Then he opened them again. His hands were safely at her shoulders now, holding her as he pulled away slightly. It was all she could do not to whimper plaintively at his retreat.

"We can't do this," he said.

He didn't sound like he meant it. She frowned, still spinning a little, and off balance from his quick withdrawal. She felt cold without his heat, although the room was perfectly warm.

"Why?" she asked simply.

"You want a list?" he asked, his voice steadier now.

"If you're going to stop now, I may need it," she said. She knew she sounded a bit sharp, but she was reeling a little.

"You're vulnerable right now. You're hurting. You're not thinking straight."

For some reason this list irked her. She scrambled to her feet. "Have you taken up mind reading, or did you just decide you know better than I do how I feel?"

"You want cold, hard facts?" he asked, getting up as well. "You're a client. You barely know me. And…I'm not prepared."

She had the odd sensation of feeling her cheeks heat when

she would have thought they couldn't, she was already so flushed.

"I won't always be a client. And I know more about you than you probably realize. I know what kind of person you are, what kind of man you are."

She left unsaid the fact that his unpreparedness, the lack of the proverbial condom in his wallet, ever at the ready, actually endeared him to her even more. He obviously didn't make a habit of this any more than she did, or he would have been prepared.

But he backed up then, took that critical step away. He meant it, she realized. He really was going to stop.

"You're the one who isn't sure of her judgment anymore."

That stung. Seriously. But maybe he was right. Her judgment apparently sucked.

"All right. I get it. Sorry."

It was all she could do not to grab up her discarded shirt and hold it in front of her like some character in a romantic comedy. Except there was nothing romantic about standing here half-naked with a man in the same state, but who clearly didn't want to be there. And certainly nothing funny. She yanked the shirt over her head, pulled it into place. Then she turned her back on him, picked up both coffee mugs and walked to the sink. She turned on the hot water, thinking she should have picked cold, and stuck her head under the faucet. It would have been easier. And more pleasant.

"You get what?"

Couldn't he just let it be? Was he going to make her say it? And this time she didn't even have Amber's vital, gorgeous presence to blame.

"That you're not interested. Sorry for the…" Embarrassment? Awkwardness? Misunderstanding? What did you call something like this?

"Not interested?"

Something in his voice, some sharp, slicing edge of incredulity, spun her around. He was holding his sweater, looked as if he'd been about to put it back on, and she had to force herself not to just stare at all that bared skin. He yanked the garment on rather fiercely before he spoke, his voice tense.

"You had your hands on me. If you believe that was 'not interested,' then your judgment really is impaired."

"You just said it was."

"I didn't. I said you weren't sure of it anymore. Entirely different thing."

"Semantics."

"Words. They mean things."

She played back what he'd said in her head, had to admit she saw the difference. And she had been doubting herself, wondering if there was something she'd somehow missed about Edward, some sign or clue that he wasn't the nice guy he appeared to be.

"I'm sorry," she said, meaning it this time. "I don't usually do that, take things personally, I mean."

"You're off balance right now. Worry will do that."

Perversely, his gentle understanding only made her feel worse.

"And I don't usually have to spend so much time telling someone I'm not usually like this," she said wryly.

He blinked. She thought she saw his mouth quirk, just barely. "That made sense to me. Should I worry?"

In spite of everything, and despite herself, she smiled. "Maybe you should."

He was quiet for a moment, studying her, and she had the oddest feeling he was assessing what to say next. Not trying to guess what she wanted to hear, as some men did, but if he should say what he was truly thinking.

"After this is over," he finally said, "after we find Amber and your life gets back to normal, you'll be glad we stopped."

She liked that he put it that way, that they would find Amber, but she couldn't fathom ever being glad they'd stopped. In fact, she could more easily see her spending the rest of her life regretting it, wondering what it would have been like. And it really had been silly, to accuse him of not being interested; it wasn't like she could deny the obvious fact that he'd been a fully, completely aroused male.

But that realization was followed by a flood of self-recrimination. How could she even have thought of doing this, of indulging in this, when Amber was God knows where with a possibly crazy man who might have abducted her?

Teague's cell phone chirped a by now familiar sound, the arrival of a text message. She wondered rather vaguely, as if she only wanted the distraction, if Foxworth had a protocol for what rated an actual phone call as opposed to a text.

He reached for his jacket—Drake's jacket—and pulled the phone out of the pocket. She wondered what it must feel like, to have that constant reminder, to put it on every day, to wear what his dead friend had worn. Was it solely in tribute, to honor his memory, or was it out of fear of forgetting?

Honor, she thought, even before the question had fully formed in her mind. Teague Johnson would never forget, and he wouldn't need a daily reminder to make sure of it. But honor? Yes, that fit. That was who he was. He was a man of honor. Hadn't he just proved that to her, in a rather vivid, painful way?

Not, she thought sourly as he tapped through screens to get the text, that she agreed with him. Maybe she was a little off balance, maybe she was worn down a bit with worry, but none of that accounted for the way she'd responded to his touch, his kiss. No, there was more to it than simply needing comfort in a storm. Much, much more.

His brow furrowed as he read. Just slightly, so she guessed it wasn't horrible news. He texted a quick answer, so short it had to be just an acknowledgment that he'd gotten the message, then put the phone back into the jacket.

"News?"

He looked at her. "Not about Amber, directly."

"But something."

He nodded. "The sick relative Edward was supposedly off to stay with?"

Laney nodded, remembering the information Quinn had gleaned from his contact with North Country Enterprises. "His other aunt. She was in the hospital, they said."

"Yes. Except she's alive, well and gave a talk at her local garden club last week. And she hasn't seen or heard from her nephew in weeks."

She felt a chill overtake her. Edward had lied about where he was going and why. Lied to his bosses. Risked his job if he was found out.

She wondered why Teague had reacted as if this weren't huge. Then she remembered. This just confirmed she'd been right about what he'd already been thinking.

That Amber was dead.

Chapter 22

"I know you've been through it what must seem like a hundred times," Hayley said, her tone sympathetic, "but—"

"I get it," Laney said. "Each time there might be something new I remember."

"You already have," Quinn pointed out. "You remembered you saw Edward twice at the sporting goods place near your old work, so we knew he might frequent the place."

"Not particularly useful."

"But it was. One of the clerks there remembered him. And that the last time he was in, a few months ago, he tried to buy some nylon rope but his credit card was rejected."

"But that's long before he even met Amber, how does that help?"

"It doesn't, yet. But it might."

Teague stayed quiet. He had nothing to say. And he wasn't about to point out that Edward's attempted purchase could mean he'd planned this out before he'd even met his victim. Knowing there would be a victim, before he'd picked her out.

And he especially wasn't going to mention the first intended victim could well have been Laney herself. The thought put him even more on edge than he already was.

"At least the police are taking it seriously now."

"Yes, they are. The unused plane ticket and that he lied about the sick relative at least got their interest. The kid having the phone and being paid to text you really made them curious. And with Detective Dunbar prodding them, it may get more attention than it otherwise would."

"So…you turn it over to them now?"

Teague felt a sudden chill. Is that what she wanted? Had she had such second thoughts about what had happened last night that she wanted to be free of him, of Foxworth?

Yeah, make it all about you, that's good thinking.

The words dripped with sarcasm in his mind. But he couldn't deny he sensed Laney was wavering. Even though she wouldn't look at him, hadn't looked at him at all this morning. Not that he could blame her. And he'd expected it, after she'd coolly told him she could find her own way to Foxworth now when he'd said he would pick her up for this meeting.

"We can do that, if that's what you want," Hayley said, her tone carefully neutral.

He opened his mouth, shut it again; nothing had changed, he was better off staying out of this discussion. It was a lose-lose for him. He'd already gone way across the line in this case. If he tried to urge Laney to drop the case, she was liable to think the same thing he just had, that he wanted out because of what had happened between them last night. If he urged her to let them stay with it, she was liable to think he wanted to pursue what had happened between them last night. Whatever the hell it had been.

Besides a raging inferno, you mean?

That inner voice that usually saved itself for warnings and assessments of dangerous situations was full of biting wit this morning. Probably brought on by the long, sleepless night he'd spent pacing and cursing at himself, in between thoughts of a long, icy cold shower.

He should tell Quinn. Ask to be taken off this one. Tell him he was over the line, that he'd become too personally involved. And then he nearly laughed out loud at the vague words to describe what had been anything but. It didn't get much more specific than stripping half her clothes off her and nearly going all caveman when she touched him in turn.

And the bottom line never changed; if Laney thought he wanted to pursue what had leaped to life between them, she would be right. But he wouldn't. He couldn't. Not even for that, whatever that fiery explosion had been, could he risk the trust Quinn had put in him.

Of course, that was easy to say when he wasn't half-naked on the floor with her, her luscious breasts bared to him, her nipples taut and glistening from his mouth, his own body raging under her touch.

Just the memories were enough to send him careening toward the edge. He clamped down on his recalcitrant body, and the effort it took convinced him anew that he had to do it. He just had to trust Quinn would understand. The man knew something about uncontrollable passion, he thought. But at least Hayley hadn't been a client who had put her trust in them.

"—maybe that would be best," Laney was saying, and he wondered what he'd missed with his out-of-control, undisciplined thoughts. He obviously should have been paying more attention to what was going on instead of sitting here in a haze of sexual arousal over a woman who was—or should be—off-limits.

"It's up to you, of course. But remember, we don't quit unless you tell us to," Quinn said.

He'd been right, then. She was wavering, thinking it would be better to leave it to the police now that they were involved.

A sudden woof and a scramble of paws broke through the seemingly never-ending swirl of his thoughts. Cutter had been napping quietly in his spot on the floor, but was now on his feet. And Teague realized somewhat uneasily that the dog with the piercing gaze had it fastened on him.

Unexpectedly the dog rose up and put his front feet on the table. Even Hayley looked startled. Cutter focused on the folder that held Amber's file, the paper file they used because it was easier to pass around the table than the laptop. The dog batted at it rather fiercely with one paw and the contents scattered across the table. What was he up to? Teague wondered. With any other dog, it would be just an accident, but with Cutter that was never a safe assumption.

Even as he thought it, Cutter managed to isolate the photo of Amber, and nosed it toward Teague until it was right in front of him.

"Well," Quinn said.

"Yes," Hayley said.

"What was that?" Laney asked.

"That, I believe, was an opinion expressed," Hayley said.

Laney looked at Hayley, then Quinn, then back at Hayley. She still hadn't met his gaze once this morning.

"You know I love dogs as much as anyone, and more than most," she said. "But he is just a dog."

"If you say so," Quinn answered wryly.

She looked doubtful.

"We've learned it's not a good idea to ignore him," Hayley said. "Right, Teague?"

"More like impossible to ignore him." It was the first thing he'd said, not that anybody had asked for his input until now.

"That, too," Quinn agreed.

"And he did start this," Teague added.

"Yes," Hayley said. "Which makes it kind of his case, right?"

"And he's obviously not ready to quit yet," Quinn said.

Laney stared at them all in turn, Teague last, meeting his gaze for the first time. He kept his expression even.

She shifted her attention to the dog, who seemed to sense her doubts. He went to her, sat down and plopped his chin on her knee as he stared up at her intently. Teague knew what it was like to have that intense gaze fastened upon him, and wondered if it would have the same effect on someone who hadn't really seen what the dog could and had done.

"I…"

She shook her head, almost sharply, and Teague knew why. Cutter's steady gaze was an almost palpable thing, something you felt like you could shake off if you tried.

"Makes you feel for the sheep, doesn't it?" he said.

She chuckled. It was short and held a slightly puzzled note, but he'd take it. At least she wasn't avoiding even looking at him anymore.

"You really believe this," she said to Quinn, who probably seemed to her the most unlikely to put his faith in the whimsy of a clever dog.

Quinn nodded. "And I'm a very hard sell. But he's piled up enough stats by now that I'm convinced."

"We don't know how he does what he does. Only that he does it," Hayley added. "And he clearly thinks there's more for us to do here."

"You know there are those who would insist he doesn't think at all," Laney said.

"And they," Teague said, "would be wrong."

Laney leaned back in her chair. She looked at Cutter again, reached out and stroked his head, scratched the spot below his right ear that everybody who met him eventually learned about. He let out a soft *whuff* of sound, turned his head to swipe his tongue over her fingers.

"All right, my furry friend. You win."

This time Cutter let out a yip of happy acknowledgment, the sound of a dog who knew he'd won. At least, that's what it seemed like. And that assessment was reinforced by the fact that he went placidly back to his spot on the floor and resumed his nap, just that quickly.

"I should sleep so easily," Teague muttered.

He heard Laney move at his words, didn't dare look at her for fear of what he'd see in her eyes at the implications. He hadn't meant it that way. At least, not consciously. But memories of last night, of the sweet taste of her, of the driving need he'd had to marshal resources long unused to fight back assailed him now that he'd spoken so unwisely.

"When you run at a hundred miles an hour while you're awake, I guess you sleep when and where you can," Hayley said.

Relieved at the lighthearted words, Teague glanced at her. His relief faded when he saw her watching him, then Laney, and vanished when he recognized the assessing look in her eyes. Whatever that female instinct was about people and relationships, Hayley had it. She knew, in the same way Cutter knew about people in trouble. Like Cutter, she was rarely wrong.

And he didn't like her turning it on him. Or that he'd obviously betrayed enough to trigger that instinct in her.

But what he didn't like most of all was the twinge of regret he'd felt when Laney decided to continue. It was faint, and he quashed it instantly and easily, but it had occurred just the same. For just that moment, he'd wished she would tell them to drop it, to leave it to the police now that they were involved. Because then he'd be free to finish what they'd started last night.

Last night she was an emotional wreck, he told himself in self-disgust. *You know what kind of woman she is, do you really think she'd have been so willing so fast if her head had been on straight?*

He stopped his thoughts before he lurched into the morass he'd been mired in last night. Besides, he should have known she wouldn't quit, not really. She'd want every possible asset working on finding Amber, and she'd go to the wall herself to do it. Even if it meant spending time and money she didn't have, because she put no price on loyalty.

In a twisted sort of way, the very things that attracted him to her were the things that had her so tangled up that she was vulnerable. It was amazing she was still speaking to him at all.

She'd said nothing at all to him about last night. She'd barely said hello when she'd arrived this morning. She'd spoken only of Amber and the status of the case now. If he'd truly wanted to forget about what had happened last night, she was reacting perfectly. He should follow her lead, he told himself. Just act as if nothing had changed.

But it had.

And there he was, back at the twitchy, agitated place he'd spent most of the night. He hadn't been restless, pacing the floor last night simply because he'd gotten all revved up and had to stop. It hadn't been because his body had been awakened after a long dry spell. It had been, he'd finally had to admit at about 3:00 a.m., because he'd never experienced anything like what had leaped to life between him and Laney. And it was a little stunning to have to admit, after thirty years of living, he had never realized sensations like that were even possible. He'd never even looked for that kind of feeling, because he'd never known it existed.

And if it was that intense even when they'd stopped short…

Teague had the sinking feeling he was only beginning to realize the full extent of this. And no amount of telling himself it was just some kissing that had gotten out of hand could change that.

No matter what happened from last night on, he was afraid his life had been changed forever by a few searing minutes with the woman sitting across from him. He glanced at Quinn, caught him looking at Hayley with what the team jokingly called The Look.

He got it, now. If this was what Quinn had felt when he first met Hayley, Teague was sure of one thing.

He hadn't felt nearly enough sympathy for his boss.

Chapter 23

"It's not your fault, Laney."

Hayley's tone was reassuring, but Laney wasn't in the mood to be reassured. Although she had to admit, sitting here in the sun on the patio outside Foxworth's back door was relaxing. Not enough to stop her wondering what Hayley was up to by asking her to join her out here for a light lunch, but still, relaxing.

"I feel like it is," she said. "I should know more about the guy, I should have listened better. Been more aware. But I just floated along in my safe, quiet life, not paying much attention to anything outside my own little world."

"We all do, until something—or someone—comes along to shake us out of that. Sometimes good, sometimes bad. Sometimes both."

"Both?"

"My mother's death shook me, badly. But then Quinn came along."

"And kidnapped you?"

Hayley looked startled, but then grinned. "Teague's been talking."

She thought she kept her expression even, but something flickered in Hayley's eyes that told her she hadn't quite been successful. She'd wondered, by the way the woman had looked at them both during the assessment meeting this morning, if she suspected something. Now she was almost certain.

"He said I should ask you about it."

"It's a long story, involving the proverbial black helicopter," Hayley said, and gave her what she said was the digest version of what had happened after a midnight trek with Cutter.

"And now you're engaged," she said, shaking her head in wonder at the tale.

"We'd be married already if Quinn had his way."

"It's obvious he's crazy about you."

"And I'm crazy about him. But a girl needs time to prepare, right?"

"Not to mention enjoy being engaged," Laney said.

"Exactly."

"Especially when she gets to show off a man like Quinn."

"That, too," Hayley agreed with a laugh. "He is pretty impressive."

Laney hesitated to ask what was really on her mind. But she remembered the way Hayley had looked at them so consideringly and figured she wouldn't be giving anything away the very perceptive woman hadn't already guessed.

"After all that drama," she said at last, "how were you sure it wasn't just…all that drama?"

"How did I know it was real, and not just the circumstances?" Hayley asked.

"Exactly," Laney said, relieved she wouldn't have to explain further.

"Quinn," she said simply. "He's been doing this for a while, and he's helped a lot of people, including women. Some very attractive women. But nothing ever happened between them."

Laney drew back slightly. "Until you."

Hayley nodded. "So even if I didn't trust my own judgment, I trusted his. He knew the difference, knew it was real." Her mouth quirked. "And the fact that he wasn't thrilled about it at first helped. It's a lot easier to believe when you see them fighting it."

Fighting it. As Teague had last night.

As if she'd heard the thought, Hayley said softly, "Teague's a good man. A very good man."

Laney stared at the can of soda she held, watching a drop of condensation track down the side, wondering inanely what law of physics determined the path it took. Anything but look at Hayley.

"Yes," she finally said, "he is."

She hoped Hayley would leave it at that, but in her way she was as tenacious as Cutter.

"He's been through some true hell in his life," Hayley said. "And I won't say he doesn't carry scars from it, because he does. I think that's why he jokes so much, as a sort of camouflage."

Laney's brow furrowed. Hayley had mentioned that once, some time ago, that Teague was the most cheerful guy she knew. The one who lightens the mood with quips and teasing. She'd heard him do that a few times, when they'd been with Hayley or Quinn or Tyler, or even with a couple of people when they'd been at the airport. But rarely when it had been just them.

"He doesn't do that with you?" Hayley asked. "Interesting."

The woman was really too perceptive for comfort, Laney thought. "Not often. He's being professional, I guess." Like he had been last night, belatedly.

"He always is," Hayley answered. "At the core he's unchangeable. He's good, solid, honest, strong and above all honorable."

Laney's mouth tightened and her eyes stung. She blinked a couple of times, thinking how humiliated she'd be if she who rarely cried started now. With some effort, she managed a light tone.

"Was that an assessment, or an endorsement?"

"Yes," Hayley said simply.

She sighed. That's what she got, she supposed, for all that sailing along on the surface, enjoying her easy, peaceful life without much thought about it. The stress of starting her business had been the toughest thing she'd ever had to deal with, and she looked at it as more of a challenge than anything. But she should have known there would be a price…that no one got through life unscathed.

It seemed the bill for that peace had come due.

Teague found Quinn in the warehouse that served them as storage and also as a hangar for the helicopter. His boss was standing next to the gleaming black craft, studying something intently. He was looking at the bullet hole, Teague realized.

The rest of the damage incurred the night they'd ended up kidnapping Hayley had been repaired, parts patched or replaced. But this hole, in a harmless place that had no effect on flight, Quinn had opted to keep. Usually looking at it made him smile . Every time they piled into the thing, Teague could count on a moment when Quinn would glance at it and his mouth would curve slightly, and his eyes would warm.

Teague would tease him about it. And inwardly marvel at how at-ease he felt with his boss. At what a wonder it was to him still, to work for a man he not only respected and admired, but liked. One who was solid, steady and even and always had his back.

One who would take the teasing with a smile that spoke volumes of the strength of his relationship with Hayley. And Teague believed it; nothing could shake those two apart.

Yes, he knew how Quinn felt. What he didn't know was how it felt to feel that way.

An image of Laney, half-naked on the floor, wanting him, offering herself, shot through his mind. That was just sex, he told himself. It had been a while, she was a beautiful woman, inside and out, she'd been willing; it was only to be expected. Natural. Nature. Trying to take its course.

And he wasn't sure if he'd done the right thing by stopping, or just been a stupid fool not to take what he'd wanted, wanted so much it had nearly killed him to pull away.

"Teague? You all right?"

"Yes." *No.* "I'm fine." *I'm insane.* "What next?" *Find a cure?*

He was very much afraid there was no cure, except the one he couldn't, wouldn't take.

"Ty's still working on tracking Edward. If he's out there and moving, there has to be a trail."

Teague forced himself to get his head back in the game. "And if he's not, if he's gone to ground, with Amber," he began.

"Then we really have our work cut out for us."

"What do you want me to do?"

"Stick with Laney. There's always a chance she might remember something that could be key, something she doesn't realize could be important."

And there it was. The order he'd been dreading. And the time to ask to be taken off this one. All he had to do was say it. Simple. *Sir, you should send somebody else. I'm too—*

Too what? Stupid? Too slow to wake up? Too in lust?

No, he'd just suggest someone else. Send Liam, who was due back tonight from the tech seminar Foxworth had sent him to to help keep his skills sharp. Liam's family had raised dogs; he and Laney would get along great.

Or Rafe. Now, that would be something. Laney would bemuse the taciturn, solitary Rafe. The man had little faith left in mankind in general. Laney's sweetness and loyalty would not only win him over, but probably do him a lot of good.

That was the solution, he thought. He opened his mouth to make the suggestion.

"I think…"

The words wouldn't come. And Quinn spoke before he could force them out.

"Take some food. Or take her to lunch. Hayley's worried she's not eating enough."

Great. Now he was under orders to take her out.

"Problem, Johnson?"

The use of his last name warned him, told him he was acting too oddly, that he was getting very close to tripping Quinn's radar, and if that happened, there'd be no way out of explaining every last damned detail of why he wanted off this case. Not a prospect he savored.

"No, sir. Sorry. Just…thinking." His mouth twisted ruefully. "Probably too much."

"Get on it, then."

"Yes, sir."

And with those two words, acknowledgment and promise in one, he was committed. Not for anything would he let this man down. The escape hatch was closed, and he'd done it to himself.

Hayley watched as Quinn threw the ball for Cutter. It warmed her as always to watch them together. He made time for a session almost every day he wasn't actively out on a case, something she appreciated, as the dog got twice as much exercise from his long throws than her own efforts. She could throw hard, but he had long down pat.

And a Cutter who didn't get enough exercise was a Cutter who'd burn off that astonishing energy some other way.

"Fun?" she asked the dog as the game finally came to an end, Cutter signaling he'd had enough by bringing the ball back and dropping it beside his water bowl before taking a long, noisy drink. His tail wagged at her words, but the drinking continued.

"He especially liked the part when it hit that muddy spot and he got to wade in knee-deep to get it," Quinn said wryly as he rinsed off his hands at the outdoor spigot.

"Might have to take him to Laney again," Hayley said.

"She might like the distraction."

"Yes. And she hasn't been as focused on her business as she would be if it weren't for Amber."

Quinn smiled, put his arms around her. "First her eating, then her needing distraction and now her business. You worry too much."

"I like her."

"And that's all it takes for you, isn't it?"

"Look who's talking. Besides, Cutter started this, not me."

He laughed. "Yes, he did."

"So," she said, "how deep do you think Teague is?"

He drew back slightly to look down at her. "What?"

"Teague. With Laney. How far do you think it's gone?"

He frowned. "I'd be able to answer that better if I knew what you were talking about."

She sighed. "Come on, you can't tell me you didn't feel that snap, crackle and pop between them this morning."

His gaze narrowed. "What are you saying?"

"And Cutter. He didn't push that picture of Amber to you or me, he pushed it at Teague."

Quinn opened his mouth as if to speak, but then stopped, a thoughtful expression crossing his face.

"What?" Hayley asked.

"He did seem…a little odd today. When I told him to stick with Laney, keep prodding her memory."

Hayley smiled. "And there you have it."

"You're saying he, she, that they're— What are you saying?"

Hayley's answer was to crouch beside Cutter, who had finished his water intake and come to sit at their feet.

"Is that it, boy? Is this about more than Amber in trouble?"

The dog's tail started wagging madly, and he gave her a quick lick on the chin. Then he made that sound they'd come to know, a low, happy, half bark, half *whuffing* noise.

"That's his 'you finally figured it out' sound, isn't it?" Quinn asked, sounding a bit rueful.

"Yep. Besides, with Cutter, isn't it always more than it seems?"

"Ain't that the truth," Quinn said, pulling her up and back into his arms.

"He was right about us," Hayley said.

"That he was."

"He—"

She never finished the sentence. Didn't even try. Quinn was kissing her, and nothing else mattered.

Chapter 24

"You should eat."

"I did."

"Not enough," Teague said.

"Somebody appoint you my mother?" Laney asked, knowing she sounded like a cranky child but somehow unable to stop it.

Her plate sat still half-full, even though the salmon she'd ordered was delicious. She just wasn't hungry, even though Teague had somehow known her favorite local restaurant and given her little choice about coming with him. Even though sitting out on the restaurant patio in the summer sun usually fired her appetite for the fresh, locally caught fish that could well have come off one of the boats she could see at the dock from here.

"Yes," he answered. "Hayley."

That took the wind out of her annoyed sails. "Hayley?"

That explained the restaurant choice, she guessed. She and Hayley had discussed it once when she'd brought in Cutter.

"She's worried about you. Thinks you're not eating enough."

"So that's why you showed up and insisted we come here."

He'd been under orders. She should have known. No way he would have done this on his own, not after last night.

He'd told her she'd be glad, later, that they'd stopped. She still wasn't. But she was embarrassed. She'd had time, too much time, to think about what had happened. And what hadn't. Most of all, how ready she'd been to have sex with a man she barely knew.

But the whiny part of her insisted she knew the important things. She might not know his favorite food, or color, or sport, but she knew the important things. She knew his character, didn't she? Because if he hadn't been who she knew he was, he wouldn't have stopped in the first place. He would have taken advantage of the situation and they would have ended up in her bed.

And she still wasn't convinced she didn't regret that they hadn't.

"Where do you live?"

He seemed startled at the question out of the blue. She didn't explain. Somehow saying "I feel like I should at least know where the guy I was ready to jump last night lives" didn't seem right or wise.

"Over on Puget View Drive," he said after a moment. "I rent a guest house. Used to live in an apartment, but the noise got to me."

"Alone?"

She hadn't meant to say it, but once she had she wasn't sorry. His fingers, in the midst of tracing the curved handle of the spoon beside his own plate—he'd ordered the same thing she had, but he'd managed to finish most of it—stilled. His eyes came up, his gaze locked with hers.

"Is that really what you think of me?"

She sighed. "No."

It wasn't what she thought of him. And she realized belatedly she'd already known the answer to the question. If he'd had someone at home, last night never would have happened. He wouldn't. Teague Johnson just wouldn't. That honor thing again.

"Then why did you ask?"

She wasn't sure herself. Maybe she wished it had been something that simple. That clear-cut. Something that would keep that barrier between them, nice and solid. Something other than just doing it—or rather, not doing it—for her sake, because he thought she'd regret it later. Because that just made her want him more.

"I guess," she said slowly, "it's hard for me to believe the real reason you stopped."

"You are damn near irresistible."

She gaped at him. Then heat flooded her face and she knew her cheeks must be glowing. "No, I didn't mean that, I never thought that!"

"Teasing, Laney," he said with a wry smile.

Did that mean he didn't think she was irresistible?

She nearly groaned aloud at her own contrary, mouse-in-a-maze thoughts, darting, dodging, from one idiocy to another.

"Sorry. I just meant I don't know many men who would have stopped for that reason. Which I suppose says as much about the caliber of men I've encountered before as it does about you," she ended rather glumly.

Teague's brow furrowed for a moment. Then he picked up that spoon he'd been toying with. "I think," he said tentatively, "if I dug deep enough with this, I might find a compliment in there."

That one made her lower her gaze, but honesty made her say, "Yes. You would."

"Didn't see that on the menu, or I would have ordered it up sooner."

Her gaze shot to his face. He was smiling, nice, warm, friendly.

He was joking with her. Teasing.

Hayley's words came back to her again…*always with a quip, the one who lightens the mood.*

More importantly, Hayley's words from this morning echoed in her head. *He doesn't do that with you? Interesting.*

But now he was doing it. Because now she was no different than anybody else? Because he'd mentally put her back into the category of merely a job, an assignment?

And again her insides twisted, knotted. And no amount of chastising herself for being an idiot seemed to make any difference.

"If you're not going to eat, tell me again about that day you and Amber met Edward."

Oh, yes, she was right back in the pure business category.

The instant the thought formed she hated herself for it. He was trying to help find Amber, and shouldn't that be her focus, too? Here she was stewing over the fact that a man had nearly made love to her but stopped, for praiseworthy reasons, when her best friend was still out there somewhere, maybe in trouble, maybe serious trouble.

With a serious inward shake, she shoved her own concerns down, telling herself bitingly that she could whine later, in private.

"I don't know what I can say that I haven't already."

"Maybe nothing. But maybe something. Close your eyes. Walk through it in your head."

Like the detective had done with the kid who had Amber's phone, she thought. It had worked with him, so why not? Besides, she liked the closing her eyes part. Looking at him sitting across the too-small table from her was unsettling.

When she did, when the distraction of his face, the strong jaw, the clear blue eyes, was gone, somehow all she could think of was his bare chest, how he'd looked, what his skin had felt like, stretched over taut muscle.

Where on earth had all her self-discipline gone? She knew she had it, and had the history of long, hard hours working to get her business started and keep it going to prove it. She just couldn't seem to find it at the moment.

"What day was it?" he prompted, and she barely managed not to open her eyes just to look at him.

She tilted her head back, let the sun warm her. Soon it would be gone and the long, wet winter that was the price they paid for such glorious days as this would set in.

"Saturday," she said. "I had gone down and walked on the ferry to Seattle, and Amber picked me up on the other side."

"What were you wearing?"

She did flick her eyes open then. This question was new, and as far as she could see, irrelevant. "Me?"

"Close your eyes," he said again. "Going through the small details you do remember might trigger others."

"Oh."

That made sense, she supposed, although she'd tried so hard to remember every little thing that she couldn't imagine anything else would be lurking in some corner of her mind that she'd missed.

"Khaki-colored jeans," she said. "Red sleeveless blouse. Tan shoes, the comfortable ones. I wanted to wear sandals, because the weather was great, but we were going shopping, so I didn't want to walk that much in them."

"What was Amber wearing?"

She'd given them that in great detail more than once, but she didn't point that out. She'd been foolish enough already this afternoon. This was professional Teague, and she was going to act accordingly from here on.

"Blue. Her best color. Dark blue shorts, lighter blue knit top. She did wear sandals. She'd just had a pedicure and wanted to show it off."

"Where did you go?"

"To brunch, first. Her favorite place, right near the waterfront. Her plan was to eat a lot, then walk it off."

"Shopping for what?"

"Nothing in particular."

"Just…shopping?"

At his tone, again her eyes opened. She could do this, too, she thought. "You're such a guy," she teased. "I'll bet you only go to a store for something specific, find it, buy it and get out."

"Well…yes. If you don't need something, what's the point of going?"

"What if you don't know you need something until you see it?"

He blinked. "But if you didn't see it, you wouldn't know you needed it, so in effect you don't need it."

She managed a genuine smile at that one. And repeated his own words back to him. "That made sense to me. Should I worry?"

After a split second a grin spread across his face. "Touché," he said. "Now where were we?"

"Shopping."

"Where?"

"At the mall near Amber's place. And close to where I used to work."

"Walk me through it. Everything, don't worry about if it's relevant or boring or seemingly meaningless. Tell me."

She closed her eyes again. It did help. She brought up the day she'd thought so much about.

"It was crowded. We had to park way out. We heard a dog

in a parked car, and I was worried because it was so warm. But Amber spotted it, and there was a girl in the car with it, I guess waiting for someone. She had all the windows all the way down, and a door open while she was giving the dog water, so it was okay. It was a pug. Cute."

"Keep going," he said when she paused.

"There were Girl Scouts at the door, selling flavored popcorn. We bought a bag to share, just because the kids were so cute, so earnest in their pitch, and so excited about the camp they were raising the money for."

This had to be boring him to tears, Laney figured; he'd been there every time she'd gone through this, but she kept going.

"It was nice to get inside, where it was air-conditioned. Amber loves malls. She always has."

"But not you?"

"I went to hang with her," she said. "And that was where she wanted to go. I didn't mind. Sometimes we went for hikes like I wanted, and I know she didn't like that, but she went because it was my turn to choose."

"Good friends."

"Yes. The best."

Tears threatened again. She had to open her eyes to blink them back. Decided not to mention it, not to call attention to the fact that she was crying again, although he could hardly miss it.

"Go ahead," he said, gently.

Back in her mind again, she went through it all, every stop she could remember, the two purchases Amber had made: makeup and a pair of sparkly, dangly earrings. Walking down toward the shoe store at the far end of the mall, where Amber had her eye on a pair of stiletto heels that made Laney's feet hurt just looking at them.

And coming out of the big, anchor department store had

been a familiar face. Edward. He'd been talking to someone a little behind him and then spotted Amber. As many men did, he stopped in his tracks. Then he'd seen and recognized her, and if Laney thought that some of his smile was for the fact that she could introduce him to Amber, she kept it to herself, then and now.

The chatting up, the tentative flirtation, all took place there in the relative safety of a public place full of people. Nothing untoward was said, in fact, she'd watched the exchange with some amusement; men tended to get a bit silly around Amber. Even Edward's friend was rolling his eyes a bit. But in the end Edward played it smart; instead of asking for Amber's number he gave her his, and asked her to call him. Anytime. Anywhere. Please.

She shifted in her chair. This was where it got uncomfortable, and it didn't matter that she'd been through it a few times before.

"He left. Amber asked me about him. I told her what I knew." She took a breath to steady herself. "I said he seemed nice enough, from what I'd seen. She asked if she should call him. I said sure, why not. We finished our shopping. She took me back to the ferry, I came home. That's it."

She opened her eyes, aware she'd hurried through that, but it was the most painful part, and she'd had to say it so many times. And each time it etched her guilt more deeply.

"And she called him."

"Yes. She told me she was going to. And she seemed quite happy about it when they agreed to go to dinner."

"And she called you that day."

"Yes. She was fussing about what to wear. Normal Amber. I told her it didn't matter, she'd be gorgeous in anything. She kept fussing. Our usual routine."

"And that was—"

"Yes." She couldn't bear to hear him say it. "The last time I spoke to her."

It hit her hard, the realization that that laughing, teasing conversation might well be the last she ever had with Amber. She didn't realize she was shivering, even in the sun, until Teague put a hand over hers. The warmth steadied her, just as that new awareness, that electric charge tingled along her nerves.

"We'll find her," he said.

"I know." She believed that. Foxworth would not quit until they did.

She just wished she could go back to believing they'd find her alive.

"Walk with me."

Laney looked across at him, feeling a little drained.

"You need the distraction," he said. "After that."

She hesitated. But he was still holding her hand, and if she didn't walk with him he might let go. And at this moment in time that seemed like the worst thing that could happen. So she rose, and they started to walk along the peaceful, pictur-esque waterfront.

She didn't pull her hand free, although she considered it. But right now she felt as if he were her anchor, the only thing keeping her from, as he'd once said, going airborne.

You're my anchor, Laney. Without you to keep me cen-tered, remind me of who I am, I'd be lost.

Amber's oft spoken words came back to her with a poignancy that struck hard.

"What?" Teague asked.

Most women would kill for a man this observant, Laney thought ruefully. And here she was wishing that, for once, he wouldn't notice every little change in her expression.

Or wishing it wasn't because he was a trained pro at it. Something she'd do well to remember. Especially when he was holding her hand and her body was all too aware of the fact.

"Just something Amber used to say."

"What?"

"That I was her anchor. Kept her sane, centered."

His fingers tightened around hers. "I can see that."

"She worried about something happening to me. Neither of us ever thought it would be her, not Amber, the golden girl who had it all—" She stopped dead, shaking now. "Oh, God. I'm using past tense."

He didn't say anything. He simply pulled her into his arms and gave her shelter.

Chapter 25

She was steadier by the time they got back to her apartment. Teague had driven mostly in silence. It didn't matter, he was there, and that in itself was comforting.

She appreciated that he hadn't tried to soothe her with false hope. That he hadn't assured her Amber was all right. He'd only said what he'd always said, that they'd find her. But he must have known all along, and more certainly the more time passed, that there was a chance it would be too late.

As she opened her door she managed not to look at the spot where they'd ended up on the floor last night. But it took an effort that was almost embarrassing, and as observant as he was, Teague was likely noticing how carefully she was avoiding it. Her discomfiture made her voice a little sharp when she turned back to look at him.

"I'd invite you in, but I don't want a replay."

He winced, made a small, compressed sound that matched the expression. "That never should have happened."

"I didn't mean that it happened. I meant the abrupt stop."

He looked disconcerted then, which gave her a small bit of satisfaction.

"It wasn't right. You're—"

"A client? I know that."

"Quinn—"

"Wouldn't approve of you getting involved with a client? Yeah, I got that, too."

He shifted uncomfortably.

"Not sure Quinn has room to talk, though," Laney said.

Teague's mouth quirked wryly then. "And he knows that. It's not that he'd say anything. Except to be sure."

"Of what you want?"

"Oh, I know what I want," Teague said, and a new undertone had crept into his voice, a note that sent an entirely new kind of shiver through her. "He'd be worried about you. Because you're not in a real good place right now."

"I'm also a grown woman capable of making decisions."

"That's obvious. Look at what you've accomplished."

"But you think me incapable of making this one? Incapable of knowing that I know what I want, too?"

She heard him suck in a deep breath. His jaw tightened as if he were fighting some internal battle. She hoped he was. She hoped he was losing. Or maybe winning? Was he fighting to go, or to stay?

"Not incapable. Just situationally off balance."

"Is that an official military term?"

He blinked. And then one corner of his mouth quirked upward. "No. But maybe it should be."

"Have you ever been…situationally off balance?"

"Often. But I've also been trained to adapt."

"And you've made decisions in those situations?"

His brow furrowed. She waited. "Of course."

"And how did they work out, given you're still here to talk about it?"

His mouth quirked again, and she suspected he'd figured out where she was going with this.

"Laney—"

She cut him off before he could stop her. "So you're saying you can make a rational decision while situationally off balance, but I can't?"

"Remind me never to get in a battle of words with you," he said dryly.

"Gladly."

"Probably wits, too."

"Maybe," she said. "Does this mean you surrender?"

He sucked in a harsh, audible breath. "Speaking of words," he muttered.

"If I were Amber," she said slowly, holding his gaze, seeing, savoring the heat burgeoning in his eyes, "I'd try to wind you up tight and then send you on your way wanting, lesson learned."

"But you're not Amber."

"No. I love her like a sister," she said, very consciously using the right tense this time, "but we're very different. But I finally remembered that, thanks to her, I'm prepared. She's always telling me a girl should be, and I'd forgotten she gave me a box on my birthday, as a joke. Or a nudge."

"Laney," he began then stopped as if he didn't have a clue what to say.

Somehow this reassured her, made her bolder. And in the back of her mind she could hear Amber egging her on. She had always said this was the only part of her life where Laney was afraid of taking a chance, and maybe she'd been right.

And underneath it all was another driving motivation. Amber's disappearance had rattled her quiet world, had brought reality crushingly home to her. You really never knew what might happen and assuming you would have endless tomorrows was not the way to really live.

She reached up to touch him, her fingers lightly stroking that clenched jawline.

"Go or stay," she said. "But don't treat me as if I'm fragile or breakable. Or make decisions alone that we should both make."

"Damn."

It exploded from him, sounding more like prayer than curse. And then he turned his head, pressed his lips to the palm of her hand. Decision made, she thought, exhilaration slamming through her.

The fire sparked, caught. Nerves already tingling sent messages of heat and need, awakening every part of her in a fierce wave. And then his mouth was on hers, urging, demanding, and she knew he'd thrown that caution to the winds. She wasn't sure there wouldn't be a big price to pay, eventually, wasn't sure he hadn't been right all along, but she didn't care. Not now, not when he was holding her, not when she had vivid, searing proof that what she'd felt last night hadn't been some kind of fluke born of her unsettled state.

It was fire, pure and scorching, and unlike anything she'd ever felt before. Her heart was hammering in response to his touch, her body both demanding and offering. This, this was what they wrote about, sang about. She'd never been sure, feared she was lacking whatever something that enabled people to experience this. But it had just been the wrong person before, that was all. Teague was right, even if only for this moment in time. Maybe she'd regret this someday, maybe he would, but now, now it was all that mattered.

Whatever this was, it was worth any risk.

They made it as far as her couch this time. It made shedding clothes more difficult and the entanglement more frustrating. She thought she heard something rip as he yanked at her shirt. She didn't care. And he didn't even notice, which somehow thrilled her.

He was as beautiful as she'd remembered. Taut, lean and strong. Then his hands, just a little rough and very, very male, were on her, cupping her breasts, lifting them for his mouth. She nearly cried out at the searing sensation that shot through her, as if the nerves he aroused were connected to her entire body. His tongue flicked nipples already hardened by his touch, and she arched helplessly. He suckled her gently, and this time she did cry out as the heat and sensation flared. Harder then, drawing that eager peak into his mouth until she thought she would forget how to breathe. He switched to her other breast, repeating the sweet attention until she gasped out his name. Her body seemed to ripple of its own accord, and she felt the ridge of thoroughly aroused male prodding her lower belly, hot, hard, silken, ready.

Just the thought of taking him inside her had her heart pounding until she thought she would die if he didn't move, now, right now.

He slid a hand downward, not in a rush, at least not the rush she seemed to be in. Leisurely, as if there were all the time in the world, as if she wasn't about to be consumed by the fire he'd lit. He traced each rib, stroked over her waist, slid out to linger at the curve of her hip, as if he thought someday he might have to reproduce that curve and wanted to get it right.

She understood that if her own urges were any indication. She wanted to trace every inch of him, to savor, remember, wanted her hands and body as well as her eyes able to summon up the memory of this, in case he went all noble on her again and this was the only time they would have.

And then, as his mouth came back to hers, his hand moved, and in the moment before his lips took hers again she felt his touch in that most intimate place. Realized by the ease of his stroke how ready she was for this man, in the instant before the feel of it made her cry out again as he captured the sound with an ever deepening kiss.

He lifted his head, breaking the kiss. She made a small sound of protest.

"Point of no return, Laney," he said, his voice so low and rough it sent a shiver through her, and the counterpoint to the building heat somehow made it all explode. "Are you sure?"

"What I'm sure of," she whispered, "is that if you don't hurry I'll go insane."

He made a harsh sound somewhere between acknowledgment and relief. He moved then, reaching down to the floor to wrestle with discarded clothes. A condom, she realized.

He'd come prepared this time.

As if he'd read her thought he said ruefully, "I almost didn't. Thought maybe it would keep this from happening."

"But you did."

"Just remembering how last night felt told me that was useless."

The husky, quiet admission released any last reservations she had; all she'd needed was to know this was the same for him, this growing, consuming inferno they created together.

"Bed?" he asked.

"Too far," she answered.

"Yes," he agreed.

When he finally slid into her, slowly, carefully, she thought she would scream if he didn't hurry. She wanted all of him, as deep as she could take. And yet the sensation of the slow, steady invasion was so wonderful she wanted it to go on forever.

And then he was there, and her name escaped him on a whispered groan, sending another shock wave through her. She lifted to him, wrapping arms and legs around him, pulling him as close as she could.

He groaned again and finally began to move. Tentative at first, as if unsure.

"Not fragile," she reminded him, the words taking all the breath she could manage.

The sound he made then was fierce, low and utterly male. And then he gave her what she'd been aching for, a powerful steady rhythm, stroke after stroke after stroke, driving her higher each time, until she was clutching at him, on the edge of spiraling out of control.

Something shifted awkwardly, and she vaguely realized the couch wasn't quite wide enough for this kind of energetic activity. They were slipping.

"Hang on," Teague said in her ear, pausing for a nibble that made her shiver anew after he spoke. He moved her arms around his neck, then tightened his hold on her hips. And rolled.

Still joined, they hit the floor. He'd done it so he landed on the bottom, taking the brunt. It drove him even deeper into her, and she gasped more out of pure pleasure than the shock of the impact.

He urged her up slightly, shifting her weight until it was centered on the connection.

"Over to you," he said.

He was giving her control, she realized. A new, different kind of flame kindled in her, low and deep and hotter than anything she'd ever known. He was hers now. For this moment in time, he was hers. Surrendered. Willingly. This man she doubted knew the meaning of the word in the fighting sense had done it without hesitation for her.

She would see to it that he didn't regret it. She began to move, slowly, then faster as he urged her on. Every move that ratcheted up her own pleasure seemed to give him just as much, so she quit thinking and just moved as it pleased her.

She knew the moment when he reached the precipice, felt

it in his body, heard it in his warning gasp of her name. She leaned forward just enough, felt him shudder. It was the last push she needed and she cried out his name in turn as she went up and over, spiraling, flaming, and not caring if she ever came to earth again.

She woke slowly, sleepily. Opened her eyes to her small bedroom, the dawn coming early this time of year, seeping around the edges of the blinds designed to keep it out. Familiar, unchanged. She lay still for a moment, letting her fuzzy brain slowly rouse.

And then she was jolted wide-awake by some very unfamiliar changes. In almost the same instant she realized two things. Her body was most pleasantly sore in a few unusual places, and there was a heater snugged up behind her.

Teague.

She was tucked into the curve of his body as he slept, half-wrapped around her.

It all came back in a rush. The couch, hitting the floor. Then he'd picked her up, brought her in here. Good thing, since the box of condoms Amber had gifted her with was here. And now open and less full than it had been.

It was all she could do not to jerk upright and stare at him, just to be sure it had all been real.

But it had been. She knew it had. Her body knew it had. Incredibly, impossibly, magnificently real.

He was still asleep, so she tried to stay still. He had, after all, worked hard last night. She smiled—a silly, pleased, self-satisfied smile. And why not? She was pleased. She'd been pleased to within an inch of her life, and that last time, just after midnight, she wasn't sure they hadn't blasted that last inch out of existence.

She lay there in the faint light, luxuriating in the feeling, letting herself remember it all. She had no idea how this morn-

ing after was going to go, but right now, at this moment, she
didn't have to think about it. She could allow herself to re-
live it, from the moment he'd unexpectedly shown up insist-
ing she needed to eat, to the meal itself—which, she thought
now, she should have eaten more of, but she'd had no idea she
would be burning off so much energy later.

She could have done without the wearying walk-through
of that last day with Amber, but she was sure he could have
done without hearing it again, especially since she'd come
up with nothing new. Nothing had changed from what was
said to the fact that Edward had seemed a gentleman who
would let Amber decide, from Amber's flattering sandals
to Edward's rather battered ball cap with the fastener in the
back that was tearing.

An image flashed through her mind. That cap, with the
plastic snap strip that had started to tear. It had been nearly
halfway through the half-inch strip…that tear. She remembered thinking he was going to lose it eventually. The image
was clear in her mind.

And so was something else.

She sat up abruptly, heedless this time of waking Teague.
And she did; barely seconds later, she heard him.

"Laney?"

She turned, looked at him. But instead of taking the long,
romantic look at him she'd wanted moments ago, she cut to
the chase.

"I remembered something," she said.

Chapter 26

"You're sure?"

"Yes."

She grabbed a T-shirt from a hook near the bathroom door and tugged it on. It was blue and long, covering her to midthigh, and he had the feeling she normally slept in it. He was glad she hadn't last night. But then, there had been nothing normal, at least for him, about last night. Something he was going to have to process later, obviously.

"I only got a glimpse, and the broken snap band distracted me, but it was there. Embroidered on the back, right over the hole they leave to adjust the hat size."

"And it said Clamshell Marina."

"Yes."

Teague gave up his disappointment that she'd covered up. No matter how much he liked looking at her, or how much he'd wanted a different kind of morning, especially after a night that had been nothing less than epic, this was more important now. He tugged on his own jeans before following her into the living room. She went to the small desk in one corner of the room, turned on the laptop that sat there, then grabbed up her phone from beside it.

He let her do the search. His own Foxworth smartphone might be quicker, and have some extra bells and whistles courtesy of Tyler and Liam, but he sensed she needed to do something, and since she'd done the remembering, this seemed only fair.

In moments she had the location mapped. He looked over her shoulder. "Over the bridge?"

She nodded, then turned to the now booted laptop. He studied the map on the phone she'd set down. The Hood Canal was what made where they were a separate peninsula rather than simply part of the larger Olympic Peninsula. The two were connected by a rather remarkable floating bridge that opened to allow marine traffic, including the occasional submarine his former navy brethren were piloting to or from their home base.

"Here it is."

He switched his gaze to the laptop screen where a simplistic website showed an image of a small, picturesque cove with a few structures and modestly sized boats of various types. Masts poked up from occasional sailboats among the powerboats that took up most of the space at the three docks.

"Small," he said.

"Yes." She was reading the page quickly. There were no links, so it seemed the single page was all there was. "No services except a small fuel dock, and no available boat slips."

"Full of locals, maybe," he said. He leaned in over her shoulder, schooling a body that recognized her all too well after last night to behave.

"Then why would Edward have gone there?"

"He ever talk about fishing when you used to see him?"

She thought for a minute. "No. And the only boats he ever mentioned were the ferries."

"As in looking or riding?"

"Riding. He missed one once, and was complaining about the traffic."

"So he uses them."

"Yes."

"Meaning he comes to this side of the sound, somewhere."

"Apparently."

He looked back at the web page, scanning. Judging by the description, the little cove didn't even have a name, it was so small.

"Moorings," he said.

"What?"

"They have a few moorings, it says. Offshore, for transient boats."

"So, if he has a boat, he could be there even if the slips are full?"

"Could be."

She grabbed for her phone, clearly intending to dial the number for the rather grandly titled harbormaster. He stopped her with a touch on the arm. A mistake, since even that mere contact reawakened senses that had been on a slow simmer since he'd awakened naked beside her and memories of the night had swamped him.

She stopped, looked at him. God, those eyes, he thought, distracted by their warmth. With an inward shake and more discipline than it should have taken, he steadied himself.

"It's a lot of ifs, but if he does have a boat, and if he is there, and if Amber is with him, it might be best not to risk warning him."

She set the phone down abruptly. Clearly she hadn't thought of that. "Then, what?"

"It's not that far," he said.

"We're going?"

"Seems the best plan to me. It may be nothing, he may just have bought, found, or been given the hat, but it's something to check out."

He didn't add that he thought any action, even useless, would be better for her state of mind than just waiting yet another day. And much as he would like that action to be staying here and further exploring that fire that erupted between them at the slightest touch, he doubted that would be met with approval on several fronts, including his own judgment.

"While we're on the way," he said, "I'll get Ty working on finding out if the guy has a boat. It should have turned up on our basic info run, but maybe he just bought it or something."

"Maybe he just bought it for this," Laney said, sounding grim.

"That would be an elaborate plan, but possible," he said, adding silently, *and I don't put much past the machinations of twisted minds anymore.*

She was on her feet without another word. She started back toward the bedroom. Then she stopped. Turned back, looked at him. And then came back.

His breath jammed in his throat when she put her arms around him, leaned in and kissed him.

"Thank you," she said.

"I… For what?"

She backed away then. And gave him a smile that made him wish they were both naked and back in her bed again.

"A whole list," she said softly.

And then she vanished into the other room.

On second thought, he mused, feeling pinned in the spot where he stood, this wasn't that bad a morning after all.

"Ty says he rechecked, still nothing in the system on a boat in Edward's name. He's checking under the aunt's name now."

Laney nodded. "If she bought him his car, she might have bought him a boat, too."

"If Ty comes up empty, we'll contact her again directly."

"She got pretty defensive before," Laney said.

"Then Quinn and Hayley may do it in person. They make a good tag team. Quinn intimidates, Hayley commiserates."

That earned him a smile that warmed him probably far more than it should.

"I wonder how long it takes to get stuff into the licensing computers?"

"A while, I'm guessing, knowing the pace of government. But even if he bought it the day before, it should be in there by now." He hesitated, then decided he had to say it. "This may well turn into a dead end, Laney."

"I know that. It's the tiniest of clues that may not even really be a clue. But we won't know that if we don't do this, right?"

"Yes. Sometimes it's all about eliminating possibilities."

"Sherlock Holmes."

He laughed, liking that she felt light enough to make the reference. "Something like that, yes."

"My parents used to love going over there," she said as they passed a road sign indicating they were headed west. "Dad said Olympic National Park was the most amazing place he'd ever been."

"Did you go with them?"

"Of course. We went every year for a while. Camped out a lot."

"Sounds nice."

"You should meet them sometime."

He blinked. Had she actually suggested he meet her parents? He had no idea what to say to that, and the way his pulse had leaped at the simple suggestion made him edgier than he had been.

"Then at least you'd know what normal, real parents are like," she said, promptly pushing the whole idea back into feeling-sorry-for-him territory. He didn't like that, either, so ended up saying nothing.

They were at the bridge now, the long, floating span unrolled before them. The sun was bright, reflecting off the water, and he pulled a pair of sunglasses from the visor and slipped them on.

"Weird to think it's a fjord," she said.

"Does sound a bit exclusively Scandinavian."

"No big boat delay today." The bridge was built so most small craft could cross under at one end of the crossing, only having to open the center for larger vessels.

"No."

"Did you know it's the third-longest floating bridge in the world?"

Okay, so maybe she wasn't feeling exactly light. "No, I didn't."

"I had to wait for a submarine to pass once. It was kind of exciting. I mean, you see all kinds of navy boats coming and going, even carriers, but the subs, they're...different."

"It's the stealth," he said. Then he reached out and put a hand over hers. Hers was cold.

She sighed. "I'm chattering, aren't I?"

"Yes. For you, anyway."

"Sorry."

"It's all right."

They cleared the bridge and headed up a rise onto the Olympic Peninsula. It wasn't far to where the GPS on his own phone told him to make the turn onto a country road, and then farther on onto a local road. They ended up on a narrow, downward-tracking side road that looked as if it had been fairly recently built, making Teague wonder if the marina was new also. That might explain the Spartan web page and the lack of a name for the tiny cove.

They reached the water and they could see the marina farther on, where the road curved around the other side of the cove. There were few other buildings; this wasn't a town, not even a village, unless you counted a small general store, gas station and boat repair combination as such.

They cleared the store building but Teague kept driving. He slowed when they were at an angle where they could better tell the layout of the small marina. And could see there were two boats at offshore moorings.

"Narrows it down," he said.

"Unless he keeps the boat here, in a slip," Laney said. "Assuming this isn't all a wild-goose chase."

"Then we talk to the harbormaster. They'll have records."

"Not much of a harbor to be master of," Laney said.

"But his domain nevertheless," Teague said with a grin.

They came to a widened spot where it appeared people frequently pulled off the road. He guessed it was because it gave a nice view of the little cove, and so it wouldn't look unusual if they did the same.

"Let's take a look," he said.

Laney looked puzzled but said nothing as he got out and went to the back. He quickly unlocked the metal case that was fastened to the side of the cargo area. He selected the smaller of the two weapons inside, in a clip-on belt holster, and slipped it into place on his hip under his shirt. Better safe, he thought. He didn't really know what he'd be dealing with. It was his absolute last resort, especially if Amber turned out to be a hostage.

Laney got there just as he grabbed the second, heavier go bag, his equipment bag. He had the minimums in both bags, clothes and food, but specialized stuff was in this one. Including his goal: the high-powered spotting scope. He unzipped the largest side compartment.

Pulling it out, he uncapped the ends as he walked back to the front of the SUV. Laney had realized what he was doing now and came to join him. He liked that she didn't ask a million questions, but waited and watched. It made her easy to be with. Everything about her made her easy to be with.

What happened between them when they touched made it hard to think about being without her.

The thought rattled him. He wasn't ready for thinking that way. He didn't look at her as she stood beside him. And it wasn't, he told himself firmly, because he didn't dare.

He leaned forward to use the hood as a platform, put his elbows on the sun-warmed metal and brought the scope up to his right eye. It was a matter of seconds to get it focused on the marina. He scanned that first. It was quiet on this weekday morning. Early-morning anglers already out and at it, pleasure boaters apparently not yet ready to cast off. There did appear to be a light on in the small building at the head of the first dock, so somebody was around.

He shifted, focused on the first boat on a mooring, a sailboat that, he gathered from the model designation on the side, was a twenty-seven-footer. The sails were furled, covered with bright blue canvas, and there was no sign of anyone aboard. He shifted to the second boat, a low-slung, racy-looking cabin cruiser that was a bit smaller than the sailboat, not quite the size people tended to call a yacht.

But the style and function wasn't the only difference in the two boats. The sailboat was clean, well-maintained. The lines on deck were neatly coiled, there was nothing out of place or strewn about, the wood he could see was shiny with fresh varnish, well protected. Shipshape, he thought.

The cruiser by contrast was battered, the wood dull and open to the elements, a ding in the fiberglass hull near the bow sloppily patched over. The canvas cover over the rear cockpit area was faded and worn. Unless it was a sleeper, like Rafe's battered car, a boring-looking sedan that nevertheless purred like a big cat and could run like one, too, he'd guess the engine was in no better shape.

There was a small dinghy that looked in no better shape than the boat, strapped rather haphazardly to the roof of the cabin. Did that mean the owner was still aboard? Or did this marina, even though small, have a water taxi of sorts to transport people from the offshore moorings? He would tend to doubt it, given the small size, but couldn't discount the possibility. He was shifting the scope back to the marina to check when a movement caught his eye. He moved it back, refocusing on the cruiser.

Someone had come out of the cabin, into the cockpit. A woman.

A blonde woman.

He handed the scope to Laney. "Look. The powerboat."

She looked at him first, and he kept his expression neutral. She put the scope to her eye and looked. His answer came in her first, heartfelt exclamation.

"Amber!"

Chapter 27

The relief that flooded her left her almost shaky.

Amber was alive.

She looked away to glance at Teague.

"It's her?" he asked.

"Yes."

"You're sure? The scope's good, but it's still kind of far."

"It's her."

She put her eye back to the scope, afraid somehow Amber would have disappeared in those three seconds. But she was there, looking rather bedraggled for the usually put-together Amber. Her hair looked tangled, windblown, the pink shorts and cropped top she wore wrinkled in a way Amber would never have permitted normally.

But she was there. Alive. And willing?

Had all this really been for nothing? Was Amber truly on some romantic getaway?

Embarrassment flooded her. She lowered the scope, not

knowing what to say. All the time and effort Teague and the rest of Foxworth had put into this, and here Amber was, perfectly alive and kicking.

"I feel so stupid," she said.

"Don't."

"But I was obviously so wrong."

"You weren't."

"But she's here, and apparently fine."

"Everything you told us is true," he said. "It just happened that the innocent explanation may have been true."

She looked up then, meeting his gaze for the first time.

"May have been?"

"We're going to make sure she's here voluntarily."

She couldn't make herself believe it. But she was also honest enough to admit the embarrassment could be part of that. And Teague's insistence this was not yet over helped ease that.

Besides, why on earth would the water-hating Amber be out on a boat? Especially one that didn't look particularly seaworthy?

She turned back and lifted the scope once more.

Amber had walked to the back of the boat and now stood staring down at the water. Something about the way she was standing, the way her shoulders were slumped and her head was down, made Laney doubt her own doubts.

"She's not happy," she said.

"Maybe this didn't work out like she thought it would," Teague said.

"It's more than that." Still peering through the scope, Laney watched as Amber lifted her head. "She's crying."

Teague didn't say anything, and she supposed that even without the scope he could have seen Amber wiping at her eyes.

"You said she hates the water."

"Yes. That's why this boat thing is so weird."

"Can she swim?"

"Not well." She lowered the scope to stare at him. "You think she's considering trying to swim to shore?"

"Or maybe regretting she can't swim well enough to try."

Laney looked back, assessing the distance from the boat to the nearest dock. She shook her head. "She'd never try it. The water's too cold, she knows that. We grew up hearing how a person can only last a few minutes in the sound. And she really can't swim well at all."

Someone appeared at the head of one of the docks and began to make her way down the gangway to the boat slips. Amber seemed to see her, too, because she turned quickly and began to wave rather frantically. Laney thought she heard Amber's voice even from here, in that way sound carried farther across the water. It seemed the woman coming down the dock saw or heard, because she waved back as if Amber had been merely sending an ordinary greeting. Then she climbed aboard a boat just three slips from the head of the dock and quickly disappeared inside.

And Amber froze.

Laney put the scope back to her eye. Amber's head turned until she was staring back toward the cabin, and this time there was no doubting it. Certainty flooded back. She hadn't been wrong.

"Teague, she's scared."

"Laney, from this distance—"

"I know her like a sister. She's scared."

And then Amber slowly, with obvious reluctance, walked back toward the cabin of the cruiser. She disappeared inside, leaving Laney staring at an empty cockpit.

Teague had his phone in his hand, was already dialing.

"Quinn?" he said after a moment. Then, "I'm putting you on speaker. I'm with Laney, out at a small marina on the Olympic Peninsula. We found Amber."

"Alive?" Quinn's voice came through with remarkable clarity. They might be in a rather remote spot, but there had to be a cell tower somewhere close. Or Foxworth had some kind of technology no one else did, which seemed to her equally possible.

"Yes," Teague answered. "But there's definitely something wrong."

Laney felt an entirely different kind of warming as Teague accepted without question suspicions based on her gut feelings and her knowledge of her best friend. He'd never made her feel as if she were being silly, even if he'd doubted some of her interpretations.

Teague quickly explained what Laney had remembered, where it had led them and what they'd seen so far, including a reiteration of Amber's fear of the water.

"Any signs of injuries?"

Laney hadn't thought of that, and her stomach clenched.

"Not from here," Teague said. "We're on the opposite side of the cove, and my scope was enough to make sure it's her. And for Laney to say she's scared."

"Laney," Quinn asked, "you're sure it's more than just her fear of boats and the water?"

"I think so," she said. "But since she has that fear, I've never really seen her on a small boat before."

"Teague? Options?"

"I think some closer recon is in order."

"Agreed. And in the interest of maintaining good relations, I'll notify authorities."

"We're out here a ways," Teague said. "Their response time may not be the best."

"And you're in a different county, so there'll be some time spent bringing them up to speed. I'll see if Dunbar can help, he might know someone over there."

"And in the meantime?"

"Give me the details of the location."

Laney listened as Teague rattled off a description of where they were in terms that were oddly technical, including wind conditions, the shape of the cove, estimating the width of the entrance at the widest part, and how far in the target was located. For a moment she felt absurdly ignorant. She would have given him generalities like where it was, the trees, maybe how big it was, but nothing like the detailed report Teague had rattled off.

"Copy. Turn on your GPS when you're in position," Quinn said.

"Roger that."

And just like that the conversation was over, no goodbyes, just two men who knew what they were doing, even if she had no clue.

Teague saw her looking at him as he put the phone away, and she must have looked perplexed because he said, "He's on his way."

"He is?" What hadn't been in that recitation of details were any driving directions. It hit her then. "The helicopter?"

Teague grinned. "Quinn's not one to pass up a chance to fly. Besides, he talked Charlie into buying it, so he figures he has to log enough hours to make it seem useful."

Something was different about him, Laney thought. He was…energized. Amped or something. She'd thought perhaps he'd decided to come here just to make her feel as if she were doing something, but even if that were true, it wasn't now. They'd actually found Amber.

And now he was in, what? Action mode?

That fit, she thought as they got back in the car and continued down the road that curved around the top of the cove. Things had changed, dramatically, and so had he. They were no longer looking, they'd found, and now he had a specific objective rather than a general goal.

"Now what?"

"A closer assessment," he said.

"How?"

"Not sure yet. I want to check out the marina close-up, see what's there and available."

The parking area for the marina was fairly small, and Laney guessed they gambled on the probability that not everyone who had a boat here would all show up at once. Although some bright, high-summer weekend days it seemed as if every boat on Puget Sound must be out at once.

Teague picked a spot and backed in. He did that often, she'd noticed. As if he wanted to be ready to roll at a moment's notice, and even backing out and turning around took too much time. A small thing, but different than most people.

Once parked, he opened the center console between them and flipped a switch on a small, rather odd-looking box fastened to the inside. A light came on, a bright blue LED, blinking first, then glowing steadily.

"GPS," he said when he saw her glance.

"Oh." There was that feeling again. "I thought he meant the GPS on your phone."

"No. This is Foxworth. Liam and Tyler put their heads together and developed this. Signal's scrambled, unless you've got one of our trackers."

"I'm surprised Foxworth doesn't have its own satellite," she said dryly.

Teague's head snapped up. That had startled him, for some reason. "Charlie jokes about doing that all the time, despite all the hoops we'd have to jump through. Mainly to get a rise out of Quinn, I think."

"He's not for it?"

"He doesn't want to get to relying on something we don't control." Teague grimaced. "He doesn't trust the people who do."

"Not surprising, given his history." She contemplated him for a moment before adding, "Or yours, I'm guessing."

He met her gaze then. She saw the hesitation there, his natural reticence about talking about his history, warring with… with what? The new intimacy between them? Was he afraid she would demand to know everything about him, thinking she now had the right?

Did she? Had last night, even as amazing as it had been, given her the right to know everything he thought and felt? She didn't know. It was all too new, too powerful, and she didn't want to mess things up by pushing for something he might eventually offer on his own.

"What do we do now?" she asked, letting it go.

She thought she saw a flicker of relief cross his face. "Look around. We're just looking for a place to park our boat, if anybody asks."

She liked the sound of that "we" and "our" enough that it made her edgy.

"What kind of boat?" she asked, trying to shake off the feeling; this was obviously just some sort of cover, and meant nothing more, and she'd better remember that. She was already in deep enough. "In case anybody asks."

"Just like that one," he said, nodding toward the boat on the mooring.

That made sense, she thought. Opened a door for discussion of said boat, in case anyone knew anything.

"Only ours is in better shape," he added.

She laughed. It felt odd, a little giddy even. Not surprising, she supposed. Not only had she had the most amazing night of her life, with the most amazing man she'd ever met, they'd done it. They themselves had found Amber. Here, now.

Now the only question was, was she really in trouble, or not? Was she going to welcome their arrival, or be embarrassed? At this moment, Laney didn't care. She wasn't going to apologize for worrying about her best friend.

Especially since it had brought Teague into her life. The man who'd all along promised they'd find her.

And he'd kept that promise.

"We're not going to just ask?" she said as they walked toward the small building at the head of the first dock.

"Not yet," he said. "If she's that scared, there is something wrong and no sense in warning anyone why we're here."

The giddiness faded. Seeing Amber alive had been such a relief she'd put the rest out of her mind for a moment. But she couldn't deny what she'd seen, Amber had been frightened, and by more than just being on a small boat on the water she was afraid of.

She felt Teague's hand on her arm, warm, strong, comforting.

"We won't leave here until we're sure she's okay."

She looked up at him, meeting his gaze, seeing the steadiness in his eyes. "Thank you."

"It's what we do," he said.

"But you're the one who listened to me from the beginning."

"I think," he said with a crooked grin, "that was Cutter."

She laughed; she couldn't help it.

"That's my girl," he said, linking her arm through his as they kept walking.

It might have been part of the facade, might have only been to put a smile on her face, as befitted a happy, boat-owning couple out on a lovely day, but she didn't care. It felt good, after last night she felt amazing, and she was happy just to be with this man. All seemed right with her world at this moment.

And they'd found Amber.

Chapter 28

"Got a waiting list," the man in the baseball cap said, sounding rather proud.

Teague smiled. "Good for you," he said. "Popular place."

He hadn't had to ask when they'd walked into the small office. Laney had immediately whispered, "That's the hat!"

"Yep, folks had their doubts, we're such a small place, but it's paying off."

"Always good to hear. What's your turnaround time on that list?"

"Depends. Some folks, they pull their boats out for the winter, dry storage, you know? If they want to keep their spot, they have to pay for it without using it, so lots just take their chances on getting back in."

"What about your offshore moorings, in the meantime? Our boat's about the size of that cruiser."

"Those are just for transient boats," the man said.

"So those two haven't been there long?"

The man pulled off the cap Laney had recognized, and Teague caught a glimpse of the embroidered name she'd remembered, exactly as she'd described it. He ran a hand through gray hair before settling the cap back on his head.

"Sailboat just pulled in yesterday. Other guy's been here a few days now. Gonna have to up his rate he stays much longer."

"You have a water taxi, or he have to make his own way ashore?"

"Not yet. Trying to talk the owners into that, but they say most folks have their own dinghy or runabout, if they need it. Like those two vessels have their own. Not that the guy on the cruiser's been onshore once after the day they got here."

"They?"

"Oh, yeah." A flash of what Laney would call a leer went across his face. "Mind you, I wouldn't be comin' ashore, either, if I had that pretty little blonde aboard."

"I prefer brunettes, myself," Teague said.

Laney reminded herself he was playing a part here, but the words warmed her nevertheless.

"I can see why," the older man said appreciatively. Laney resisted the urge to point out she was standing right here.

"So they didn't say they'd be staying so long? When they got here and came ashore?"

"Oh, she never did. I just catch a glimpse now and then. She doesn't come out much, either."

"Seems odd, the nice weather and all," Laney said, speaking for the first time.

"Well, they're on their honeymoon, you know. Other things on their mind."

"Honeymoon?" Laney tried to keep her tone even. At least he hadn't leered again.

"Yeah. Newlyweds. You know how they are, like to keep to

themselves." He glanced out toward the moorings. "Not much of a boat, it's true, but I suppose it's the thought that counts."

There was no way this was true, Laney thought. Even if Amber for some reason had stopped communicating with everyone she cared about, she would never, ever do something as momentous as get married without telling her or her own parents.

"So, you want to put your name on that list?"

"I'd like to look around a bit first. Afloat. You got something I could borrow or rent? Like one of those?"

He gestured at a rack just outside the door of the office where several kayaks were stowed. The man frowned. "Those are privately owned. But my son and his wife keep theirs here, I guess you could borrow them. Not too long," he warned, clearly uncertain.

"It won't be. And I'll be happy to rent. You might as well get something out of it."

Teague pulled out his wallet and handed the man a crisp one-hundred-dollar bill. Laney thought that was a bit much, but it certainly mollified the old man's concerns. He even helped them remove the long, narrow craft from the racks before a ringing phone called him back inside.

"I assume you know what you're doing with one of these?" Laney said.

He glanced at the placid water of the cove. "Enough for this, yes. It's only a reconnaissance run."

"No white-water kayaking on your list of life experiences?" she asked as she hefted the second kayak, which was slightly shorter and therefore she guessed lighter than the flatter, wider one Teague had still easily picked up. She'd seen people fishing off kayaks like that.

"No," he answered. "Thought about it. Seems like a fun ride."

"It is. Makes this seem pretty tame."

He paused in gathering the double-ended paddles to glance at her. "You've done it?"

"A little. Enough to know I could get addicted and I don't have time right now."

"Maybe someday we could—" He stopped. He looked down, back at her face, then started to speak again and stopped again.

"What?"

Suddenly he was all brisk business. "I'll take the fishing kayak. It's more stable if I have to make a quick move. Keep your phone handy, you may have to call Quinn if something goes haywire while I'm out there."

"Wait a minute," Laney protested. "I'm going with you."

"You need to stay here—"

"I'm perfectly capable of kayaking less than a hundred yards in calm water."

"I never said you weren't."

"Besides, you might need help. If he's really abducted Amber, he's dangerous."

He gave her a steady look that told her to him, that was all the more reason she should stay behind. But instead he said merely, "I need you here to call Quinn if anything happens."

"Teague, if he's a kidnapper, he could be armed."

"That's all right. So am I."

For a second she just gaped at him. She should have paid more attention to what he'd taken out of that go bag of his.

"Don't worry. I don't plan on using it. Hopefully I won't need to."

"But if you do, I should—"

"I get it, Laney. We're so close to resolving this, I understand you're anxious. But you have to stay here."

She bristled at that, despite the fact that it made simple sense. He was trained to handle such things, she was not. She wasn't sure quite why this was getting to her so much.

This was what Foxworth did; she should just let them do it. Besides, he was just going to check things out.

"So I'm supposed to just sit here on the sidelines? That's my best friend out there."

"I know that. But I think you're forgetting something."

"What?"

"Edward would recognize you. He'd know something was up."

Laney drew back. In the heat of the moment, the excitement of actually finding Amber, she had forgotten that.

"Let me check things out. Then we'll decide."

She wondered if the "we" was just to placate her. She didn't think so. And she knew he was right. It only made sense that he be the one to make the approach.

It wasn't until he lowered the kayak into the water and began to paddle away that the cold clutch of worry that tightened her chest made her realize the other reason she'd reacted so strongly. A kidnapper was dangerous, and Edward could indeed be armed.

She was as worried about Teague as she was about Amber.

And suddenly it was white-water kayaking that seemed tame compared to what she'd let herself in for now.

It had been a while, but Teague got into the rhythm of the double-ended paddling and the smooth glide of the tiny craft fairly easily. He made a show of inspecting the docks first, pausing to look around, and checking out the other boats and the slips. He was just a guy checking out a marina to see if he liked what he saw, that was all.

A guy with a not-too-happy woman back on the dock, he thought wryly. Funny how none of the reasons to stay behind that dealt with her own safety had convinced her, but the one that might endanger Amber had. It said a lot about her. Not that he hadn't known those things already.

He had to fight back a rising tide of heat as memories from last night threatened to swamp him. He'd never known anything like what had happened between them. When he'd been with women before, it had been pleasurable, but they'd always parted without much drama on either side. Sometimes it felt like he either really liked a woman or was physically attracted to her, but never both at the same time.

Until now.

It may have been foolish, maybe unethical, but he wouldn't trade it now for anything. And if Quinn found out, if he got mad at him over it, well, it was still worth it.

And he needed to get his head back into what he was doing. He couldn't let hot, persistent memories distract him, or let the quiet peace of this wooded cove lull him into thinking this couldn't go south on him at any moment.

He headed farther out toward the moorings. He went slowly past the sailboat, scrutinizing it long enough to justify equal curiosity about the powerboat several yards away.

He went slower as he got close to the bow of the power boat.

It was in even worse shape up close than it had looked from a distance. The fiberglass was dulled and scratched and dinged in many places. The wood was indeed weathered and in some spots visibly rotting. Even the mooring lines were worn, salt-encrusted and fraying in spots. And he'd tied off on the mooring buoy with a clumsy, ill-advised square knot, and every shift in wind and current had likely pulled it tighter. The guy was no sailor, that was for sure.

And unless the inside was in markedly better shape than the outside, he couldn't imagine any woman, let alone one like Amber, putting up with this willingly for a guy she'd just met.

The small porthole-type windows on the side were closed. What looked like a blanket or fabric of some kind was blocking any view, out or in.

He heard nothing from inside.

He reached the back of the vessel, moving as slowly as he thought he could get away with. As he came alongside the cockpit, he gave it a quick look-over as best he could from the low vantage point of the kayak. The hatch into the main cabin was closed. A fishing pole lay dangling over the side, a knotted tangle of line showing the probable reason for its abandonment.

He eased past until he could see the transom. The first thing he noticed was the blackened pattern where dirty exhaust had exited an engine obviously in no better shape than the rest of the boat.

Breezin' Through was the name painted across the stern. And below that was the name of its home port, a small place Teague had been through once on his way to somewhere else. A broken ladder leading up into the cockpit hung crookedly, half-submerged, above a swim step.

Aware of the time passing, Teague kept going, maintaining the look of someone just checking things out. He paddled out to the entrance of the cove, made sure there were no surprises Quinn would need to know about, then turned to start back.

There was a man standing in the cockpit of the cruiser.

From here it appeared he was merely stretching. But he was facing this way, so Teague assumed he was eyeing him and kept paddling, all the while keeping his eyes on the shirtless man, glad of the sunglasses that hid the direction of his gaze. As he neared, the man didn't try to hide that he was watching him.

Soft, Teague thought as he got close enough to tell. Bit of a belly. Big, though. Enough that a woman wouldn't be able to fight him off. Dark hair, longish, to him at least. Pale skin, but that was normal up here in the land of much rain. So, captor, or new lover? His gut was saying the former, but he had no proof.

Nothing more than the same kind of gut feeling that had told Laney there was something wrong.

He paddled closer. Put a smile on his face. Just a guy out on a nice, sunny day, getting what he can before the weather turned.

His smile faltered. He paddled a little closer, to make sure, but he already knew.

All their assumptions had just been blasted out of the water he was floating on. The man in the cockpit wasn't Edward Page.

Chapter 29

"Morning," Teague called out as he neared the back of the moored boat. For a moment he thought the man wasn't going to respond, but he finally gave a short nod. "Nice place," he added.

For that he got a one-shouldered shrug. He dragged the paddle to slow to a stop. He'd had to do a swift reassessment of the entire situation, and had to do it with absolutely no data on this new element. He had no idea who this man was, other than not the man they'd expected. But he couldn't pass up the chance to do a little poking now that he was out here.

"Thinking about moving my boat out here."

He jerked a thumb toward the marina where a few more people had arrived and were heading toward boats in various places. All the while Teague's eyes never stopped moving. The back door from the main cabin was again closed. Who did that, if you were just stepping outside? Unless, of course, there was someone else aboard you didn't also want stepping outside.

"You like it? Or is it too remote?"

The man looked at him, suspicion sharp in muddy brown eyes. "Not remote enough," he finally said.

Teague could almost hear the "Since you're here bothering me" he was sure the man was thinking.

"What if you needed a repair or something? Doesn't look like there's much around here," he said, pressing on as if he were truly that casual kayaker and oblivious to the real situation. And the man's mood.

Of course, looking at this man who so obviously wasn't the man in the picture he had memorized, now he wasn't exactly sure what the real situation was. Other than down here, seated in a craft that somewhat limited his mobility, he was vulnerable. He preferred the high ground and room to maneuver, but sometimes you took what the conditions gave you.

"Good luck," the man finally said gruffly. But he sounded more irritated now, less suspicious.

"Yeah, I figured. Probably better over in Harborside," he said, his gaze fastened intently on the man's face now. He saw the slight furrowing of his brow, the narrowing of his eyes, even though the expression lasted only a split second.

"Maybe," he answered after that moment's hesitation.

"I thought about there, too, but I'm not sure I want to dodge that ferry all the time. It must get annoying. Bet you have to have their schedule memorized, right?"

"No." Then, shifting his feet restlessly, the man added, "It's not a problem."

Teague nodded like a guy who'd just been reassured. But in fact he'd just been given an interesting fact. He decided to probe a bit more. With a silent salute to Cutter, he said, "But I worry about the Coast Guard outpost there, too. They hassle you much?"

Teague knew he wasn't imagining the sudden new spike

of suspicion in the man's eyes at the mention of the armed military unit. "No."

"Glad to hear that. Guess they have bigger fish to fry." He grinned. "Those chase boats they have there are cool, though."

"If you like that kind of thing," the man said. "Now if you don't mind, I have bigger fish to fry, as you put it."

The signal that the conversation, one-sided as it had been, was over couldn't have been clearer. And yet he didn't turn away and go back inside, putting a final end to it. Instead he stood there, waiting.

For me to realize I've been dismissed and leave? Teague thought. *To be sure I really go?*

And to make sure I don't see anything when he opens the door to go back inside?

Teague was tempted to say something about what the harbormaster had told him, about the pretty blonde he had stashed aboard. But he didn't want to scare the guy into doing anything, maybe hurting Amber any more than he already had.

His phone *pinged* the arrival of a text message.

"Damn," he said with a grimace. "Wife can't leave me alone for five minutes, I swear."

The man on the boat snickered. Apparently the image of harassed husband tipped him solidly in the harmless category. Which told him a little bit more about the man himself. He checked the screen, saw the message from Quinn that he was at the warehouse with the chopper and would be lifting off shortly. Acknowledged it with a quickly typed "Roger."

And took advantage of having the phone out to snap a couple of surreptitious photos of man and boat, including the registration number, which he immediately sent to Ty. He didn't dare try to send a second message of explanation right in front of the guy, but Ty would understand there would only be one reason he'd send images in the middle of a case. He'd be tracking the guy down the moment they arrived.

"Thanks for the info," Teague said, stuffing the phone back in his pocket and trying to look like that harassed husband. "I'd better get back to the wife, or my life will turn to misery. Enjoy the nice weather while it's still here."

He paddled off, aware every moment that he was presenting his back to the man, offering a choice target. But while suspicious, he hadn't seemed scared or worried. Especially after the wife jokes. Teague doubted he'd take a shot at him out in the open, especially now that there were more witnesses around. If he was even armed at all.

Teague wasn't sure about that, but he was now sure of some other things. The guy was wary. Cautious. And although he could be just a guy wanting to keep his gorgeous new girlfriend all to himself, he could also be keeping an unwilling woman locked away. And while he himself was no judge, he didn't look like the type a woman would drop everything and run off with. Laney had said Amber liked a man who took care of himself, and this guy looked like he'd been down on his luck about as long as that boat had been.

And that was the big thing he'd learned, he thought as he paddled past the sailboat and headed back toward the docks. As soon as he got out of sight he was going to call Foxworth and have them start checking for stolen boats from Harborside. Because this guy didn't have a clue. There was no ferry out of that small place, nor was there a Coast Guard station.

So at best, he was a liar. At worst, he was a kidnapper, probably rapist, and who knew what else. And Laney's best friend was trapped with him.

His jaw set, he angled the kayak to head back the way he'd come along the first dock near the office. He could see Laney now, pacing near the gangway. For a moment he just watched her. The way she moved, that fluid strength coupled with a very womanly grace, warmed him even at this distance. He remembered those long, lithe legs wrapped around him, remembered the feel of her body against his, around his, demanding and offering, taking and giving, surrounding him, driving him to an explosive place he'd never been before.

His body cramped with need, and he wondered where the hell all his vaunted discipline had gone to. He never allowed himself to be so distracted on a case.

But then, he'd never run into anyone like Laney, on a case or anywhere else, before.

He tried to shake it off, to rein in his unruly body. Focus, he demanded silently. And quit wondering how it would feel if she really was the fictional wife he'd just concocted. He could think of worse things. A lot worse.

Uh-oh.

That alarm sounded in the back of his mind again. And he was going to listen, he told himself. Otherwise he might as well just keep paddling this damned kayak off the edge of the world.

She was holding something as she paced, he belatedly realized. Maybe his scope. She probably had been watching the exchange. Which meant she knew it wasn't Edward. That would save him explaining that, anyway.

When he got close enough to see her clearly, one look at her face told him he'd been right, he wasn't going to have to tell her about this new and unexpected development.

"Teague, you copy?"

Ty's voice crackled in his earpiece. "Go ahead."

"Boat's registered to a Carl Reed."

Teague frowned. "Reed? Like Nancy Reed, the rich aunt?"

"Exactly. Same address. Maybe the late husband. Registration's expired now."

Teague's brow furrowed. So there was still some kind of

connection between this guy and Edward Page. But what was it?

He edged the kayak to the dock. She was there, waiting. She waited until he was safely back on solid decking before she spoke. Even now, alert, aware and thoughtful. She was something.

"Did you see her?"

"No. He kept it closed up the whole time."

"My God. How could I have been so wrong?"

"We all were. We all assumed it was Edward."

"Because I told you it was."

He brushed that off. He wasn't about to let her take the sole blame for that. It had been a natural assumption, Amber starts dating a new guy and then vanishes; anyone would have connected the two.

"Not your fault. And it's Page's late uncle's boat, according to the registration."

"But Edward's not there?"

"Not unless he's hiding below. Puts us back a bit, it turning out to be a stranger."

"But he's not a stranger," she exclaimed.

Teague set down the kayak he'd just picked up. Stared at her. "Tell me."

"I know him," she said, sounding as wound up as if she'd like to start pacing again. "I mean, I don't know him, but I've seen him."

"Where? When?"

"He's the guy who was with Edward that day I introduced them."

Chapter 30

Laney tried, fiercely, but she couldn't remember anything more about the man. Edward hadn't even bothered to introduce him to them, so focused had he been on Amber. While she herself had been noticing how quickly he had switched his intentions. Which hadn't been fair. She had turned him down, more than once. It was completely illogical, really, since she would have said no again anyway.

But she had to admit now that seeing how quickly he switched had actually made her feel better about saying no.

But not enough to warn Amber off.

Guilt stabbed through her again. It wasn't as biting, now that she knew Amber was alive, but it was still there.

"Amber never even spoke to him that day, and Edward never introduced him. And she never mentioned him after, that she even knew his name let alone that she was seeing him. She would have. I swear, she would have. She would have made a joke out of it. 'My life could be a corny movie, girl meets guy, falls for his best friend' or something."

He didn't look at her for a moment as he dug out his phone. Probably thinking what an idiot she was for jumping to wrong conclusions.

"Teague, there's still something wrong," she said.

"I know," he said as he hit a button on the phone, but still held her gaze. "Maybe even more than we thought."

Before she could ask what he meant, he spoke into the phone. "Hayley?" A pause, then, "Good. Tell him there's been an unexpected development."

He went on to relay what they'd learned. He listened for a moment, then said, "No, don't know if he stole the boat or just borrowed it from Page." Another pause. "All right. We will."

"Will what?" she asked when he disconnected.

"Watch and wait. Quinn's on his way with Rafe."

"Rafe?"

"You haven't met him yet. He's a little intimidating, but he's a good guy."

"Intimidating? Next to Quinn? Hard to believe."

That crooked grin flashed for a moment. "Rafe's a whole different kind of scary. You'll see. But he's the best there is at what he does."

"Which is?"

"Lots of things. He's got the best instincts I've ever seen. Better even than Quinn, on some things. I swear he can sniff out a bad guy practically as well as Cutter."

She smiled at that, but it had a rueful edge. "And no doubt better than I."

"You had no way of knowing."

He said it so definitely it eased her guilt a bit.

The kayak secured for the moment, he headed back to the car. She followed, although she was torn between going with him and watching the boat. She compromised and took the scope with her so she could watch while he was doing whatever he was going to do.

"And when you already know who the bad guy is, what does your Rafe do?" she asked as they went up the gangway.

Teague seemed to hesitate for a moment, then said, "Among many other things, he's our sniper."

She blinked. Somehow just the use of that word instantly took this to an entirely new level. "Foxworth needs a sniper?"

He glanced at her. "Occasionally."

"Oh." She wasn't sure what was showing on her face, but when Teague spoke again, it was gently.

"If it comes down to it, Rafe will take the guy out if he has to, to keep Amber from getting hurt."

Laney suppressed a shudder. "And who decides he has to?"

"Quinn."

"Only Quinn?"

He opened the back of the SUV, reached for the bigger bag the scope had come out of and pulled it toward him. She lifted the scope to her eyes to check the boat; all quiet, no sign of Amber or the new part of the equation.

"If it's optimal," Teague answered.

She lowered the scope, looked at him. "What's optimal about shooting someone?"

"I meant, if the circumstances allow, he's the one who makes the decision."

"And if they don't?"

"He trusts us to make the best decision for the situation. But if it comes to deadly force, he wants to be the one, in case there are repercussions. If there's any heat, he takes it."

It was all she could do not to gape at the things he was taking out of the pack. More ammunition. What looked for all the world like a small explosive device. These he put in the pockets of the vest he pulled out next. A knife went into a small slot at the top of his right boot. And here she'd thought he just wore the combat-style footwear because he liked them, or they were comfortable.

He must have sensed her unease.

"I have to go in prepared for anything, Laney."

"I know. I just... I never thought... The police are coming, right?"

He nodded. "But we're in a remote area here. Their response time could be as much as an hour, maybe more."

And by then Amber could be dead. She thought of how she'd feel if that happened, if she was reduced to just sitting here safely onshore while her best friend was murdered just a hundred yards away. It didn't bear thinking about. She would paddle out there alone and unarmed before she could let that happen.

But Teague would make sure that didn't happen. And these were his tools. Only as good, as effective as the man who wielded them.

She was feeling more foolish by the moment. And yet thankful, too. She lifted the scope once more. Still quiet.

"Have there been repercussions? When Quinn has made that decision?"

"A couple of times."

"Did he get in trouble?"

"Quinn has a lot of friends, and even more goodwill to spend, in a lot of different places."

She pondered that answer. Thought of how she would feel when this was over, and Amber was safe.

She'd do anything she could to help Foxworth, if they asked. She didn't expect there was much she could do, but if they asked, she wouldn't hesitate. And she guessed everyone they helped probably felt the same way. That was, as Teague had said, a lot of goodwill.

She also knew he was talking more to distract her than anything. And she was letting him, in fact was glad of it, because it felt so wrong to just sit here safely while Amber was...

Was what?

She lowered the scope once more to look at him. "What did you mean, when you said maybe more was wrong than we thought?"

For the first time he looked away. Dodging her gaze? "I just meant this guy is a whole new element, and we don't know how that changes the picture."

That made sense. What didn't was why he was avoiding looking at her.

"You mean because we don't know anything about him?"

"Yes. With what we knew about Edward we could make a reasonable guess on how he might react. With this guy in the mix now, the whole dynamic could change."

"And I'm no help. I can't even give you a name." Frustrated with herself, it came out sharply.

"Stop, Laney. None of us expected this. And that," he said ruefully, "will teach us."

His words, and especially his tone, eased the knot in her stomach a little. But then something he'd said spun back to the front of her mind. "You said with him in the mix now," she said, the implication only now registering. "Do you mean you think *both* of them might be involved? Edward and this guy?"

"We can't discard the possibility. We've already made one wrong assumption about this case. We can't—"

He stopped, tilting his head as if listening. Before she could absorb the ramifications of what he'd said, she heard what he'd heard, in the distance, the sound of a helicopter nearing. Quinn. The cavalry had arrived. At least, she thought so, but just when it got so loud she couldn't believe it wasn't within view, the sound changed, lessened, and seemed to stop moving. For a couple of minutes it stayed the same, puzzlingly growing neither louder nor fainter.

Maybe it wasn't Quinn yet after all, she thought. Lots of helicopters, including navy and Coast Guard, flew around here.

She looked at Teague. He straightened up, closed the back lift gate. Looked back at her. And again, read her expression.

"It's Quinn."

"But it stopped, how can you be sure?"

"He's dropping off Rafe. He'll be here momentarily."

Even as he said it the sound changed again, roaring as if the craft were taking off again. "Dropping off?"

"I'm guessing that rise just across the road. High ground, and best angle on the marina."

She glanced that way. "But it's covered with trees, where could he land?"

"He probably didn't."

She blinked. And stared as the small black helicopter indeed came into view over the trees she'd just been speaking of. "You meant literally dropping him off."

"Like a hot rock," Teague said cheerfully. "Fast rope insertion. Piece of cake when no one's shooting at you so you can keep both hands on the rope."

Feeling ever more out of her depth, Laney watched both the approaching chopper and Teague as he pulled out his unusual phone, pressed a series of buttons, fiddled with a small device in his hand that he then put in his ear.

"Hey, boss," he said.

He must have gotten an acknowledgment, because he spoke again. "Rafe? You copy?"

A pause, then he said, "No, no change. Laney's been watching while I gear up. They're holed up on board."

He listened for a moment. "Copy," he said then. "I'm not thrilled with the kayak, it's not exactly stable for boarding, but it's the best shot. He's seen it, and has me pegged as a henpecked husband. Harmless."

Laney wondered how he'd managed that. She couldn't imagine Teague Johnson as a henpecked anything.

"It's a small boat, close quarters. I'm going in armed, but it'll be last resort, too easy for Amber to be hurt in a cross-fire."

Laney suppressed a shudder. The helicopter seemed to go past them, then turned beyond the cove and headed back over the water. It slowed, not quite a hover but certainly not moving quickly, near the entrance to the cove.

"Copy that," Teague said to whatever he'd just heard in his ear. A little bothered that she had no idea what was actually happening, Laney watched the chopper a moment longer. But when Teague moved toward the kayak again, she'd had enough.

"I'm coming this time," she said, reaching for the second kayak.

His head snapped around. "Laney, no, you need to—"

"What I need is to be there."

He abandoned the kayak, came back to her. He put his arms around her, held her close. She let him; they'd certainly not had the slow, pleasant morning she'd hoped for, so she would take what she could get.

"We'll handle it.... We'll get Amber out of there."

"I know you will." And she did, that wasn't the issue. "Amber's terrified, I told you that."

"I know. But it will be over soon."

Laney knew he meant to be soothing, calming, and it would work under probably any other circumstances, but now it didn't even dent her determination. Reluctantly she pulled free, took a step back. Looked at him steadily.

"Amber's terrified," she repeated, "and terrified people sometimes do crazy things. She'll have no way of knowing you're the good guys. Unless she sees me."

She knew she was right. And she saw from the way

Teague's eyes narrowed, followed by his jaw clenching, that he knew it, too.

"Damn," he muttered, and something about his tone made the curse irrelevant. It made her feel valued, protected. She'd been on her own so long it took her a moment to recognize the feeling.

That it was this man making her feel that way gave her a whole new feeling. And she realized it hadn't been just those feelings she'd longed for. It was those feelings from the right person.

Teague was that right person.

And she didn't have a single minute right now to deal with that discovery. He'd told her, when he'd tried to do the noble thing and not give in to the attraction between them. He'd told her she could, and likely would, feel differently once Amber was back safe and sound. She didn't think so, but she couldn't deny he was only in her life because of what they would be facing in the next few minutes.

Whether he would be in her life after this, she would soon find out. The most important thing right now was Amber. It had to be.

She supposed it was selfish, but she couldn't help but wish she'd met him some other way.

Chapter 31

And this, Teague thought with grim realization, was why Quinn warned them not to get too emotionally involved. It messed up your thinking, had you worrying about something other than the goal. Not that he didn't want them to care, that was the cornerstone of Foxworth's philosophy: they cared when no one else did. But Teague knew if he'd been thinking straight, he would have seen the logic of Laney's proposal from the get-go.

But instead he'd been focused on keeping her out of harm's way, keeping her safe, when in fact she was right. In fact, he'd almost set it up himself, albeit inadvertently, with his nagging wife jokes. If she appeared with him, the guy would think that's who she was, that the text had been to order him back to get her. It would fit.

She was right about Amber, too. She could well be so traumatized now that she'd see another, strange man as just another threat. She might even decide a drowning death was better, and go for the water.

And Laney had the right to be there. Because the bottom line was that no matter how dedicated he and Foxworth were, no one had more at stake here than Laney. Except maybe Amber herself.

So he was just going to have to deal.

"You will stay back," he ordered. "And whatever happens, you don't get between me and him, or between the boat and where Rafe is."

It only took her a second to process that. Still quick, he thought, as she went a little pale. "I—"

He cut her off. "No argument, or you stay here."

"I was just going to suggest I stay on the other side of the boat from you. That fulfills your requirements, right? And it might distract him a little, divide his attention."

The way the boat was positioned now, she was right. Again. She was thinking tactically, in a way that both surprised him and didn't. This was Laney, after all. She might never have been in a situation like this before, but she was quick and she was smart, and she learned fast.

"All right. Just pay attention to the angle of the boat so you don't end up in the wrong place for Rafe."

"In his line of fire, you mean."

She said it steadily enough. Admiration flooded through him, not for the first time since he'd met this woman. She'd do to ride the river with, as Texas-born-and-bred Liam sometimes said, a saying he'd picked up from his Texan grandfather. Oh, yes, she'd do.

"Yes. And if that happens, if shooting starts, you are to get the hell out of there as fast as you can. Head sideways. Toward the sailboat for cover, or the rocks if you have to, just not back toward the docks or toward the entrance of the cove. Is that understood?"

"Yes. I'm not stupid, Teague. I know when to rely on the pros."

"I never thought you were stupid. Ever. Far from it."

He didn't have time to react to what flashed in those warm eyes then. Quinn was in position, so was Rafe, it was time to move.

And he couldn't let himself be the one distracted, by wondering what would happen after this was resolved. Wondering if she would indeed come to her senses and realize what had happened between them had been born out of the situation, out of circumstances, and not real.

Never mind that it had been the most real thing he'd ever felt in his life.

He made her put on the Kevlar vest he dug out of his pack. She protested, saying he'd need it if anyone did, but he insisted and she finally gave in. It was the only thing he could do to protect her, and that was the only thing that would enable him to stay focused on the job at hand.

Compartmentalize, he ordered as they paddled out. She handled the kayak efficiently, if not with familiar ease, and he could tell she'd done it before. It could be nice, under other circumstances, cruising around the sound with her, up close and personal in the small watercraft. He'd never taken the time for such leisurely exploration in all the years he'd spent here. He was more of a get-where-you're-going-and-do-what-you-came-to-do kind of guy. That he was pondering this at all told him how much trouble he was in.

Don't think about it, he ordered silently. *Don't think about anything but the job. Especially don't think about her maybe getting hurt, or worse. Just do the job. Like you have countless times before.*

So why was it so damned hard this time?

He knew the answer even as he thought the question.

Just think about trying to explain to Quinn why you had

your head up your ass, he told himself. And he dug down deep and found the focus, although he wasn't sure how long it would hold. Until the moment Laney was in real danger, he guessed.

The man was back out in the rear cockpit. Laney had told him he'd gone inside once he himself had gotten back to the docks. She'd been watching intently. But this time he was facing the other way, looking out toward the entrance to the cove.

Watching the sleek, black helicopter that was making slow, high circles above it.

A normal person might look, watch. Might wonder what the helicopter was doing there in the first place, and certainly what it was doing hanging out in one spot like that. Might wonder if there was something going on in the water below that they should be concerned about.

But a guilty person, someone with something to hide, something big, might well assume the helicopter was there for them. And react accordingly. What the guy did now would tell them even more than his ignorance of his supposed home port.

He got ready to run.

"Rabbit?" Quinn's question echoed in his ear.

"Rabbit," he confirmed.

"Rafe?" Quinn said.

"Copy."

The man scrambled up to the bow of the boat, fumbled with the mooring line fastened around a cleat. Teague saw his assessment of the man's lack of sailing skills had been accurate: he was having difficulty with the unsuitable-for-the-purpose square knots. And he was getting frantic, clawing at the knot uselessly.

After a few more seconds, enough time for Teague to get closer, he quit the battle and darted back to the cockpit, dug in one of the bench lockers and came out with a knife. Teague watched as he sawed at the line near the cleat, while calculating his own approach. Quinn had moved in closer and lower, and the man looked over his shoulder as if he'd realized it.

The line finally parted. He didn't even pull it clear of the buoy, just let it trail in the water, and Teague had the thought that if it was long enough to tangle in the prop his sloppiness could end this rather quickly.

Teague motioned to Laney to get clear. He had to raise his voice to be heard over the helicopter's noise. "If he's as lousy at steering that thing as he is everything else about it, he might run right over a kayak."

He saw reluctance in her eyes, but she did as they'd agreed and paddled away. Quinn was low enough now he was kicking up a lot of concentric waves and spray, and the noise was an effective distraction. So far, the man seemed so focused on the helicopter he wasn't paying any attention to them, if he'd even noticed them at all.

He scrambled back to the helm, slipping once as he looked over his shoulder again at the helicopter that was now barely a hundred feet away and even less off the deck. Since he hadn't started the engine first, the boat was drifting, powerless, the current and probably the wind Quinn was generating nudging it backward. Underneath the sound of the bird closing in, Teague heard the bark of the boat's engine trying to crank. And crank again, apparently in a similar condition to the boat itself. Finally it turned over. He couldn't hear it, but saw the belch of smoke from the exhaust.

Teague looked to the far side of the boat, saw Laney's kayak. The stern of it, anyway. She wasn't as far back as he would have liked. Of course, he would have liked her safely back onshore. But she should be clear unless the guy decided to turn and aim for her, and Teague doubted he even knew she was there. He'd only just spotted him, and thanks to the shift in the boat's position he was coming at him head-on.

Teague waved, casually, as if there was nothing unusual

going on, as if there wasn't a helicopter closing in just yards away. The man barely spared him a glance, clearly still thinking him no threat.

The boat started to move, turning as he tried to clear the buoy and head out toward open water. And in that moment so did Quinn, bringing the chopper down even lower and closer. The man's expression turned to pure fear. Teague moved in, paddling hard and fast. The chop from the rotor's wake made it tougher, but he dug in deeper, forcing the little personal craft through the broken water. He had to get there before the guy could get any speed up.

He wasn't sure he was going to make it. The boat began to move, to turn toward the entrance to the cove. There was no way he was going to be able to keep up if the guy got it going forward.

Even as he thought it, Quinn acted. He quit hovering. The rotors tilted, grabbed air and the bird shot forward and down. Straight at the boat. To the man at the helm, it must have seemed the helicopter was diving right at him. On a deadly collision course. It would take a tough heart and steady hand to maintain in the face of that.

This guy had neither.

He slammed the boat's engine into Reverse. The neglected machinery protested by dying instantly. He abandoned the wheel and hit the deck with a scream Teague heard even over the helicopter as it roared past, arcing back to safer altitude as it cleared the boat by a nearer margin than was sane. Quinn Foxworth was one hell of a pilot.

This was his chance, and Teague knew it. He'd have to move fast and smooth to avoid ending up in the drink trying to do this from a kayak. No time for hesitation, once he started he was committed. Momentum was key. He drove the kayak up against the swim step. Ignored the bobbing of the boat in the chop. Scrambled out, up and over.

He was on the deck of the cockpit before the man realized what had happened. It took a moment to recover from having nearly been sliced to pieces by an eggbeater flown by a clearly crazy pilot.

Teague ran toward him, hoping to take him down before he could react. But the man was too close to the cabin hatch, and he yanked it open and dived inside a split second before Teague had his hands on him. Teague started down the narrow steps after him.

And stopped dead.

He backed up slowly, holding his hands up.

"Don't," he said.

"You!" the man exclaimed. Clearly he'd been so unnerved by Quinn's startling tactic that he hadn't even realized the man who had come up over the back of the boat was the same one he'd talked to earlier.

"Hi, again," Teague said, his tone cheerful. "Sorry, didn't catch your name before."

The man opened his mouth as if he were going to give it, as if this were some kind of normal, social meeting. The mind worked that way sometimes, Teague knew, falling back on the learned forms when everything was in disarray.

And this guy's plans had certainly been chopped to bits.

"Back off," the man ordered, his voice low, shaky and edged with a wildness that didn't bode well for anyone.

"Take it easy," Teague said.

"You're together, aren't you? You and that maniac in the chopper?"

Looking at the big picture, Teague doubted Quinn would be the one considered a maniac by most people. But that was probably not the best thing to point out just now.

"Back off," the man repeated. "And tell your buddy in that damned helicopter to back off, too. Or I'll gut her like a fish."

He meant it, Teague thought. And he had the means. In his hand was the knife he'd used to cut the mooring line.

And it was at Amber's throat.

Chapter 32

"Back off, Quinn," Teague said into the headset. "He's got a knife and he's using Amber as a shield."

"Son of a bitch."

"Exactly," Teague agreed, angry with himself. If he'd been ten seconds faster, hell, even five, he would have had the guy before he got down into the cabin. But now he had Amber jammed up against his side, and the narrow but deadly sharp filleting knife already had drawn blood, a thin line that trickled down her throat.

A moment later the sound of the helicopter faded as Quinn withdrew.

"You're a cop," the man said with disgust.

"No," Teague answered. "Just a friend."

He would have tried to give Amber a reassuring look, but there was a none-too-clean rag tied over her eyes. Duct tape was plastered over her mouth and a rope tied with those same knots—much more suitable here—held her wrists together behind her back. Her cheeks were wet, tears having already gotten past the dirty rag. Her blond hair was tangled and matted. There was a bruise on her left cheek, more along her arms.

"A friend? With a helicopter?"

"A private one. It wasn't marked, in case you hadn't noticed." He doubted the man had noticed anything except that it was coming straight at him.

Teague looked at Amber. He wondered if the restraints were a result of her venturing out on deck this morning. Perhaps she really had been trying to escape, stopped only by her fear of the water and inability to swim. She had to be terrified to have even considered it.

He'd been right about the close quarters. Drawing his weapon, even the smoke grenade was out of the question; Amber would get hurt, maybe even killed. He had to find another way.

"Give it up, man," Teague said. "The cops are on the way, and they won't be as reasonable as we will."

"We? Who the hell is 'we'?"

"Friends of Amber's. All we want is her, safe."

The man snorted scornfully. "Snooty bitch doesn't have any real friends. Not that would risk this. She's all flash."

Teague heard Amber choke back a sob. "You're wrong," he said softly, thinking of Laney, the truest of real friends.

"She's a whore, doesn't know the meaning of the word loyalty. If you're one of them that thinks you're her boyfriend, you're a fool."

"I'm a fool? I'm not the one who's cornered in a boat that's adrift and headed straight for the rocks, with a helicopter pinning me down and the cops on the way," he said.

Teague had the feeling the guy hadn't realized quite how precarious his position was until he'd heard it in words like that. He looked around the small cabin as if he expected to hear the crunch of the hull hitting rock at any second. Teague guessed the waters of the cove were calm enough that wasn't likely to happen fast, although Quinn could probably blow them that way with rotor wash if it came to that.

"Back up." The man shouted the order, gesturing again with the knife at Amber's throat, drawing a little more blood and a muffled cry from behind the tape. "Get outside."

Having little choice at the moment, Teague knew he was going to have to comply. Besides, he needed room to maneuver, and he didn't have that down here. So it was to their advantage to be out of the cabin. He knew Quinn would be monitoring. And more importantly, once they were outside, so would Rafe. Now that it was clearly a hostage situation, he'd be prepping his shot carefully.

The man was a good head taller than Amber, which would help. It would still be tricky, with the boat moving in four directions at once, laterally and vertically, but Rafe was indeed the best he'd ever seen, and if it could be done, he could do it. He'd even pulled off one or two that simply couldn't be done, until he did them.

Slowly his gaze fastened on the man with the knife; he backed up, slowly, trying to anticipate what the man would do. If he wanted to try another run for it he had to go up on deck to the helm. He might try it, using Amber as leverage to keep Quinn at bay. Which meant he'd need Teague here and alive for at least long enough to relay the message.

He started up the steep, narrow cabin steps backward, never taking his eyes off the man. He focused on his eyes, watching for some expression to warn him the man had tipped over into panic, because as Laney had said, panicked people did stupid things.

"We're coming out," he said into the headset, although he was sure Quinn had heard the shouted order. He was also sure his boss was intensely frustrated at the moment, despite having done what had to be done, keeping the boat where it was. But since it took both hands—and feet—to keep the helicopter in the air in such tricky and close quarters, there wasn't much else he could do now but hang back and watch.

And, if necessary, give the order to Rafe.

Once again, Rafe was their ace in the hole, and Teague had never felt better about it. All he really had to do was make sure he got a clean chance. Get Amber clear. It wasn't even a long shot, not for Rafe. Maybe six hundred feet. He'd done shots at ten times that distance. Hell, he could probably do it with a pistol, if he was in practice.

He emerged into the open air. The man shoved Amber up the steps. Blind and terrified, she stumbled repeatedly, earning a string of curses from the man that singed even Teague's marine-corps-toughened ears.

He could hear the helicopter, but didn't want to look away. He also wanted to look for Laney, but he couldn't let himself do that, either, not now. He judged from the sound Quinn had backed up as much as away, probably thinking another dive might be necessary. This also told Teague Quinn was relying on him to make the call for Rafe, although Quinn himself would, as always, give the order.

The man edged backward toward the wheel, keeping his attention on Teague and the knife against Amber's vulnerable throat.

A flicker of movement caught the corner of Teague's vision. By training he didn't betray it by moving his eyes, but mentally shifted his focus to the edge, to his peripheral vision. And realized what he'd seen was the tip of a kayak, edging up closer, behind the man.

Laney.

He wanted to yell at her to get away, get clear, but he didn't want to betray her presence to the man who right now was focused completely on him as he finally reached the helm.

I'm not stupid, Teague. I know when to rely on the pros.
I never thought you were. Ever. Far from it.

The exchange echoed in his head. *I'm not stupid, Teague.*
Give her credit, he thought. She'd earned it. *And maybe*
it's time you learned to rely on a civilian.

"Hope you have a paddle," he said, raising his voice, he
hoped just enough.

"It'll start," the man sneered, taking it just as Teague had
hoped.

He wasn't sure if he hoped Laney had heard and understood or not.

A split second later he knew she had.

Drops of water sprayed in an arc as a double-bladed kayak
paddle swung up over the railing. The man never even saw
it until it caught him, hard, on the side of the knee away
from Amber. He yelled. Spun around as the joint buckled.
He staggered.

And let go of Amber.

Teague dove, taking him low, where he was already off
balance. The man's feet went backward; his heavy body went
forward, over Teague's back. In that instant Teague rolled to
one side. The man hit the deck. Hard. Face-first. The loud
thud was satisfying.

The man didn't move. He appeared stunned, but Teague
wasn't about to leave anything to chance. He kicked aside
the rusty knife the man had dropped when he hit. He pulled
his own blade from his boot and went to Amber, who cow-
ered away from him, muffled sobs coming from behind the
duct tape. She was close enough to the rail he was afraid
she'd go over.

"Teague?"

Laney's voice came from over the side. The bedraggled
blonde went still.

"She's all right," he called. *And thank God you are.* He

took a step toward the bound woman. "It's all right, Amber. It's over. Laney's here with me."

He reached out and tugged off the blindfold. Amber blinked in the sunlight, looked at him, then spotted the man lying on the deck. She recoiled. Teague realized coming at her with that knife out without explanation probably wasn't a good idea.

She bore little resemblance at the moment to the beautiful woman in the photographs. Her eyes were indeed that striking color, but reddened to the point of looking painful from what had probably been non-stop crying. Her hair looked as if it hadn't been washed the entire time. Teague was willing to bet she had never been this dirty in her life.

Or as scared.

He made sure his voice was gentle, reassuring. "Amber, my name's Teague. I'm going to cut that rope off you. I need it for him."

She was shaking, but after a moment she nodded. He did it as quickly as he could. He cut the rope close to the knot, to give him the most length to work with. He quickly backed off. His instinct was to comfort the terrorized woman, but priorities demanded he secure the bad guy first. In seconds he had him trussed up securely, still facedown.

In his ear Teague heard Quinn tell Rafe to stand down. He heard a sound at the rear of the boat; realized Laney had come around to the stern. She might need some help getting out of that kayak, he thought.

He glanced at Amber. The terror was fading, but she still looked scared, as if she were not certain her situation had improved all that much. She looked up where the helicopter had retreated to a normal altitude. When she glanced over the rail at the water, like someone again contemplating risking the swim, he knew just how right Laney had been.

"He's one of the good guys, too," Teague said, gesturing up at the hovering aircraft.

"Laney," she whispered.

"She's here."

He walked back to the stern. Laney was there, looking up at him from the kayak, clearly wound so tight it was a wonder she didn't explode right out of the unstable craft. "She's really all right?"

"Physically," he answered, knowing she'd understand. She gave a quick, short nod. She reached up to him.

"Help me?" she asked.

"Always," he answered.

He took her hand, pulled, and she scrambled aboard rather neatly. For a second she didn't move, she just clung to him.

"Thank you," she whispered. She was crying, as she had been the first time he'd seen her. Yet differently, because she was smiling.

"Thank *you*," he said. "You gave me the chance."

And then she ran to Amber.

And Teague stood and watched the reunion, thinking this truly was what Foxworth was all about.

And wondered just how many different ways those last twelve words they'd exchanged could be taken.

Chapter 33

"It's over, Amber. We'll have you off this boat in no time," Teague said. He took a breath as if he needed to steady himself. It reminded Laney of the day she'd met him, when she'd been the one crying. "It's all over."

His voice sounded flat, and Laney wondered if he was feeling the adrenaline crash she'd been warned about. But what either of them was feeling had to be nothing compared to what Amber was going through. She hugged her friend tightly.

"It's all right, Amber."

Laney kept her voice low and soothing, but it didn't seem to have much effect on Amber's weeping. Not that she blamed her.

"I feel so stupid. I should have known. You would have known."

"I didn't," Laney said, well aware she had been saying the same thing about herself not so long ago. Only Teague's reassurance had helped her.

Teague, she thought. Teague who had believed her, brought her help, and in the end rescued her best friend personally. Despite what he said about the whack she'd given the guy with her paddle. Which had been a clumsy affair anyway. She'd wanted to stand up and deliver it to his head, would have liked the feeling of delivering that blow, but had decided trying to stand in that kayak would likely land her in the water where she'd be no help at all.

But Teague hadn't needed much, just a bit of distraction, to take the man out with a speed and efficiency that was a bit breath-stealing. He'd never hesitated, just launched himself at the man, and it had been over so quickly she had felt a little stunned by it all.

But Amber was alive, albeit bruised and dirty. Laney didn't know yet just how bad it had been for her precious friend, but she quickly decided the best course was to assume the very worst and treat Amber accordingly, with softer than kid gloves.

"You're always so careful about men," Amber said in a tone of self-accusation. "You tried to tell me, but I just thought you were paranoid. Didn't know how to have fun."

"Amber, stop—"

"But it's true. I always fall for the guy right off, and you—you've never slept with a guy you'd known less than six months in your entire life."

Images slammed through Laney's mind: Teague, first on the floor, then in her bed, half-naked then naked, she herself wild with a kind of need she'd never experienced, so hungry for him she nearly screamed with it. And then, with his hard, hungry body driving her, she had screamed.

In that moment she was glad Amber wasn't looking at her, because she was certain every single bit of that night, every hot, delicious moment, was etched on her face.

"You always told me I'd regret moving so fast all the time," Amber said, gulping back another sob.

"Wait, Amber," Laney finally managed to get out, pushing the heated visions back for the moment. "Who are you talking about? How did this happen? I thought you were seeing Edward."

"I was."

"But him, how did he come into it?" Laney gestured at the man on the deck; he'd come around now, but Teague had rooted around and found the roll of duct tape he'd used on Amber and proceeded to tape his mouth shut, saying there was absolutely nothing the guy had to say that any of them needed to hear. He'd also added a couple of zip ties to the rope, until the man ended up hog-tied and helpless on the deck where he'd threatened Amber's life. Laney felt nothing but satisfaction about that.

Amber gave a bitter, humorless laugh. "He was always hanging around, flirting. Then they had an argument. He said Edward owed him, and he wanted me in payment. The bastard just got out of the car and left me with him. I tried to get away but he sped up and I couldn't. I tried whenever we stopped, but that's when he started hitting me. And then he tied me up."

Laney's stomach lurched. She tightened her arms around Amber, letting her cry, saying nothing simply because she couldn't think of anything to say.

Amber might be safe now, but this was a long way from over for her traumatized friend.

Laney kept her arm around her as she helped her get off the boat that had been her cell and onto the skiff that would carry them back to dry land. Laney figured that alone would help Amber's mental state a great deal.

As long, Laney had thought, as she didn't look too closely at the man who'd come for them. This was the infamous Rafe, she gathered, and she didn't think it was just her knowledge of his lethal skills that had caused her to suck in a breath when she first looked at him. She'd never seen eyes like that, shadowed, tightened by a darkness that she didn't think came just from whatever had caused the limp she noticed as soon as they were ashore.

But now it began, she thought. There was so much to figure out, to unravel. But Quinn took over, and his commanding presence made it clear it would all be handled.

With an inward sigh of relief, she mentally handed it over and turned her attention completely to reassuring her best friend.

The garrulous harbormaster was still looking a bit befuddled. Teague couldn't blame him. He was sure the guy had come in today expecting a pleasant end-of-summer day, probably vowing to enjoy the weather as the season wound down. And instead he ended up with cops in his office and a helicopter in his parking lot. And a cluster of gaping marina tenants demanding explanations.

They'd taken over the office completely. Detective Dunbar and a couple of uniforms had arrived some ten minutes after they'd made it back ashore, picked up in a runabout Rafe had commandeered from an astonished boater at the docks. He would have liked to have seen that, Teague thought. The look people got when Rafe stared them down was always startlingly the same, as if there was some deeply buried human instinct that took over when they were confronted with lethal force personified.

He'd requested the assist when the boat indeed wouldn't start, was in fact slowly drifting toward the rocks and it became clear Laney wasn't about to leave Amber to kayak back. And although Amber could have fit with him on the larger fishing kayak he had, he didn't think it wise to ask the woman to take on her fear of water that closely after all she'd been through.

Rafe had arrived, taken the line Teague threw him and tied the boat off once more at the buoy. They then climbed, Amber quite gingerly, into the smaller, open boat. Laney never left her friend's side, and Amber clung to her like a lifeline.

I get that, Teague thought. *Because Laney would never, ever break. Not when it came to someone she loved.*

His mind skittered away from the very word. *Don't even go there,* he ordered himself. And walked over to look out the window as if physically going somewhere else could prevent his mind from going where he didn't want it to go. He stared at the peaceful scene the marina had returned to, the only hint of anything out of the ordinary the helicopter Quinn had neatly set down in the parking lot.

He had no time for thinking about things he didn't want to think about anyway. There was simply too much to do, too many details to wind up, and too much explaining to do. Thankfully most of that would fall to Quinn; he'd already given his report to his boss before Dunbar and crew had arrived. He'd given a briefer, only-the-essentials report to Dunbar himself, who had studied him for a moment with a look that said he knew there was more to it but he was trusting Teague that it wasn't relevant.

First order of business now that it was all over, but the details, was Amber, and while Laney's first instinct was to help her clean up—the normally fastidious woman must feel awful, she'd said—Teague had had to hold her back.

"Evidence," he'd said. And while Laney's eyes widened, she'd only taken a split second to nod in understanding.

"She needs to see a doctor," Laney insisted now. Teague turned back to look at her; she was giving Dunbar that determined, chin-up look that said she wouldn't back down.

She hadn't looked at him since the detective had arrived.

In fact, seemed to be purposely avoiding even the slightest
eye contact. And he was afraid he knew what that meant.

"We'll make the initial statement short," Detective Dunbar
said. "Then we'll get her to a medical facility."

Laney nodded, glancing over to the office where Amber
was now seated, huddled into herself in a way that made
Teague wish he'd done more damage to her abductor.

One of the uniformed deputies was the woman who was in
there with Amber, and Teague didn't doubt Dunbar had seen
to that. The man was competent and efficient, tough when
he had to be, but with the capacity for gentleness as well, a
compassion that people responded to in the same sort of way
they responded to Rafe, albeit oppositely.

Teague had instinctively liked him the first time they'd
met, when he'd helped them with Kayla's missing brother. He
hoped the goodwill they'd built up with him then would
cover what had happened here today. He thought so; Dunbar
was a practical sort, who realized law enforcement couldn't be
everywhere all the time, especially out here in remote areas.

He just had to hope Quinn could convince him they hadn't
dared to wait for them to arrive before getting Amber out of
there. One look at the pale, bruised, dazed woman, her eyes
still wide and dark with shock, should do that. He'd seen the
expression on the female deputy's face when she'd led Amber
gently into the office to get that first statement, and knew
Dunbar had chosen well.

He'd hear the whole story eventually, he knew. And Quinn
would manage to smooth things over, although this one might
be a bit trickier than some, given they'd actually staged a hostage rescue on their own, without waiting for the authorities.
He wondered if Quinn had put in a call to Gavin de Marco, the
Foxworth attorney. He imagined how that might have gone.
"Hey, Gav, we just boarded a private vessel and knocked out
a guy whose name we don't even know."

He didn't know enough about the law to predict what the answer would be, but he'd dealt with de Marco a few times, and the man was, in his own way, as unflappable as Rafe. And, Teague suspected, as steely when he had to be. And he had a way of presenting things that made it clear to all concerned it would be best to simply accept and move on.

Foxworth's well-established policy of never taking public credit when their paths did cross with official channels helped, Teague supposed. They scrupulously avoided stepping on toes.

"Can you live with others taking credit for what you've done?" was one of the first questions Quinn asked him during the long—very long—interview process that was more of a vetting than many public officials ever got.

"I've been living with it for years," he'd said. "As long as the right thing gets done, and I know I had a part in it, that's enough."

"They're liable to be blatant about it. They often are."

Quinn hadn't had to explain to him who the "they" were. "I've served with and under the type often. Most of them had one thing in common."

"Which was?"

"They themselves have no idea what to do. I don't get envious of the clueless."

Quinn had laughed. Later, he'd told him that he'd decided then and there that unless Teague did or said something unforgivably stupid through the rest of the process, he was in.

He glanced over at Detective Dunbar, who was still talking to Laney. Or rather, listening to her. He could tell by her expression that she was earnestly pouring out what had happened. And Dunbar was indeed listening, which was all Laney had ever asked, but this man was the only cop who really had.

He looked tired, though. Still lean, and fit, but tired, and there seemed to him to be a trace more of the silver at his temples than there had been even since he'd first met him, during Kayla and Dane Burdette's case a few weeks ago.

Great, he muttered. *With all this going on, you're standing here wondering if a cop's gone grayer?*

He answered himself grimly, because he knew perfectly well that he was focusing on any and everything except what he now knew. What had been made painfully clear in the minutes after the hostage rescue. Amber's words were undeniable, and Teague found he couldn't dodge them any longer.

You're always so careful about men, Amber had said. *I always fall for the guy right off, and you—you've never slept with a guy you'd known less than six months in your entire life.*

You always told me I'd regret moving so fast....

He'd known it. Sensed it. What had happened between them was totally, completely out of character for her. His first instinct, the one that had driven him to leave that first time, when it was the last thing he'd wanted to do, had been the right one. He'd told her it was the circumstances, told her she was vulnerable, under stress.

He should have stuck with that.

And that he hadn't had a prayer, not once she'd decided she wanted him in spite of all the reasons he'd given her, of resisting.

Guilt blasted through him. *Some professional you are,* he thought. *Quinn tried to warn you, and you went right ahead anyway. And now that the circumstances are back to normal, now that everything that drove us together has been resolved, you get to deal with the fallout.*

So deal with it. Be a professional now, since you were anything but before.

He could do that much, he told himself. The best thing he could do for Laney now was save her the embarrassment of having to tell him she'd come to her senses, that she hadn't really meant any of it.

That he had meant every bit of it was something he was just going to have to live with.

Chapter 34

"The psychologist and counselors will help Amber work through it all," Hayley said, her tone reassuring. "They're very good at what they do."

Laney drew in a deep breath, having a little trouble adjusting to the fact that it was indeed all over. She looked out the window of the Foxworth meeting room, noticing with a little shock that the trees were starting to turn. There were spots of the yellow, gold, orange and red that would soon overtake everything but the evergreens for which the state was named. When she'd first been here, when Teague had first brought her here just five days ago, all had been green.

Teague. He was acting so strangely. He'd barely spoken to her since they'd gotten back on dry land, and not at all since they'd been back here. He'd spoken to Amber, telling her repeatedly it was all over and she was safe, but hadn't given her even a glance.

She was already antsy from having left Amber with strangers, but the staff at the small hospital had insisted Amber needed rest more than anything after both her ordeal and the aftermath of interviews and recounting it all, and they would be keeping her overnight. And the Foxworth counselor had already arrived and had promised she would stay, and call Laney immediately if Amber woke up. Laney was fairly sure that wasn't standard procedure, to sit with a sleeping patient, but as she'd learned, nothing was really standard with Foxworth. They exceeded expectations in all areas.

And so did their people.

She turned back to Hayley.

That they thought ahead and had such people ready, that Amber was already in very good and gentle hands, just emphasized what Laney already knew. "I have the distinct impression everyone at Foxworth is very good at what they do," she said.

Hayley smiled. "Yes. Yes they are."

A soft *woof* drew Laney's attention.

"Especially this guy," she crooned, leaning over to scratch that spot behind Cutter's right ear, glad to hide her face since she was fairly sure she was blushing as thoughts of one of the things Teague was very, very good at rushed through her mind, a flood she seemed helpless to stop anytime she thought of him. Which was about every other minute. She'd finally had to avoid looking at him at all to get her story out to Detective Dunbar.

"He has his own inimitable talents, does Cutter," Hayley agreed.

Laney continued scratching until the dog sighed in utter bliss.

I know that feeling, boy, she thought ruefully.

Quinn joined them then, taking the seat next to Hayley. Teague was with him, but hesitated to take the seat he always had before, next to her. Finally he tugged the chair around the corner of the table and sat there instead. Hayley looked at him quizzically, but he avoided her eyes. Odd, Laney thought. But then everything felt odd now. Adrenaline crash, Quinn had explained to her back at the marina. She was liable to be exhausted for a while once it was all over.

"Just hang on a little longer," he had said, putting an arm around her shoulders and squeezing gently.

Funny, she'd thought, how different it felt coming from Quinn. He was incredibly strong and it was steadying, but had it been Teague it would have been all the comfort she needed to keep going endlessly.

"We think that we have it pieced together now," Quinn said.

"Good," Hayley said. "Because I'm missing a few parts."

"You," Quinn said, "are missing no parts at all. They're all there, and arranged beautifully. I've inspected them myself."

The easy, teasing, and blatantly loving exchange made Laney smile even as Hayley blushed.

"Well, now, if you want to talk about working parts," Hayley said archly.

Quinn laughed. Laney snuck a sideways glance at Teague. He was standing with his back to them, staring out the window, ignoring the conversation as thoroughly as he'd been ignoring her. And she began to get the message he was sending.

Over.

It's all over.

How many times had he said it as they were waiting on the boat? She'd assumed he meant it to reassure the shattered Amber.

Now she was wondering if he'd meant it just as much for her.

Quinn exchanged a glance with Hayley that told Laney he was curious about the strange attitude as well. "Teague?"

There was a split second's hesitation before Teague responded, before he turned around and said, "Sir?"

"You want to run through the big picture?"

He gave a half shrug that for some reason struck Laney as if he'd slapped her. Had he really lost all interest so quickly now that it was, as he'd repeatedly said, *all* over? Was it really just a matter of giving a report that seemed to bore him? Nothing more?

His tone did little to convince her otherwise; it was short, clipped, beyond businesslike.

"Dunbar says Brady Osgood has a history. Grabbed a neighbor girl when he was a teenager. Cops couldn't prove she hadn't gone voluntarily. Couple of assaults, one rape charge. They suspect he scared the vic into dropping it. It's always their fault, not his. He bought the plane ticket online, with Amber's card, to throw off anybody who might look for her. Page turned up back at work this morning. The boat is his now, from his great-uncle. It's in that shape because he couldn't afford to fix it. Or register it. All his money went down the roulette drain. He's deep in debt. Mostly to Osgood. So he let him take the boat. And Amber."

Laney smothered a gasp at the starkness of it. Teague didn't even pause.

"Osgood said he took her to teach Page a lesson. That he owned him. Page says that was what woke him up, made him realize how far he'd sunk. It wasn't a vacation he took. He's been in rehab. We verified that. Says he had no idea what Osgood was really up to."

Teague sat down, as if to signify he was done.

"Well," Quinn said with a wry expression, "been taking succinct lessons from Rafe?"

Teague didn't laugh, didn't even smile, earning him a speculative look from Hayley. Laney tried to process it all, had the fleeting thought that this bare-bones report was in a way easier to handle than any drawn out explanation of why Brady Osgood was a twisted, evil man. She didn't really care. She'd come close to losing Amber to his twisted psyche, and why he was what he was didn't ameliorate anything in her book. Not yet, anyway. She might want more details later, and Amber might, but for now, that was enough.

Cutter was getting restless, as if he sensed the undercurrent in the room. The dog made a low, whining sound, and went to sit in between the chair Laney was in and the one Teague had pulled around to the end of the table. He looked from one to the other, intently.

Makes you feel for the sheep, doesn't it?

Teague's quip had made her chuckle then. Thinking of it only made her feel worse now; the absence of his solid comfort was a palpable thing. He was even better at his job than she'd thought, if he could disengage so completely so quickly.

And that's all it had been to him, apparently. A job. A job that was now over, as was any other connection between them.

You can't say he didn't warn you. He gave you a chance, more than many men would, when he walked away that first time. He'd tried not to take advantage. You're the one who jumped him the next time. You can't even be angry at him; he tried to tell you you'd regret it. Because he knew all along this was all it was, some stress-induced aberration.

Her thoughts careened around her brain, and she hated that it was all true. But she hated more that all the reason, logic and truth didn't stop her from feeling hurt. Hurt so badly it was a physical thing, a stabbing, searing pain that was spreading from some deep place in the pit of her stomach to every part of her.

She should have stayed with Amber. But they'd insisted she'd be sleeping. Still, there were other things she could and should be doing. She'd called Amber's parents from the hospital, and they were on their way, but she should go pick up some things for her. Clothes, cosmetics, things to make Amber feel normal. She could go to her apartment and pack a bag, or maybe it would be better to get her new things, things that couldn't be any kind of reminder.

Cutter whined and nudged her arm with his nose. She automatically moved her hand to stroke his head and then ruffle the thick fur at his neck.

Quinn cleared his throat. Teague tapped the side of his thumb on the table, the only sign that he was anything other than just bored, now that it was all over.

Suddenly it was more than Laney could deal with. She stood up abruptly. "Amber will need things," she said.

"Of course she will," Hayley said. "I picked up some basics, toiletries and things, but you'll know better what she likes, especially in clothes. And I'd guess we should take into account that looking attractive may not be quite so appealing to her just now, so maybe something plain?"

"Thank you," Laney said in a heartfelt tone that matched what she was feeling. "I wouldn't have thought of that, but you're right."

"Jeans, then. And a choice of tops. Feminine and not so," Hayley said briskly. "Underwear, somewhere in between. Let's go."

Hayley stood up. She looked over at Cutter, who had instantly gotten to his feet when Hayley did. "You want to come, or stay with the boys? We're just going shopping."

At the word shopping, the dog made a very male-sounding whuff of distaste and sat back down, this time at Teague's feet.

"Stay with the boys it is," Hayley said with a laugh at her dog's cleverness.

Maybe she should get a dog of her own, Laney thought as she gathered up her purse and started toward the door with Hayley. It seemed silly, to be a groomer without an animal herself. He could be the shop mascot or something. Greet customers. He'd have to be very mellow, laid-back, to deal with the overly alpha dog, or the spoiled rotten ones she occasionally had to deal with.

Maybe Cutter could help her pick one out. She smiled at the idea. It made perfect sense to her. The effort that smile took, and the fact that she was aware of it, told her how stiff her expression had become since they'd arrived here and Teague had so sharply withdrawn.

She looked back, and was a little startled to see Teague and Quinn walking away toward the office at the back of the bigger room.

He hadn't even said goodbye.

They went into the office and closed the door.

And Laney couldn't stop the feeling that uncurled inside her, the feeling that she would never see him again.

It really was all over.

Chapter 35

"Again?"

Teague stared at his boss incredulously.

"Too much to ask of you?" Quinn's voice was neutral. Too neutral.

"Of course not, but what about Liam, or Rafe?"

"Liam's running an errand for me and Rafe's at the shooting range."

"Funny how they're always busy," Teague muttered. "They—"

"I don't know what's gotten into that dog," Hayley said, bustling through, gathering up a folder, her purse and some knitted fingerless gloves from the table. Fall had arrived with a vengeance in the last two weeks, rain, wind and cooler temperatures were gradually taking over. "The minute the rains began, he seemed to start hunting for every possible mud hole to roll in. Not to mention that dead…thing on the beach, and that goopy resin stuff today. He'll be lucky if Laney doesn't have to shave him."

Teague managed not to react to the name. He'd gotten better, gotten to where he could hear her mentioned without wincing. Or at least, not outwardly.

Hayley paused in front of Teague. "Thanks so much for picking him up for me again. All this wedding preparation is driving me crazy."

"We could still elope," Quinn said, sounding hopeful.

"Don't I wish," Hayley said wryly. "But Charlie has made it quite clear that's not an option, not for a Foxworth."

"Charlie," Quinn said dryly, "is planning on it being a business event."

"I like to think of it as more a Foxworth family reunion," Hayley said. "You've both built a huge family, the kind you build by choice."

Quinn looked disarmed, charmed and captivated all at once. Without hesitation he pulled Hayley into his arms and planted a long kiss on her lips. And again Teague marveled at the change in the man who was his boss; he'd been tough, competent and very alone until Hayley and the irrepressible Cutter had literally charged into his life.

And now he was the happiest man Teague knew.

He thought about suggesting they get a room, but the fact that this was Foxworth sort of meant they already had. He was the odd one out, if anything. So he should probably just leave.

Oh, yeah, just hurry why don't you? That way you can spend more painful, awkward time in the one place you do not *want to be.*

Disgusted with himself, he turned on his heel and walked out.

"Do you think they'll work it out?" Hayley asked anxiously, listening as Teague clattered downstairs.

"Are you sure there's still something to work out?" Quinn countered.

"Of course there is."

"Look, I realize they got close while we were hunting for Amber, but—"

"They got more than just close, and you know it." She heard the outside door close, wondered if Teague would have slammed it if the automatic door system hadn't prevented it. "You saw the way he looked at her. And she him."

"Yeah, well," Quinn said, sounding awkward. "But you know things get crazy under stress. Adrenaline does funny things to your thought process."

"And of course any relationship that starts under stress can't possibly last," Hayley said with exaggerated emphasis.

"I never said that," Quinn answered instantly. "I couldn't, could I? I live with proof otherwise every day."

"Good answer," Hayley said, grinning at him then.

Quinn pulled her into a tight embrace. "So I'm forgiven?"

"Nothing to forgive," Hayley said, snuggling close.

"I'm just saying I know Teague. I know how he thinks. He's a good, honorable man. And he'd never want to take advantage of someone's emotional state."

"I know that," Hayley said. "Teague's the goodest of good guys, with the whitest of hats. But sometimes it's too much for even a good guy to resist. I mean, the electricity between them practically made Cutter's fur stand on end."

"I know a little something about it being too much to resist," Quinn said, nuzzling her hair. "But I also know Teague would fight it, if he thought it was just the situation, and that Laney hadn't been thinking straight."

"I think Laney is quite capable of thinking straight, even through what she went through. And I," she said, reaching up to touch his cheek, "know a little something about that."

Quinn's smile warmed her to the core. His kiss did even more.

"They're going to have to work it out themselves," he said after a moment.

"With some help from Cutter."

"What?"

"Honestly, Quinn. You don't find it rather pointedly odd that only since this case ended has he been finding ways to get so dirty and rank that a trip to Laney's is the only solution?"

Quinn blinked.

"The dog who at most needed grooming maybe once every month or two suddenly needs it every couple of days? You think that's an accident?"

"Wait. You think he's doing this on purpose?"

"You don't? This is Cutter we're talking about."

Quinn looked thoughtful, then bemused. "Yes. Yes, it is." His gaze narrowed then. "So, does this mean you really aren't quite as busy as you've made it seem, too busy to go pick Cutter up when Laney's done with him?"

"Maybe," Hayley said with a grin that gave her away.

"Well, good," Quinn said. "Then you can afford some time now."

"I might be able to squeeze in an extra few minutes," she said, reading his intent in the sudden smokiness of his eyes.

"What I have in mind is going to take longer than a few minutes," Quinn said, his voice suddenly deeper, with that undertone that never failed to send a shiver of lovely anticipation through her.

"Oh, I hope so," she said.

Teague tapped the steering wheel restlessly as he sat outside Laney's shop. There was really no good reason not to just do this. Go in, get Cutter and get out. Never mind that the dog made it a hassle every time, resisting leaving until once Teague had even had to pick him up, a process Cutter had protested with a grunt that thanks to his good manners hadn't quite turned into a growl.

Laney had been pleasant and unemotional every time, after all. Businesslike. That was it. She'd treated him like any other customer, polite, friendly and not an iota more. There wasn't the slightest trace of the Laney of before, and certainly no trace of the woman he'd fallen for like an axed evergreen.

Because he had. He admitted that now, now that it had somehow fallen apart. He'd known she'd regret sleeping with him, he'd known it was just the circumstances. And now that Amber was safely on the way back to physical health and working on the mental aspects of her ordeal—with Laney's steadfast help, he was sure—and the crisis had passed, Laney's life would return to normal. She would get past any lingering guilt, be glad she'd refused to give up her certainty something was wrong, and she would look back on those hours of insanity between them as just that.

And none of that helped him one damned bit. He wanted her just as much now as he had a month ago. And he missed her with an ache that astonished him with its depth and stubbornness.

So here he was, about to torture himself yet again. He could have refused, could have insisted he had an appointment he couldn't break, but he hadn't. He didn't know what bugged him most, that Rafe and Liam always seemed to manage to be elsewhere and not available for doggie chauffeur duty, or Cutter suddenly managing to become the dirtiest dog on record. If he was into conspiracy theories…

Dog, he said to himself. *He's a dog. Just a dog.*

And laughed ruefully out loud at himself, both for actually thinking Cutter was just a dog, and that he himself was such an idiot.

His inward-directed sarcasm drove him out of the car and actually got him through the shop door. He heard Cutter's bark from the back room, heard Laney talking to the animal.

"—such a mess. You're lucky that solvent worked, you rascal. Tree resin may smell interesting, but rubbing your head in it gets you much nastier stuff to smell." He heard a faint jingle, guessed it was the collar with the boat-shaped tag. "There. All done."

Teague heard Cutter jump down from the grooming table. A second later he trotted out into the shop. He made a bee-line for Teague and sat, looking up at him intently. Then he looked back over his shoulder to where Laney stood in the doorway of the grooming room.

She looked amazing, he thought. She was wearing scrubs, as she had been that first day. No reddened eyes, although she looked rather somber. Enough that he had to fight the urge to ask what was wrong. It wasn't his problem. Not anymore.

"The smell of the stuff I had to use on him will fade by tomorrow."

He nodded.

"I trimmed his nails."

He nodded again.

He couldn't take just staring at her, so he shifted his gaze to the dog. Who had apparently gone back to staring at him. Maybe that was why he'd had to look down. Just a confused sheep...that was him.

"I'll bill her."

"That will be quite a bill," he said, adding to Cutter, "troublemaker."

"He's been...busy," Laney said.

"Yes." He didn't look at her. Couldn't. "Thanks," he said, and turned toward the door.

He stopped at the sound Cutter made, a combination woof

and whine that sounded like nothing less than utter, human exasperation. The dog trotted to the door, turned and sat.

At least he was ready to go this time, Teague thought. Not sure what that sound was, though.

He walked over, reached for the door handle.

"You're going to have to move, boy."

Cutter just looked at him.

"Cutter, come on."

The dog steadfastly refused to budge. Teague tried to push the door open and step over him, but the dog moved, bumping his leg enough that he had to stop the motion or lose his balance. This process was repeated twice, until Teague realized it was pointless.

Once he'd stopped, Cutter looked up at him again. And then looked at Laney, who was now barely a yard away, watching with some curiosity and more than a little bemusement.

"I'm sorry," Teague found himself saying. And it was for much more than just a recalcitrant dog.

"He's the problem," Laney said. "What are you sorry about?"

Teague let out a long breath. "A lot of things."

He looked at Cutter, who was looking at him as if he were indeed that sheep who could be stared into submission. And waiting. Waiting for what? Teague knew the dog was very sensitive to human emotions, so maybe it wasn't that big a leap to sensing unresolved issues.

Issues. God, he hated that pop-psychology word.

He made one last move for the door. Again Cutter blocked him. He thought of picking the dog up again, but it never morphed into the action. This was ridiculous, he thought. If the damned dog wanted the air cleared, then by God he'd clear the air.

He turned to face Laney.

"I'm sorry," he said again. "What happened between us shouldn't have. It wasn't fair for me to take advantage when you were so worried."

Laney's brows shot upward. "Take advantage? Is that what you call it? As I recall, I'm the one who pushed you."

"I still should have—"

"Been noble again? Walked away? Left me alone? And wanting you more than I've ever wanted anyone in my entire life?"

He'd been silently saying "Yes" to each question, until she got to the last one. That one nearly put him on his knees with its simple declaration.

"Laney," he began.

"That night was my decision, my choice, Teague. I know perfectly well if I'd said stop at any time, you would have. Because that's who you are. The man you are. But give me the same credit, will you? If I'd wanted to stop, I would have. I didn't."

He could barely breathe now, the memories, the vivid images were coming at him hot and heavy. He closed his eyes.

"I still don't," she said softly.

His eyes snapped open. "Laney."

"I know you think I wasn't thinking clearly. That I was so worried about Amber that I turned to you for solace and it went too far."

That was so close to exactly what he'd thought that it took him aback.

"I gave it time," she said. "I've waited, just in case you were right, and it would fade away now that the crisis with Amber was over. It didn't."

"Laney," he said for the third time, unable to find any other words. Not sure there were any others, not that mattered, anyway.

"You can have all the time you need, Teague. All the time it takes for you to be sure what you feel is real. And if you decide it's not, well, I'll just have to live with that. But don't cut us off without even a chance just because of how we met."

He stared at her. How often had he thought of coming to her, saying just that? Asking her to give them a chance, to take all the time she needed, but give them a chance.

Cutter woofed, softly, nudged at him.

"I think," he said slowly, "I'm outgunned."

A slow smile curved Laney's mouth. It sent a shiver through him that made him throw caution to the wind. No turning back. And he didn't care. The world opened up with that smile. It was the kind of smile that made a man willing to charge bayonets.

"Outnumbered, anyway," she said softly.

"And definitely outclassed," he said.

She smiled. He was lost.

"You mean it? You're sure?" he asked.

"I do."

"I'm new at this. Feeling like this, I mean."

"Me, too. But I'm still sure."

"Help me?" he asked.

Her smile turned to something warmer, deeper, as she quoted his answer from that day on the boat back to him.

"Always," she said.

And then she was in his arms, his lips were on hers, claiming, and she yielded, then staked her own claim with a fierce response that took his breath away.

When he finally had to stop to breathe, he reached behind him without looking and flipped the Open sign around to Closed.

"Settle in, dog," he said to Cutter. "This is going to take a while."

For a moment the dog just watched the two humans who had finally found their way. And then he plopped down on the mat inside the door, letting out a sigh of utter canine satisfaction.

Another job well done.

* * * * *

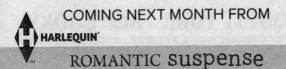

COMING NEXT MONTH FROM

HARLEQUIN®

ROMANTIC suspense

Available August 6, 2013

#1763 COPPER LAKE ENCOUNTER
by Marilyn Pappano

No one believes that Nev's disturbing dreams are coming true. But when her life is threatened, Detective Ty Gadney risks it all—including his heart—to find the truth.

#1764 COLTON BY BLOOD
The Coltons of Wyoming • by Melissa Cutler

To be with the woman he loves, Dr. Levi Colton must face the secrets of Dead River Ranch. But an enemy wants those secrets buried...no matter the cost.

#1765 LAST CHANCE REUNION
by Linda Conrad

Two stories of Chance County, Texas, have the Chance siblings fighting for justice and finding second chances at love.

#1766 A KISS TO DIE FOR
Buried Secrets • by Gail Barrett

To bring down a powerful killer, a former teenage runaway must confront her high-society family's darkest secrets—and convince a cynical ex-soldier he's the hero she believes him to be.

REQUEST YOUR FREE BOOKS!
2 FREE NOVELS PLUS 2 FREE GIFTS!

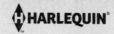

ROMANTIC suspense

Sparked by danger, fueled by passion

He saw her car before it turned into the lot. By the time she'd
parked a few spaces down from his, he was there, opening the
door, helping her out. Her coffee-with-cream eyes were filled
with concern, and she looked graver than he'd ever seen her.

"I'm not going to like this, am I?"

He shook his head. With his hand barely touching her upper
arm, they walked across the parking lot and right up to the
open door. Her jaw tightened, her mouth forming a thin line,
as she looked inside, her gaze locking for a moment on each
note. It was hard to say which one disturbed her most. It was
the stick figure that bothered Ty, the idea of taking something
so simple and innocent as a child's drawing and turning it into
a threat. From the tension radiating through her, he would
guess it was the knife in the pillow that got to her.

"The crime-scene techs are on their way over," Kiki said.
"Does anything appear to be missing?"

Nev shook her head. "The only thing I have of any value is my laptop, and it's in the room safe."

"Do you think this was done by the same boys who sprayed shaving cream on my car last night?" Nev asked, her demeanor calm, her voice quiet with just the littlest bit of a quaver.

"No." Kiki was blunt, as usual. "Gavin and Kevin Holigan are twelve and thirteen. They probably can't spell that well, and besides, this isn't their style."

"Do you have any problems at home in Atlanta?"

Nev smiled wryly. "No. I live with my mother, grandmother and sister. I work at home. I go to church every Sunday and Wednesday. I don't have any enemies there. I don't inspire that kind of passion, Detective."

Those self-doubts again. Ty didn't doubt she believed that. She had no clue what kind of passion she could inspire. He wanted nothing more than an opportunity to show her.

He needed nothing more than to keep her safe.

**Don't miss
COPPER LAKE ENCOUNTER
by Marilyn Pappano,
available August 2013 from
Harlequin Romantic Suspense.**